On the Banks
of the Irtysh River

A Novel

———————

David Funk

Acknowledgments

This novel could not have been completed except for the invaluable help of many readers/editors. To all of you I say, "Thank you!" I owe a special debt of gratitude to Angela Funk, Harold Dawes, Ksenia Nadkina, and Judii Rempel. The vital contributions of each made this novel infinitely better than it would otherwise have been. Thank you also to Danny Unrau and Dr. John B. Toews for their encouragement and support. Finally, I am grateful beyond words for Shirl, who has stood with me through thick and thin. I love you.

For Agnessa

Contents

Part One

Part Two

To live your life is not as simple as to cross a field.

—Russian proverb

mourn for Russia's gloomy savour,

land where I learned to love and weep,

land where my heart is buried deep.

Eugene Onegin,

—Pushkin

One

On Board the S.S. Melita

1

I met the Rempel family because a steward molested one of their daughters while she lay seasick on her cot in the cubicle that passed for a stateroom. As Ship's Surgeon, I was summoned immediately. Needless to say, when I arrived, I found the family gathered around their violated daughter in a state of stunned disbelief.

Her mother and older sister sat on either side of her on the edge of the bed. She was silently weeping, clutching a blanket to her breast. A younger daughter stood miserably beside, trying to comfort her weeping sister. An older son gritted his teeth in anger while trying to shush a fussing baby upset by the storm of emotions battering the walls of the room. He bristled protectively as I entered.

"We left Russia to escape such brutality!" howled the man I took to be her distraught father.

He had spoken in German.

I suggested the need for privacy. Her mother, Lena, remained while the rest of the family reluctantly agreed to wait in the stateroom the men of the family occupied next door. Lena held the girl's hand and comforted her as best she could while looking at me with sad eyes filled with great suspicion. Her pale face framed by gray hair pulled tightly back and wrapped in a bun at the nape of her neck was lined with grief and worry.

I got down on one knee on the floor beside the bed to lower myself to the girl's level. She pulled away in alarm when I got too close.

In a poor attempt to set her at ease I gently asked, "*Wie heisst du?*"

After a moment's hesitation she replied through her tears, "Joanna," in a quiet, timorous voice.

"And how old are you, Joanna?" I continued, speaking German.

Joanna glanced at me with large, fear-filled eyes, and looking away quickly said, "Fifteen."

Understandably, Joanna was emotionally devastated. She answered all of my questions while her mother held her tightly, and in that embrace she seemed to slowly regain some strength as the time passed.

Through my examination I was able to determine that Joanna had not been physically harmed. Fortunately, the devil whose threatening words and calloused hands ruptured her innocence had been interrupted when Joanna's older sister, Katarina, unexpectedly returned to the cabin. Otherwise, who knows what horrors might have occurred in the dim light of that windowless room. The villain had leaped from the bed and bolted down the corridor. Of course, he was apprehended within hours for his name was on the duty roster assigned to the Rempels' rooms. How could he have thought to get away with it? When she was later asked to confirm the culprit's identity, Joanna burst into frightened sobs at the mere sight of him. He scowled and defiantly shouted his innocence as he was taken away.

So began my acquaintance with this immigrant family from Siberia. Through a series of meetings, some planned and some by happenstance, we engaged in a weeklong conversation during which I learned the story of their escape from communist Russia. As it turned out, most of the family spent a large part of the voyage violently ill due to the heavy North Atlantic seas that tossed the 15,000-ton ship about like a stick in a millrace; they seldom were able to leave their berths. It was Heinrich Rempel, his nineteen-year-old son Henry, and the youngest daughter, Agnessa, all of whom were less affected by the ceaseless rolling of the ship, that I met on various occasions and came to know.

I soon discovered that Heinrich Rempel was a complex man of perhaps fifty. Depending on his mood, he could be genial and well spoken, or sullen and abrasive. He was of average build. His thinning grey hair was parted and neatly combed to one side. A Van Dyke beard on a strong, square jaw gave him an aristocratic look. That, and the fact that, standing or sitting, he always held himself very erect. I observed, as we met over the days to come, that he always dressed in a three-piece suit and tie, often topped off by a well-worn bowler hat. It was obvious he was a proud man and particular about his looks. Beyond the hair, the beard and the clothing, though, the most notable feature of Heinrich Rempel's appearance was his striking eyes. They were grey with flecks of green around the iris. But it wasn't their color that drew me in. His eyes had the pained, haunted look of one who has seen too many of life's sorrows and hardships. It was a look common to many of his fellow Third Class Russian immigrant passengers.

I liked his son, Henry, immediately. Once he had calmed after the shock of his sister's mistreatment, comforted somewhat by justice swiftly served, I found him to be a thoughtful and compassionate young man. Unlike his father, he was unconcerned about his appearance. His clothes were plain and showed the effects of long use, but had obviously been well made; he informed me that his stepmother had sewn them. Henry was keenly observant and quick-witted. His eyes were a deep blue-grey shade that reminded me of the color of an early evening sea under a thin layer of cloud. His dark brown hair was cut short and when he turned I glimpsed a jagged scar on the back of his scalp.

Agnessa was a precocious nine-year-old with long braided hair the color of a well-baked loaf of rye bread. Her oval face held large, sparkling blue eyes that were flecked with specks of green and gold. When her father was with her, Agnessa was very reserved and well mannered. I could never decide whether she behaved in his presence as she did out of a child's sense of respect for her parent, or because she was, perhaps, afraid of her father. Certainly, in Agnessa I saw a spark that relished and even craved independence, for in her father's absence she proved to be lively and clever. On such occasions she ceaselessly pestered me with questions about the ship and about her future home, Canada, a country about which I knew only a little, and about which she knew nothing at all. Agnessa was thin, with the pale complexion of the undernourished, so I pampered her with oranges, which she loved, exclaiming at their sweetness with each bite and enthusiastically licking every bit of juice from her fingers. She'd never seen an orange in Siberia.

Henry was very gentle with his sister. It was clear little Agnessa adored him, and he, her. She followed him, seemingly, wherever he went and he was fiercely protective of her. I suppose it was for this reason that their father had little hesitation in letting the two of them wander the ship. It was this freedom that occasionally brought them into my company as I was out and about on the decks.

It was November 1926, and we were aboard the S.S. Melita, a Canadian Pacific steam ship sailing from Antwerp, Belgium to St. John, New Brunswick. The Rempels, together with a large group of German Mennonite emigrants from Russia, had boarded during our scheduled stop at Southampton, England.

2

"People say hindsight is like perfect vision; everything becomes clear in the end. I don't believe that," Henry Rempel said with feeling. "When it comes to the events of our lives these past ten or twelve years, everyone has their own opinions about why they happened, and who knows which is right."

Henry and I were sharing a lunch of liver and onions, a staple of the ship's kitchen. I had seen the three of them in the dining hall—Heinrich, Henry, and Agnessa—and decided to join them. By the time I went through the mess line and returned with my tray, only Henry remained. He was quick to engage in conversation. The fact that I spoke his language seemed to put him at ease. He was recalling the evening before his family left their village for the last time only four weeks ago.

Henry and his friend, Anatoly Lepinov, had been relaxing amongst the willow bushes on the gently sloping banks of the Irtysh River that flowed by their town of Kulomzino, in west Siberia. The willow leaves on the ground were newly fallen, and lying amongst the stems of dried fireweed and fescue they created a crisp mosaic carpet in many shades of gray. It was late in the evening. A full moon shone brightly white in the chilly October air causing the river to become a shiny ribbon of silver that wove its way passed the town and beyond, over the Kalunda Steppe.

"Father always said that when the German armies started shooting up Europe in 1914, their flying bullets reached all the way to Kulomzino, and that's when our troubles began," Henry said in soft tones that were soon lost in the night, swallowed by the darkness and the ripples along the riverbank. "I sometimes overheard them arguing in the kitchen, in the evening after I had gone to bed. Mother always disagreed with Father. 'Long before all those armies of German boots were churning Russian dirt to dust and mud in far off Ukraine,' she would counter, 'I had already laid to rest three children in that same black Russian soil and my heart was broken into ever smaller pieces with each new death. It didn't take a war to bring trouble to our family. Trouble is a fact of life.' Father would always go silent. He had no answer for my mother."

Henry paused, nibbling on a willow twig. "Elder Ewert at our church in Tschunayevka preaches that in this world you will have many sorrows, but that whatever happens in life, whether good or evil, it is God's will. 'Faith will carry you through,' he says." Henry had mimicked his minister's voice. After a moment he said, "I think I admire people with that kind of faith, though I do not understand it."

Anatoly listened as he lay on his back looking up at the speckled night sky. His eyes scanned the vast array of stars burning in the blackness fueled by the suffering of untold multitudes of lost Siberian souls.

"I think that despite what your minister says, what God wills for us is a very complicated subject," Anatoly remarked thoughtfully. After a moment he added, "Your minister is right about the sorrows, though. Life is a long muddy road filled with many deep ruts and potholes. You know, like during the thaw."

"Ya," chuckled Henry. "I heard that a horse and droshke were swallowed by a mud hole on the road to Tobolsk last spring! The driver only managed to escape by scampering over top of the horse before it was completely covered."

"I'm sure that night he lit a candle to his patron saint and kissed his ikon a hundred times in gratitude for his escape," added Anatoly with a snicker.

The boys laughed briefly, aware that they were disturbing the reverent stillness. Their soft laughter drifted over the water and then they were quiet. Their silence stretched and covered them like a deep, protective blanket of Siberian snow. They felt safe in the cocoon of their life-long friendship.

Slowly, the boys became aware of the night life along the riverbank. The incessant orchestrations of croaking frogs calling for mates were being accompanied by the rhythmic cacophony of equally hopeful cicadas hidden in the grass. A hunting owl hooted somewhere in the distance, sending shivers along the spines of furry rodents caught outside the safety of their protective burrows. A family of pintail ducks paddled soundlessly among the reeds, leaving in their wake milky skeins on the shiny river's surface. Absorbed in its own essence, nature was unruffled by the young men's troubled thoughts.

As they sat in the darkness on the banks of the Irtysh River, the Earthmover to those who named it, the boys aimlessly tossed a few small rocks into the shallows. The muddy waters of the river flowed languidly by on the long journey from their first chaotic tumblings down the Altai Mountains of Mongolia onto the placid expanse of the Siberian steppes and from thence ever onward to the Arctic Ocean far to the north, all the while collecting in their flow from tributaries along the way the experiences and memories, the tears of joy and of sadness of the disparate peoples whose towns and villages clustered on the nurturing river's banks, until at long last the Irtysh deposited its sacred trust into the vast, frozen fastness at the top of the world. The plops of the pebbles hitting the water were challenged by frogs among the reeds rumbling their defiance at the imagined interlopers even while cautiously nestling deeper into the protective mud.

In the town a dog barked.

Henry recalled that the mood had become somber, for this was to be a night of good-byes.

"Will we meet again?" Anatoly had asked his friend in a low voice. "Tell me once more. Where are you going?"

"To Canada, on the other side of the world," replied Henry softly. "I will write a letter to you when we arrive and tell you all about it. Maybe one day you will be able to come and join us."

Anatoly made no reply. Canada? It might as well be the moon. He got to his feet and walked to the water's edge.

Gradually the boys became aware of the soft sound of muffled weeping. It was coming from the direction of a willow thicket they knew to be up the bank and to their left.

Anatoly hesitated. What was there to say? Words failed him. He turned, grasped Henry's hand helping him to stand. He embraced him and kissed him formally on both cheeks. With a nod of his head he released his friend and walked away into the darkness through the trees toward the sleeping houses and dark streets of the town. He did not look back. Henry watched him until he had disappeared into the night.

After Anatoly was gone, Henry waited for only a moment before going to the willow thicket where she stood. He had known Sonia Sarkovskaja since they were children playing together in the yards and alleyways of Kulomzino. He took her warm hands in his and pulled her close, relishing the smell of her.

3

The next morning was October 27, 1926. Heinrich Rempel was up early. He bundled himself against the cold he knew would greet him outdoors. Winter came early to Siberia. He pulled on a ragged but warm overcoat, wrapped a scarf around his neck, and placed a felt bowler hat atop his head. It was not yet so cold that he must trade his beloved bowler for something warmer. While the rest of the family slept, Heinrich made the fifteen-minute walk along Trotskaya Street to the Trans-Siberian Railway station on Prince Alexander Street. Though it was still dark, he cautiously peered to the right and left sides of the road ahead. Occasionally he looked behind in the direction from which he had come. He was grateful for the darkness that concealed him, yet fearful also of what the darkness might hide. The street was quiet but for a few peddlers who plodded along as they began their daily rounds.

Up ahead, Heinrich could see the train station. Its tall brick walls covered in white plaster reflected ominous shadows in the soft glow of the gas streetlamps. Around a corner, he discovered that there was already a line of customers patiently waiting for the office to open. They stood quietly in the cold, resigned to the fact that when one wanted to purchase anything in Siberia, it would inevitably involve waiting in a cue. Heinrich shuffled his feet nervously. Eventually, a shuttered window in the wall of the station was opened and a sleepy-eyed clerk appeared. The line began to move.

When his turn to purchase tickets came, Heinrich approached the kiosk.

"Seven tickets to Moscow, please." He had spoken softly, though he tried to make his voice firm and confident, like this was nothing new or unusual. His words sounded scratchy and hesitant in his ears. He wondered whether the clerk could sense the grinding apprehension he was feeling in his gut. The tickets were for himself, his wife Lena, and for his children; Katarina, Henry, Joanna, Agnessa, and baby Johann.

Before he would hand over the tickets, the railway employee at the counter insisted on inspecting the passports and other travel documents Heinrich had picked up the week before at Russkapa, the Russian Canadian Passenger Agency office in the city of Omsk, across the river. The agent raised an eyebrow in suspicion, but when a ten-ruble note was found tucked inside the cover of the last document, he nonchalantly passed the tickets through the hole in the kiosk window. Bribery was expected and appreciated in the new order of the

Union of Soviet Socialist Republics, just as it had been in the Russia ruled by Tsars.

As he left the station Heinrich looked anxiously about to see if he was being followed. The darkness had weakened considerably. He hurried back up Trotskaya Street, his breath forming a wisp of fog that trailed his head in the cold morning air like a bride's veil. Thoughts of his beloved, dead Katy on their wedding day flashed through his mind and dissipated as quickly as they had appeared.

The family was awake when Heinrich returned home. An unfamiliar feeling of joyful expectancy crackled in the air of the room. In barely subdued tones they talked excitedly about what the new day would bring.

Lena had prepared a breakfast of hot tea and bread made fresh the day before. Heinrich offered a prayer of thanks and asked for protection in what lay ahead. Butter and raspberry jam were spread generously on every piece of fresh bread as the family ate in silence. Everyone enjoyed tea sweetened with more raspberry jam that was stirred into the hot cups. After years of careful scrimping, the blatant luxury of the meal bore a hint of scandal. Nothing was saved, for what could not be carried would have to be left behind.

With breakfast quickly finished, last minute packing was completed. In preparation for the journey, Lena had baked dozens of buns, which were twice roasted to make rusks. Almost as hard as wood, the rusks would last for weeks without spoiling. Lena had also made kringles, donut-like pastries that had been boiled and then baked. The rusks and kringles would be their only food on the weeklong trip to Moscow and would taste good when dunked in strong tea made with boiling water bought from vendors at railroad stations along the way. They were packed tightly in a large cloth bag for the journey. As for luggage, only essential items of clothing and personal toiletries had been packed. The Soviet government wouldn't allow citizens who were leaving the country to take anything with them but the barest necessities.

At seven o'clock a *droshky* hired by Heinrich arrived on Trotskaya Street in front of their house. With a minimum of fuss, all the bags and packages were loaded onto the buggy. Heinrich anxiously glanced up and down the rutted, tree-lined road to see if there were any watchers. There were none that he could see and he hoped against hope there were none he couldn't see. A few close friends knew of their leaving, but no one else. The children, especially Agnessa, had been given strict instructions to speak about their departure with no one. It was too risky. People were always spying on each other and reporting anything remotely suspicious. Documents could be confiscated. Travel plans could be canceled; arrests made.

A last look at the rooms that had been home for so many years: the beds where his family had slept, the table and chairs where they had sat, eaten, laughed, wept, and prayed, the large brick Russian oven that had given them warmth, and the iron stove on which they had cooked their food. Heinrich closed the door and hurried to join his family huddled outside. He did not dare to pause and dwell on the memories of years gone by that unexpectedly flooded his thinking. There would be time for that later.

Snow began drifting down softly from out of the dawning sky, silent crystalline tears of regret and of parting. Without comment, the family filed onto the dirt road. Walking behind the *droshky*, they set off along Trotskaya Street. They silently passed by their neighbors' unpainted, dilapidated houses with shuttered windows like eyes closed and hidden behind decaying fences. Quietly they made their way to the railway station. Heinrich carried baby Johann while Lena held Agnessa's hand. Katarina, Henry and Joanna followed behind.

The muted light of morning had taken a firm hold of the sky to the east when the Rempels arrived. Heinrich and Henry quickly unloaded their bundles, while the driver in his thick sheepskin coat waited impatiently on his perch. With rubles in hand as payment, as soon as the *droshky* was empty the driver clicked his tongue and his horses pulled gladly away, perhaps hoping for home and fresh hay. Horses and buggy soon disappeared in the dim light and the swirling snow.

A small group of close friends had gathered on the sidewalk in anticipation of the Rempels' departure. After the droshky had gone they wept and held each other in long embraces in the manner of those who know theirs is a final good-bye. When it could no longer be avoided, they shuffled homeward down the road, waving last farewells that were lost in the falling snow.

Nervously the Rempel family entered the station's cavernous reception hall. Its high imposing whitewashed walls and vaulted ceiling loomed over them with the gaze of a disapproving judge. Sensing animosity, they quickly made their way through the weary throng of waiting passengers until they found a small space on the floor where they could put down their burdens and rest. There was little excitement in the crowd. Rather, the mood of those who waited was a depressed sense of anxious urgency. At nine o'clock in the morning Train Number Three of the Trans-Siberian Railway would leave for Moscow. Would the train arrive on time? Would there be enough room for everyone? What would happen if the train did not come at all?

The Early Years

1

Heinrich Rempel was born in 1875, in a village in the south Russia colony of Yazykovo. The villagers called their town, Hochfeld. Their Russian neighbors called it Morosovo.

As Heinrich told me about the village in which he grew up, the fact that it was called by two different names highlighted an issue I had been pondering.

"Your village has two names: one German, one Russian. You are Russian," I observed, "yet you speak German."

Heinrich bristled. "We lived in Russia, yes, but we were never Russian. You may think that odd, but to us it was vitally important to hold on to our German heritage. It was the language of our faith, the essence of our identity in a foreign land. We learned Russian only so we could do business with our neighbors."

He then explained that his family belonged to a religious community basing its beliefs on the teachings of a sixteenth century monk from Friesland named Menno Simons. Simons' followers managed, in a time when religious dissidents were labeled heretics and were burned at the stake or executed in some other similarly hideous manner, to get on the wrong side of both Lutheran northern Europe and the Catholic south. Among other things, their problem was that they did not recognize baptism at birth, which carried along with it automatic membership in the church and state. That, of course, was treason. Baptism, they believed, should be based on a personal confession of faith. So, Simons' followers were rebaptised as adults. And that was treason as well.

Consequently, the Mennonites, as they were called, were hounded throughout Europe for more than two centuries. Because of persecution they tended to stick together and, in their wanderings, eventually adopted German as their common tongue.

I asked, "How did the Mennonites find their way into Russia?"

"Well," Heinrich said, stroking his Van Dyke, "another history lesson. By the 1780's, the Mennonites had gained a reputation as industrious farmers who were skilled at reclaiming flooded land. The Tsarina of Russia, Catherine the Great, a German herself, heard about us and invited us to come and farm her empty south Russian steppes. She promised free land and exemption from paying any taxes. We were also given complete religious freedom and, because we are pacifists, exemption from military service. The Tsarina gave us the right to self-government and the freedom to teach our children in our own language—all of these things for a period of one hundred years. It was becoming difficult to find good land for purchase in Prussia so you can imagine how we jumped at the opportunity. Mennonites flocked to the fertile land of the Ukraine. My ancestors made the journey in 1789. We have been there ever since."

It was obvious Heinrich was extremely proud of his heritage.

I found it puzzling. If country of origin means anything, being born in Russia, the Rempels were Russian. Yet, they never thought of themselves as being Russian. Heinrich's description of the Mennonites in Russia reminded me of the Jews of Europe, living in the midst of but separately from the cultures that surrounded them, practicing their own traditions, keeping their own identity.

"Did you know," he concluded, "that the language of business in Omsk has long been German?"

2

Heinrich Rempel was born into a family where it was understood the inheritance would go to the eldest son. The Rempels had made a name for themselves in the manufacture of buggies, farm wagons, and sleighs. From that beginning they had expanded into the business of milling fine flour and seed oils. They were known to the people of Hochfeld as the Factory Rempels. From childhood Heinrich began learning the art of running a business so that one day he too would be able to make his fortune through hard work and determination.

When he was eighteen, Heinrich's apprenticeship in the family business was interrupted. He was called to serve in the Tsar's Imperial Army. Conscription of all able-bodied young men had been instituted by the Tsar after some embarrassing Russian defeats in the 1850's during the Crimean war. Old promises were forgotten and necessity now dictated policy. The Mennonites were no longer excluded from conscription. However, coming from a religious community that forbade the taking up of weapons and violence against another human being, training in the arts of war was not an option for Heinrich Rempel.

Fortunately, an acceptable form of alternative service had been negotiated by church leaders. Instead of training as a soldier, Heinrich, along with one hundred seventy other 'objectors of conscience,' served Tsar Nicholas' Russia by planting trees and caring for orchards in a forestry camp specially built for that purpose at Anadol, about fifty kilometers north of the Sea of Azov.

Returning to Hochfeld after his two-year term of service ended, Heinrich once again threw himself into the consuming atmosphere of the family business. As he matured through his twenties, he gradually found himself becoming one of Hochfeld's most eligible bachelors. At five and a half feet he was a little on the short side, but he was strong and handsome. He was also energetic and had a creative flair. Unlike some of the young men in the village who preferred a life less encumbered by work, Heinrich labored diligently and made his way up the management ladder of his father's companies. More than a few of the young women of Hochfeld secretly contemplated the dream of a comfortable future with Heinrich Rempel.

One happy day late in the autumn of 1901, Heinrich met Katarina Epp. Katy, as everyone called her, was raised in the neighboring village of Franzfeld. She was fine featured, friendly, a little shy when in company, and loved by all who knew her. Already as a twenty-year-old she was accomplished in the kitchen; in the Epp family her beef borsht and apple pies were legendary. What struck Heinrich immediately about Katy, when they met, was the sparkle in her soft brown eyes and the way she drew out of him the capacity to simply enjoy the present moment. They fell in love immediately with an intensity that surprised them both and would remain through all the years of their life together.

Of course, the way had been well prepared before Heinrich and Katy met that first time. The Rempel and Epp families were aware of each other through the informal network of friends and relatives that made communication in the close-knit villages of Yazykovo as reliable as heat in August and frost in February. The fathers discussed the possibility of the union and the children were consulted regarding their willingness to consider the marriage. The mothers baked copious amounts of zweiback and pirozhki. Katy supervised the preparation of large tureens full of borscht flavored with soup bones and meat that had simmered overnight, loaded with vegetables and spiced with parsley and dill. All was to be consumed on the joyful day when the families and their guests met to witness the young couple's wedding.

At this point I interrupted Heinrich for the obviously required explanations. Zweiback, he told me, are buns of a particular recipe baked one on top of the other, like two-layered snowmen. Pirozhki are pastries containing apples, cherries, or some other fruit. I must say that, with the dreary diet we are served on the Melita, those two delicacies sounded like they would make a very welcome addition to our table.

The happy couple was married at their Mennonite church after the regular worship service on February 19, 1902. It was an icy Wednesday evening on which the wind chill dipped to -20 C with a blustery northeast wind and clouds dark with the threat of snow. But the church was warm, thanks to a well-stoked furnace, and the sermon was inspirational, thanks to the well-prepared minister. The hearts of all who were present rejoiced with Heinrich and Katy.

The couple was quick to prosper. In December, to Heinrich and Katy's great joy, their first child, a baby girl, was born. Two years later a son was added to the family. Aided by a loan of seed money from his father, Heinrich ventured out on his own. With his partner, Isaac Huebert, he built a fine flourmill in the south Russian town of Kamenskaya. They called the mill, *Nadyezhda*, Hope.

Then came the year 1905. Tragically, both children died, one in January, the other in February, both of the kinds of illnesses that took all too many children in those days before antibiotics. That spring, a third baby was expected, but that daughter also died, shortly after birth. Heinrich and Katy were devastated. Such experiences can bring people together or drive them apart. For Heinrich and Katy, grief only strengthened their love as they sought comfort in each other's arms.

In 1906, Heinrich learned the Tsar was giving free land in Siberia to encourage settlement on the steppes. European Russia was crowded and plagued by unemployment. The Trans-Siberian Railway from Moscow to Vladivostok had just been completed and a vast country was being opened up for the brave of heart and strong of limb to forge new lives for themselves. Looking for new opportunities in a place far from bad memories, Heinrich sold his share of the Kamenskaya mill. Hoping to make a fresh start he and Katy, who was again expecting, made their first trip to Kulomzino.

Two months later, a daughter was born. Katy wanted to name the infant Margaretha, after her mother, but Heinrich insisted that his daughter should be given the name of her own mother. Katarina, or Katyusha, as her parents liked to call her—both her parents liked the Russian form of endearment—was a happy, robust child who quickly brought back some of the joy that had fled her parents' hearts.

After a few months in Kulomzino, it soon became apparent that there was no free land of any value left to be had in the area surrounding the town; it had all been allotted long before the Rempels arrived. For people without good land, there was only poverty, and the poverty the Rempels saw in west Siberia was alarming and soul crushing.

Heinrich packed up his young family and moved to Arkadak, a town on the Ryazan-Ural Railway line in the Saratov region of south Russia. There he entered into a partnership in the building of a much larger mill than he had previously owned. The flourmill was a huge, red brick building, four stories high, with arched, white brick cornices over each of its many windows. It boasted a red brick smoke stack that reached into the sky high above the mill's peaked roofs. The mill towered over the other buildings in the area. It signaled to all the prosperity its owners enjoyed.

In 1907, the family rejoiced in the birth of a son. Heinrich again insisted the infant must carry his father's name, as dictated by tradition. But Katy didn't have much patience for traditions carried on for their own sake. She argued that it would be confusing to have two Heinrichs in the same house. Who would come when she called? In the end, they agreed to name the baby Henry, using the English form of his father's name. They had learned of the name in a letter from Heinrich's cousin in Canada and thought it quite exotic.

Four years later, Joanna was safely added to the family. Joanna's dark hair and blue sparkling eyes made her an immediate favorite. Everyone doted on her, especially Katarina who was thrilled to have a baby sister.

All three children were healthy and flourished as they grew. It seemed that finally the Rempels were being spared the cruel childhood illnesses that so regularly robbed young families of their infants.

As their family grew, so also did Heinrich and Katy's fortune. The mill sold high quality flour and seed oils. There were markets aplenty where their products were sought after and routinely sold for a handsome profit. Heinrich and Katy prospered and were content.

First Lessons

1

The Rempels' move to Kulomzino on the west bank of the Irtysh River across from the city of Omsk began like all moves of its kind, full of hope and promise.

Heinrich had become restless. His heart was no longer in the milling business. He was bored and wanted a new challenge. His thoughts kept returning to west Siberia and the endless opportunities the booming agricultural heartland afforded an astute businessman. After many letters to and from business acquaintances in the Omsk area, Heinrich came to a decision. He would open a farm implement store in Kulomzino. His shares in the prosperous Arkadak mill were quick to sell. The family turned its eyes to the east.

It was the end of May 1913. Spring had come to south Russia. The bright sun was shining out of a clear cerulean sky. Its energizing warmth wakened the somnolent land. Cherry trees along the roads were a riot of tiny pink explosions. Myriad hues of fresh-grown green blanketed the fields surrounding Arkadak as tender shoots of silky bentgrass, wormseed, and Russian thistle competed with the newly planted seeds of wheat, oats, sunflowers, and sugar beets for nutrients and moisture in the rich soil. The air was filled with a chaotic clamor of birdsong, the hopeful avian invitations to courtship and nesting.

On the way to the railway station the Rempel children chattered with excitement. They had seen the train pass through their town all their young lives. From time to time they had watched passengers getting on and off at the station platform. They had even been to the station to pick up travelers, like when Oma and Opa Rempel or Oma and Opa Epp came for a visit. Often, as they watched the trains chug by, they wondered where the people on them had come from and where they were going. For Henry, the aura of mystery surrounding the towering wagons had led to summer afternoon dreams of climbing aboard and traveling to exotic unknown places. And today was the day! Today it would be their turn to look out of the high train windows down onto the passenger-loading platform. Today they would experience the luxury of traveling in the huge, elegant coaches pulled by the massive, smoke-belching, steam-powered locomotives. For children who had always walked wherever they went, or at best had occasionally traveled in a droshky or, in winter, on a horse-drawn sleigh, today was a dream come true!

The family watched the noisy train rumble into the station. Its workhorse was a steel behemoth of a black engine topped by a huge funnel-shaped chimney before which sat a large driving light. Two more large lamps were mounted on the platform at the base of the boiler. Steel railings guarded a catwalk along its length above three huge drive-wheels that stood almost as tall as Henry. The engine's cab was enclosed, to protect the crew during the long cold Russian winter, with windows that opened on the side and a moveable partition at the rear to allow access to the tender behind, on which was carried the cord wood that fueled the boiler's ravenous fire.

The engine pulled eight coaches. The first, for first-class passengers, was painted blue. Two cars for second-class passengers were painted yellow. Five cars for third-class passengers were painted green.

At the end of the train was the post-wagon. It had two brass horn ornaments on its side panels. A green letterbox bearing a picture of a sealed letter was painted on the wall. Using the new rail system, mail from St. Petersburg could now reach Siberia in a matter of weeks rather than the months it had taken by horse-drawn coach on the old Trakt, or Post, Road.

Henry had made his way down the line of wagons and had examined each one by the time he heard his father call him back. He ran to where his family waited to board, breathless with exclamations about what he had seen.

The call went out for passengers to board the train. According the Russian railway regulations of the time, if all the coaches designated for second-class passengers were full, those passengers without a seat were entitled to travel first class. Heinrich was aware of this regulation. He noticed a few passengers hang back as boarding began. Let them try for the greater luxury, he thought. He and his family would be content to travel in more humble comfort.

As their turn to board came, Heinrich waited until Katy had climbed the steep stairs. He then handed Joanna up to her. Katarina was next. Henry stumbled on the second stair when it was his turn. He picked himself up quickly but later saw that he had bruised his knee on the metal step.

Together with the crowd of other harried locals boarding the train, Heinrich shouldered his way into the second-class car with his excited family in tow. An empty compartment was quickly found. It had two benches with padded seats and backs facing each other on either side of a large window. Two fold-down bunks on the walls above could be lowered and used for sleeping. Soon their baggage was stored under the benches and everyone got settled in their places.

As they waited for the train to begin to move, a bell in the station clanged loudly once, then twice. "Last call!" it said. There was a last minute scramble by passengers, especially those in the crowded third-class cars, where the latecomers were trying to find unoccupied spots. Suddenly, the station bell rang three times. "Here we go!" The train's steam whistle gave a long, shrill blast of warning. Many passengers were hanging out of windows saying last farewells to those who remained behind. Together with their loved ones on the station platform they crossed themselves in a communal prayer for a safe journey.

The children's hearts skipped a beat as, with a lurch and a squealing of steel wheels on steel track, the train lumbered off. All eyes peered out of the window to watch the world seemingly begin to fly by as the steam locomotive slowly powered its way to full speed.

As the train chugged north and east, the children marveled at the vastness, and emptiness, of the Russian steppe. Looking out of their window, they noticed that the further north they traveled, the fewer the farmers they saw working the land. At the same time, everywhere on the prairie, swaths of snow grew larger and more numerous. The snow on the steppe gave the impression of a white and black patchwork quilt stretching all the way to the horizon wherever they looked. The train passed endless expanses of these quilted fields, the stitching created by innumerable tiny streams of snowmelt gathering together and pooling into puddles and ponds, or joining together to form rills that noisily gurgled through dips and ditches. The land was shaking off its snowy mantle, awakened by the warmth of the days, the hope of spring and the coming time of rebirth. Occasionally the children glimpsed stands of white Russian birch and larch trees dotting the landscape, with green-budding stunted undergrowth tangled around and amongst their trunks. In the distance, small stands of pine grew straight and tall in small groves that formed dark tableaux on the steppe.

It was on the second day, as they watched the countryside slide by their window, when Henry noticed that, like clock-work, every kilometer there was, next to the track, a small rustic yellow-painted cabin. He asked his father about them.

It happened that just then the conductor was passing by. The conductor was a tall man with mutton-chop whiskers on his long cheeks. He was immaculately dressed in his starched grey uniform with gold piping and wore his astrakhan hat of Persian lamb's wool with the coat of arms of the Ryazan-Ural Railway proudly displayed on its front. He was only too happy to pass his knowledge on to the family before him.

The cabins, he explained, were the railroad's signaling system. Because the land was flat from horizon to horizon, each cabin was always in sight of the next. In the cabins lived good-conduct convicts, prisoners who were able to serve out their sentences with little or no supervision. As the train approached, it was their job to hold up a green flag to signal that the way ahead was clear, though if truth be told, he said, most often it was the convict's woman who held up the signal flag. Rarely was the flag unfurled, and if it was, it merely hung limply or snapped half-heartedly in the wind, making a sad and timid appearance, looking tattered and faded in the sunlight. In the dark of night, a green lamp was displayed. Seeing the light or the flag, the engineer knew it was safe to continue on up the track.

The train the Rempels rode in was a local carrier, not an express. They couldn't count the number of small villages and towns they passed. The children tried, but after a couple of days lost interest. There were too many. Almost without exception, the villages were poor collections of randomly placed, decrepit dwellings with mud walls and thatch roofs in desperate need of repair. Occasionally a cow or goat could be seen poking its head out of a window or standing in a doorway. People in the villages would stop what they were doing and stare dully as the train clattered by. The children watched in silence as the poverty of rural Russia paraded by their window.

Stations were located in every village and sometimes in places where there was no other building in sight. The train was slow and stopped at each station along the way, exchanging one group of ragged locals for another. Inexpensive fares for third-class made the railway a popular way to travel, even for the impoverished Russian peasants.

As the days passed, cities became the Rempels' real standard for measuring the distance they had covered. They looked forward to arriving in each one and ticked them off their list as they left them behind. In this way they passed through Penza, Kazan, and then beautiful Ekaterinburg. Ekaterinburg lay at the junction of the Ryazan-Ural and Tran-Siberian Railways. There they changed trains and headed east into Siberia.

It was at the Ekaterinburg station that the family, and especially six-year-old Henry, received an object lesson that demonstrated for him just how wide was the gulf that lay between the rich and the poor of Mother Russia.

It was early evening on the sixth day of their journey. In the dimming light the gas lamps outside the station were being lit. The Rempels had transferred all of their baggage to the eastbound train and were comfortably settled in their new coach. Leaving Katy with the girls, Henry and his father walked across the spotlessly swept sand platform toward the vendors who lined the walls of the station, intending to buy food for their dinner. They always chose to purchase their meals from station vendors rather than eating in the station buffets, which Heinrich considered to be an unnecessary luxury. At nearly every station, peasant women sold roasted or boiled chicken. Hot dumplings filled with ground meat and spices were a favorite. Other women sold crusty loaves of dark bread with homemade butter, and fresh milk. Depending on the time of year, fresh fruits and vegetables could also be found. Boiling water for tea was always available at the stations for free. It was served from huge steaming samovars fussed over by white-gloved attendants. Henry's job was to fill the kettle while his father shopped for food. Whatever treats Heinrich bought were always taken back into their compartment where the family enjoyed their meal as they waited for the train to move on. That, of course, could only happen after the passengers eating in the buffets would finally return.

On this particular evening while Henry was waiting his turn at the samovar, he found that he could peer through an open door and look right into the First-Class Buffet. His eyes were just beginning to take in some of the fancy delicacies arrayed on tables close to the door when, to his surprise, a small barefoot boy wearing a pair of ragged breaches and red top darted in, grabbed some bread, and ran from the room holding his prize tucked under his shirt. It happened in a flash; the boy had passed Henry and disappeared down the platform and into one of the Third-Class cars before he could say, "Tsar Nicholas."

Right about this time, Heinrich returned to where his son was standing. Rich scents were emanating from the bag he carried. Henry immediately told his father about what he had seen. He wasn't sure why he told; he couldn't explain it. Henry knew what the boy had done. He knew stealing was wrong. In Arkadak, his father had often complained of how things about the mill that weren't tied down were constantly disappearing. But Henry had never stared thievery in the face before. He felt distressed and excited all at once in a jumble of mixed up emotions.

By this time, of course, the alarm had been raised. A group of incensed onlookers was standing by the door to the buffet, together with a tall man wearing the red uniform of an army officer. Everyone was gesticulating and speaking loudly—no one seemed to be listening—while they looked this way and that, trying to make sense of where the young thief had gone.

Heinrich approached the group. When he got the attention of the army officer, he told him what Henry had seen. Much to Henry's dismay, the army officer came over to him. Feeling like he had done something dreadfully wrong, Henry was at first very hesitant to say anything in answer to the questions that were fired his way. He stood, hands by his sides, looking up with wide eyes at the frightening man.

Heinrich finally got stern. "Tell the man what you saw!"

Reluctantly, Henry found his tongue. "I saw a boy run out of the buffet," he said quietly, eyes focused by his feet on a green leaf lying out of place on the carefully tended sand platform. And then he looked up and pointed to the Third-Class car into which the thief had disappeared, the last before the post wagon. "I saw him go into that coach."

Without further ado, the officer took Henry by the shoulder and marched with him to the Third Class wagon. He grabbed Henry under the arms and hoisted him to the top of the stairs, then climbed up himself.

"Look in the car and see if you can find the vermin," the officer growled.

Henry cringed at the insult the command contained. He suddenly felt sorry for the boy. He looked into the darkened interior; the wagon had only a few small windows. Candles stuck to little shelves by their own tallow at each end of the car added a dim, flickering glow. Everywhere in the car people were crammed together, resting on benches or sleeping wherever space could be found on the floor. Bags and baskets were piled higgledy-piggledy in the crowded aisles and on the cramped benches beside the tired travelers.

Henry put his hand to his nose; he was startled by the rank smell pervading the crowded car. As his eyes became accustomed to the gloom he began to see more clearly. He noticed there was no padding to be found anywhere in the wagon and the thought crossed his mind of how uncomfortable it would be to ride in here. He saw men with matted beards and long tangled hair slouching against the walls and slumped on benches. Some were wearing dirty sheepskin coats. He could see that most had on the red shirts common to peasants, open at the throat and hanging over their breeches with a belt cinched overtop. The women wore drab, shapeless skirts with gaudy kerchiefs covering their heads. The children's clothing was ragged and dirty. Some of the peasants were chewing on chunks of sour black bread that they had softened by dipping in tea. Some of the peasants were smoking cigarettes. Because they preferred to travel with the windows closed, between the cigarettes and the mass of unwashed bodies and clothing, the stale air in the car was a foul cloud of reek and smoke that made Henry feel like he would gag at any moment.

Henry could think of nothing but getting out of the car as quickly as he could. His eyes darted back and forth; he could not see the boy. It was hopeless. But then, wait a minute. He looked again. There he was! He was sure of it. Against the far wall, partially hidden by a stack of sheepskins. He had raised his head for a peek and then ducked back down.

Henry pointed to where he had seen the boy. The officer gave a loud cough. Everyone in the car fell silent.

Knowing the game was up, an adult reached behind the pile. He stood up, bringing the boy with him, holding him by a handful of his hair. With his other hand the man grabbed the boy by the right ear and twisted hard. The boy gave a sharp yelp.

"You worthless piece of sheep's dung!" the man shouted. "What have you done now, you filthy little abomination!" And then quieter, under his breath, his lips barely moving, "Mother Mary and all the Saints, protect us!"

The man dragged the boy, still clutching the loaf of bread, to the officer. Both of them immediately fell to their knees in supplication.

"Your Honor, have mercy!" the man pleaded, looking at the officer's shiny black boots. "This boy is an imbecile. He didn't know what he was doing. He is too stupid! Have mercy!" His eyes darted to the side and he glanced over at Henry with a quick malevolent glare. Henry felt as if he had been kicked in the stomach, his breath knocked right out of him.

"Is he your son?" asked the officer.

The man gave a slight nod.

"You will come with me!" commanded the officer.

By now two policemen had climbed the steps into the car. They took the man and his son between them and exited the coach. As Henry climbed down the steps with shaky knees he saw them disappear into the station by a side door. As he returned to where his family waited, Henry began to cry. He angrily wiped the tears from his face lest anyone should see his weakness.

Henry was trembling as the train left the station a few minutes later. He watched for them, but the man and his son had not returned. He could not help but wonder at their fate.

When the train stopped at a station the next morning, the conductor knocked on the door of the Rempel's compartment. The air around him fairly sparked with his feeling of self-importance.

Without so much as a 'good morning,' he announced, "Madam von Rennenkampf, requests that your son join her for a few moments in her coach." He was looking at Heinrich. "Madam von Rennenkampf's husband is General Paul von Rennenkampf. He serves on the Tsar's General Staff," he proudly added. He looked at Henry. "Be quick! She must not be kept waiting!"

Heinrich nodded his permission and Henry followed the conductor to the First-Class coach. Inside he was led to a compartment much the same as those in the Second-Class car, but he was astonished to see how much more luxuriously it was decorated. It contained an upholstered chesterfield with fancy hardwood side-tables on each end. Ornate mirrors hung on the walls. The floor was covered in plush red carpet.

A stately matron of, perhaps, forty-five or fifty—Henry couldn't tell her age, she simply appeared to him to be old— wearing a green velvet dress was seated in a brown leather easy chair. Though the morning air was quite pleasant, she was nonetheless expertly wielding an intricately decorated Japanese fan. Her husband had brought it as a gift from the Far East where he had distinguished himself fighting in the Russo-Japanese war.

She smiled at Henry. "So you're the young man who caught that wretched thief yesterday! Good work!"

Awed by her aristocratic demeanor, Henry could think of nothing to say. In answer to her praise, he blushed scarlet. He was not so sure that his actions had been good. What had become of the boy and his father? The question irked him.

Madam von Rennenkampf eyed Henry for a moment. She saw a shy, somewhat frightened boy. He was cleanly dressed with neatly combed hair.

Having raised a family, Madam von Rennenkampf knew boys.

She asked, "Are you hungry?"

Still speechless, Henry could only nod. Without another word, Madam von Rennenkampf got up and took Henry by the hand. She walked to the door of her coach and called to the conductor. He briskly stepped forward. In response to her instructions he lifted Henry expertly from the top of the coach's stairway and placed him on the hardened yellow sand of the station platform. He then took the lady's hand and guided her down the stairway. Madam von Rennenkampf again took Henry's small hand in hers. Together, they marched through the doorway, into the First-Class buffet.

Henry could hardly take in the feast that greeted his eyes. Before him there was a table covered with white linen and loaded with platters of choice beefsteak, roast chicken and arrayed with bowls of boiled potatoes and vegetables. Henry noticed a basket of loaves of bread; it gave him a start to see them, but he quickly put any thoughts of the boy-thief aside. Another table held tureens of soup and china plates with slices of white and rye bread covered by serviettes. Bottles of Russian beer and wine stood to the side with prices clearly marked. Looking to his left he noticed a few people were eating at small tables spread with white linen. They held silver forks and knives in their hands. They glanced at Henry, but quickly forgot him as they returned to their meals and conversations.

On one table Henry saw bowls of shiny red and yellow apples. He looked up at Madam von Rennenkampf for permission. She smiled and encouraged him.

"Go ahead!"

Henry looked over the bowl of apples and chose the biggest he could find. Madam von Rennenkampf chuckled. She picked out three other apples, wrapped them in a serviette and gave them to Henry.

"Here, these are for your family," she said lightly.

Madam von Rennenkampf led Henry out of the Buffet. The conductor met them at the door. He took Henry back to his family in the Second-Class coach. When Henry proudly displayed the apples he had been given, his mother smiled broadly and his sisters squealed with excitement.

"Where does one get such fresh apples at this time of the year!" his father said in amazement.

As they rode the Trans-Siberian Railway toward the east, the Rempels occasionally caught glimpses of the remnants of the great Siberian Post Road that wound its way between the villages they passed. For hundreds of years the Post Road had been the path camel caravans carrying bricks of tea and other exotic wares from China to St. Petersburg and the great cities of Europe had traveled. It was also the road to exile for the criminals and dissidents of Tsarist Russia who walked eastward to Siberia in a march that would take months. Mail wagons overtook them and left the trudging convicts choking in the dust of their wake. Posting stations were spread the length of the Road at regular intervals of about forty kilometers where weary travelers would rest and eat.

There was constant activity on the road. The Rempels saw tarrantasses, four-wheeled wagons made of wood and held together with rope, and they also saw many telegas. The telega also was four-wheeled, but it carried its occupants in a large basket. The telega was infamous for its bone-jarring ride and penchant to break apart, but also for the ease with which it could be repaired. The horses pulling the wagons plodded through the dust and mud of the road, encouraged by the threat of the iemschik's whip, and the praises and insults of his tongue. They pulled their burden along the Trakt with the remembered whiff of hay in their nostrils drawing them over the barren steppe toward the rest and feed they knew awaited them at the next post.

Finally, at the dawning of the tenth day of their journey, the grand stone structure of the Kulomzino Railway Station was finally spotted faintly in the distance. It heralded the Rempel's arrival at their new home. As the train slowed for its approach, the station loomed before them in the early light and fog of the morning. It appeared to them mysterious and fortress-like.

As soon as the train stopped a ragged troop of porters in blue shirts and white aprons clambered into each car looking to carry luggage for the passengers. They scrambled about, fighting each other for clients. One porter made straight for Katy who was holding Joanna while gathering up her belongings. The porter quickly grabbed for her bags. With a wink and a smile on his grizzled face, he stated his price and proceeded toward the door with the bags firmly in his grasp.

But Katy would have none of it.

"No," she insisted, "I don't need you to carry my bags! We can manage!"

"*Pozhalujsta*. It is my pleasure, you're welcome Mother. The bags are heavy. You have your child and you are tired after your long journey." He turned toward the door.

"Give me my bags!" Katy cried sternly.

But the porter was not to be dissuaded. "*Nyet*! Allow me. I will carry them for you." He was almost at the door of the carriage. "See, I've almost done it already."

Heinrich had been busy collecting the rest of the family's baggage and so was slow to react to the situation. Before the porter could move any further toward the doorway, Heinrich abruptly stepped forward. He took the bags from the porter's hands.

"We don't need any help. *Spasiba*, thank you!" His words were spoken firmly.

Seeing he was defeated, the porter angrily shouted, "You rich people are all the same! You deny an honest worker his kopeck! Because of you my children will go hungry tonight!" He glared angrily at Heinrich. "Just wait! Your time is coming!" he exclaimed venomously.

The porter turned savagely and tripped over some luggage that had been left in his way. As he sprawled on the floor of the hallway between the compartments some watching passengers laughed. The porter got up and made a hasty retreat out of the car cursing loudly as he went.

As the Rempels stepped out of the car and down onto the station platform their fellow passengers reassured them.

"Don't be alarmed," they murmured as they passed by in the brisk morning air. "He's just a troublemaker. Think nothing of it. We Siberians are a much politer lot than that fellow. You'll see."

44

Kulomzino

1

The day after we first met, Henry came to the infirmary. He wanted to see if anything could be done to alleviate the suffering of his seasick family. He told me his mother and the two older sisters were in a very bad way.

Unfortunately, there was little I could do to bring relief from seasickness. I made a few suggestions and he looked defeated even before trying to implement them. He knew his family was not up to taking some fresh air on deck, away from their stateroom beds. And attempting to restore one's system's equilibrium by resting the eyes on the far horizon is difficult when the horizon is constantly hidden by fog. The best cure for seasickness is a calm sea.

He sat in silence for a moment and then looked at me. "May I ask a personal question?"

I nodded.

"You're English, yet you speak my language fluently. Where did you learn to speak German?"

I was not surprised by the question. All our conversations had been in German. I thought for a moment before I answered. I do not make it a practice to become personally involved with patients. I could make an off-hand comment about enjoying languages and finding them easy to learn, which would have been true. But there was something about Henry that appealed to me. Perhaps in Henry I saw a figment of the son I never had. I decided to open up a bit.

"Not only do I speak German, but I speak Russian as well."

He gave a start of surprise and smiled. *"Vy govorite po-russki?* You speak Russian?"

"Da!"

"We never spoke Russian at home," Henry said. "I learned it on the street, playing with the neighborhood kids."

That led to a conversation about the Russian language and the nuances of meaning it so cleverly conveys. The

Russians have a wonderful way of capturing life's truths in simple phrases that at the same time display their dry sense of humor in the face of life's calamities. God knows they've had lots of opportunity to practice! I gave him my favorite, a saying as old and as true as Time itself.

"*Kazhdij po svoemu s uma shodit.* Everyone goes crazy in their own way!"

We enjoyed a good laugh.

I told him how I came to be fluent in German and Russian. I learned both languages when I was a prisoner of war, from 1914 to 1916. I had been serving as a doctor with the Portsmouth Battalion of the Royal Naval Division. Toward the end of October 1914, the battalion was sent to Belgium. The war was barely two months along. We were attempting to hold Antwerp against a German attack. No sooner had we arrived than we discovered we were vastly outnumbered and poorly equipped for the fight. During the battle our communications lines quickly disintegrated. It was a shambles. The end result was that I was captured by the Bosch, along with nine hundred Portsmouth marines, .

We were taken to the detention camp at Doeberitz, about a hundred kilometers west of Berlin. Because I was a doctor, I was put to work in the camp hospital as an aide to the lone German physician. Very quickly I learned that if I wanted to work with the Germans and help my fellow prisoners, I would need to speak their language, and speak it well. There's nothing like adversity to focus the mind. After about three months, I was dreaming in German.

I learned Russian because there were more Russian prisoners of war in the camp than there were English. The suffering experienced by the Russians was far worse than what the rest of us had to endure because they had no help from the outside. To supplement the meager food given us by our keepers, most of us received packages from home and from the Red Cross. The Russians didn't. They got nothing at all. The conditions under which they lived were atrocious. As a result, they were a hungry, dirty, ragged lot. They were poorly fed and were plagued by bug infestations and disease. In fact, prisoners of other nationalities complained to the camp administrator so loudly about the dirty condition of the Russians that the Russians were kept separate from the rest of us. They were crowded into their own little ghetto within the camp. Many became sick with influenza and tuberculosis and were patients in the hospital. Many died. On more evenings than I care to remember I found myself writing a letter from a dying Russian to his mother, or his wife, or girl friend. I doubt if any ever got mailed. The Germans treated the Russians worse than animals.

After a moment, Henry remarked thoughtfully, "Many Mennonite men became medical workers in the Russian army. Many of them did not return home after the war."

That's when he told me about his father's opposition to war and his years in the alternative service forestry camp at Anadol.

"The Bible teaches us to love our enemies," Henry said without conviction. And with a dark look he concluded, "I could never love the bastard who molested my sister. If given the chance, I think I would strangle him."

He received no argument from me.

2

The year from the summer of 1913 to the summer of 1914 was a time of hard work and happiness for the Rempel family.

Because of the success of the Heinrich's Arkadak mill, the circumstances of their arrival in Kulomzino were completely different than they had been in 1906. Two months before moving to the town, Heinrich Rempel had gone ahead to make preparations for their arrival. He purchased a plot of land—what we might judge to be about a third of an acre—on the corner of Irtysh and Ermak streets where the family would live and operate the farm machinery business. Heinrich was very excited that their location was close to the railway station; it was only about a kilometer away. Their plot of land was an excellent location from which to run a business dependent on the railroad for the transportation of its inventory. Heinrich's plan was for the family home to be the last structure built on the property, so he also rented a furnished dacha in which to live in the meantime.

When they arrived in Kulomzino a hired droshky carried the family from the railway station to their temporary home. When they got there, they saw that it was completely surrounded by silver birch trees so that, in order to get to the front door, it felt like the family had to walk through a short path in the woods. Along the walkway, sprays of brown grass poked out of a thin blanket of rotting snow, last autumn's decay displayed in the last gasp of winter's siege. Green sprigs were beginning to bud on low bushes growing among the birch. Though it was the end of May, spring came late in Siberia.

As they viewed the dacha for the first time, the family was completely taken in by its charm and beauty. It was built of logs with six shuttered windows on its front wall, three on either side of a wide wooden door. Above each window was a triangular, intricately carved cap painted white. The whole length of the house was decorated with similarly carved and painted barge boarding on the fascia. On the wall immediately below the overhang of the roof was a narrow row of vertical batten siding. Another row of carved designs below that were seated just above the window caps. The combination of white painted decorations, brown siding and weathered log walls on the dacha had a magical effect; the dacha looked like a cottage out of a fairy tale!

Heinrich unlocked and opened the front door. The family gasped in wonder as they stepped inside. The walls were covered with elegant striped wallpaper topped by elaborate scroll-carved borders. The ceiling was divided into symmetrical, rectangular sections framed by crown moldings and was painted in pastel shades of green and blue. At the center of the dacha was a huge brick Russian oven, large enough to heat the entire house during the cold Siberian nights.

Looking out the back door, Heinrich discovered the house had been built right next to the banks of the Irtysh River. That evening, as they relaxed under the trees in the back yard, the family thought of their good fortune, surely the result of God's blessing. They marveled at the beautiful vista looking from their new home, over the Irtysh, to the twinkling electric lights of the city of Omsk on the other side of the river. The sun was setting in the west, but in the eastern sky above Omsk, the clouds seemed a riot of flames while below them the river burned with the reflected reds and oranges of the sunset.

3

Almost immediately, construction began on Heinrich Rempel's warehouse. Spring is short in west Siberia. Two or three weeks and the transition from winter to summer is completed. Only four months from mid-May to mid-September can be counted on to be relatively frost-free. A short autumn is followed by six months of snow and temperatures regularly dipping below minus 45. There was no time to waste. The warehouse would provide the space where the farm implements Heinrich planned to sell could be displayed as well as an apartment that would house a hired man and his family. By building the warehouse first, Heinrich could open his business and begin generating an income while the family's home was being built. The warehouse would face west along Irtysh Street.

Their dacha was an easy thirty-minute walk on the flat streets of Kulomzino to their lot at the corner of Irtysh and Ermak. In the days and months that followed, Heinrich and Henry would arrive at the property early each morning, just as the crew of workmen began their work for the day. He had hired them on the recommendation of Peter Wiens, a Mennonite pioneer and respected businessman in the area.

Sundays were the only days when work was halted at the Rempel site. They were a day of rest, if rest it could be called. The family would get up early, dress in their Sunday best, clothes worn on that day alone: suits, dresses, coats and hats, and shoes carefully polished the night before. At nine o'clock, Butcher Giesbrecht would come to collect them in his troika, a droshky pulled by three horses. They would travel the twelve kilometers to Tschunayevka, a small Mennonite village southwest of Kulomzino, to attend the worship service at the Mennonite Brethren Church. After church they would often go to Pastor Heinrich Ewert's home for lunch. Ewert's wife, Maria, would serve lunches of cold roast beef and potatoes with pie for dessert.

Adult conversation around the table would stretch well into the afternoon while the children played games in the yard. Discussions often centered on theology and the morning's sermon, before straying to other issues of concern. The political situation in Russia weighed on all of them, for lately the news was seldom good. The disappointing showing by the Octobrist Party in the fourth Duma elections the previous year was alarming because it seemed to show a loss of confidence in the ability of moderate political policies to improve the lot of ordinary Russians. There were rumors of strikes and unrest among miners and workers in factories. The radical Bolsheviks seemed to be gaining in popularity. Equally as alarming was yet another war over possession of the Balkans being waged between Bulgaria, Greece and Serbia in Macedonia. The war began in June and though it was settled by August the peace was, apparently, an uneasy one. In their conversations, sometimes theology and politics became muddled, as when they pondered whether God had really healed the Tsar's son by means of a telegram sent by that strange monk Rasputin, as had been reported in the newspapers.

It was on one such Sunday that Heinrich met Johann Isaak. Isaak was another prosperous Mennonite pioneer in Kulomzino, who, in 1902, had sold land to a group of businessmen who then built the Kulomzino railway station. Among his many enterprises was a five-storey steam-driven flourmill in Kulomzino. It soon came out that Isaak wanted to sell shares in his Kulomzino mill in order to raise capital to begin another business venture. Heinrich immediately jumped at the idea. With the projected opening of his farm implement business at least a year away, his interest in the mill would provide his family with an income during the interim.

On a Tuesday afternoon in June, Heinrich and Johann Isaak met with their banker, Jakob Hildebrandt, in his office on Atamanskaya Street in Omsk. The deal was made. Profits would be shared equally between the two partners.

In the meantime, construction of the warehouse continued. It would be built of red brick atop a stone foundation and measure eighty feet by twenty. The front would feature four windows on each side of a large double door that was centered on the wall and would be used for moving farm implements into and out of the warehouse. Smaller doors would be installed on each end: at one end for warehouse use and at the other end to access the hired man's apartment. The back wall would have eight small windows spaced along its length. They would be higher on the wall and provide extra light as well as air circulation on hot summer days. The roof would be covered in corrugated tin.

One of Heinrich's laborers was a small, wiry Siberian named Sergei, whose weathered skin folded in wrinkles around eyes that were as dark as his scruffy black beard. Sergei was a skilled bricklayer. He was also a bit of a peacock. Consequently, his hapless helper, Vasily, who was eager, but a little dim, was often the object of ridicule and abuse.

"Vasily Vasileyevich, *ty durak*! Ya numbskull!" Sergei would shout, "How many times must I show ya how to make a straight row of them bricks? See this'n? An' this?" He would jab his gnarled finger at a brick that wasn't perfectly aligned. "We are not buildin' an elbow to follow the banks of the Irtysh River. We're buildin' a wall. It's gotta be straight! Straight, I tell ya!"

And as he spoke Sergei would administer a firm clout to the back of Vasily's head. Sergei would then tear apart the substandard work and redo it carefully, exclaiming as he did so how much better it looked.

"There, Vasily Vasileyevich. Take a lesson from the master," he would crow.

Vasily, with his bristly eye-brows sticking out like bunch grass on the steppe and his crooked teeth protruding from beneath his bushy grey mustache, would grin, shuffle his feet, and continue working slowly and methodically, if also imperfectly.

4

The summer passed quickly as the warehouse was built. Heinrich, always dressed to the nines in his three-piece suit, tie, and bowler hat, watched closely to ensure that things were done to his liking. Henry enjoyed playing imaginary games in the grass, in the shade created by the wide-spreading leafy branches of the large Siberian elm tree that grew right in the center of the lot. Often he shadowed Sergei as he worked. He was awed by the Siberian's skill with brick and mortar and quite taken in by his strong personality.

One day, Henry announced proudly to Sergei, "When I am grown up, I am going to be a bricklayer. I am going build Mama and Papa the best house in all of Russia!"

"Oh, will ya now!"

"I will build many big houses and I will become very rich!"

Like most Russian muzhiks, Sergei was a very superstitious man. He also loved to tell stories.

Sergei laughed aloud. "Be careful what ya say, ya little fool! Ya don't wanna get too far ahead of yerself now! There's many afore ya done the same and lived to be sorry. I've got a story for ya, so listen close.

"A poor muzhik saw a rabbit sittin' under a willow bush and was extremely happy. He said to himself, 'I'm the luckiest man in all of Russia! I will catch this rabbit, kill it with a club, an' sell it for ten kopecks. With my ten kopecks I'll go out an' buy a sow. She'll give me ten piglets. The ten piglets'll grow up and from each one of 'em I'll get ten more piglets. Think of all the piglets that'll be born. I'll start slaughterin' pigs and I'll have more meat ta sell than I'll know what to do with.' And he rubbed his hands together with glee. 'With the money I make sellin' pigs I'll buy a fancy house an' get married. My wife'll bear me two sons, Sasha and Yasha. I'll hire some workers ta plow the field. I'll sit by the window every day an' enjoy the afternoon breeze. I'll shout to my boys as they drink tea an' laugh at the workers. 'Hey, Sasha and Yasha,' I'll say. 'Apparently ya've never experienced poverty!'"

Sergei winked and continued, "Well, let me tell ya. The muzhik shouted the words so loudly as he ran ta catch the rabbit that the rabbit heard him and ran off. Along with the rabbit went the muzhik's pigs, his house, his wife, his sons and all his riches."

Henry blinked his eyes in surprise and frowned.

"Ha, ha, ha!" laughed Sergei, enjoying the effect of his story. He looked Henry in the eye and wagged his sausage finger in this face. "So, dream a little, boy, but remember, dreamin' don't put bread on the table!"

Henry determined that he would never be like the foolish muzhik. He would work hard, just like Sergei. From that day, he watched Sergei closely to learn all he could from him.

On another day, they were eating their lunch. Henry had noticed that when Sergei had an apple he ate it all, including the core and seeds. Sergei kept urging Henry to do the same. Henry tried, but the thick skin of the core and the hard seeds turned his stomach. He could not get himself to swallow.

"Ya must eat all o' yer apple," Sergei said. "Ya never know. One day there may be no apples, and yer stomach will shrink from hunger. Ya must never waste food, boy."

Henry looked worried. He had always had enough to eat in Arkadak. "Do you run out of food in Siberia?"

Sergei lifted a handful of dirt from beside where he was sitting.

"Look at this rich, black earth. It is God's gift ta us. The food we can grow here, ha! Ya've never seen the likes of it!"

Sergei waved his hand in the air to emphasize his words, spraying the soil about, and promptly launched into another story while Henry brushed off the bits that had landed in his hair.

"There was an old muzhik and his wife who lived just down the street from here. Of course, there was no street back then, ya know, just the old peasant and his wife, with a few miserable neighbors nearby. They all lived in mud huts with dirt floors and thatched roofs. That was in the days when the only real business around here was the post station for the Trakt road.

"One year the old muzhik and his wife put in a garden, as they always did, plantin' peas, carrots, turnips and potatoes. They carefully watered the seeds and watched as the tiny green sprouts began ta grow. All through the summer they watered and weeded until, in fall, it was time to harvest their crop. They picked the peas and pulled the carrots and turnips. They carefully stored them in their root cellar and were very happy that they would have vegetables ta eat in the coming winter. But, the darndest thing was, they couldn't find no potatoes. There were three rows of potato greens, but as they dug, there just weren't no potatoes. But that didn't slow them down. They continued ta dig through the potato patch until one day they got the surprise of their life. What should they find, but one potato! One!" Sergei clapped his hands together to emphasize his point. "And what a potato it was! It was enormous! Humungous!"

Sergei got up and walked around in a circle, making a mark by dragging a stick on the ground to show how very big the potato really was.

"The muzhik and his wife called their neighbors ta have a look. No one had ever seen anythin' like it. The potato was so huge they soon realized they could not hope ta pick it out o' the ground. All of them together could not lift it! It was that big and that heavy! What should they do? They scratched their heads as they talked about the problem." Being a showman, Sergei scratched his head and tried to look perplexed. "The next day, after doing some serious thinkin', the muzhik told his wife, 'Let's cover the potato with enough dirt so that it won't freeze in winter. Then, when we or our neighbors need potatoes for our borscht, we can go and cut out what we need.'

So that is what they did. And all of that winter they had enough potato and ta spare and their neighbors had plenty as well!

"*Da*, the fine black earth of Mother Russia will take care of you if you work hard, little one."

Sergei looked over to where Vasily was lounging.

"Hey durak, *chaj pit' nje drova rubit'*. Drinking tea isn't chopping wood. There's work to be done. Get to it!"

5

A week after their arrival at the dacha in late May, Katy discovered a large patch in the back yard that had once been used as a garden. She and Katarina worked hard preparing the soil and then planted rows of cabbages, potatoes, beets, carrots, cucumbers and onions. As summer turned into autumn, they were kept busy preserving vegetables. Some were pickled. With the cabbage they made sauerkraut. The potatoes were stored in sacks in the cold cellar, reached by climbing down a ladder under a cleverly disguised trap door they discovered beneath the kitchen table.

With the end of summer also came the time to enroll Katarina and Henry in school. Since there were quite a number of Mennonites living in Kulomzino and on the surrounding steppes, a school had been opened on Nicholsky Avenue, at the corner of Prince Vladimir Street in 1911. It was a two-storey building with a low-pitched roof and fancy brickwork decorations above and below the windows on each floor. Tall broad-leafed maple trees stood along the street at regular intervals.   The school provided the Mennonite children with an education in German that included, not only the basics of reading, writing, and arithmetic, but also the foundations of their faith. Much to Henry's dismay, days were now spent seated at a desk copying exercises from the blackboard into a notebook or listening to his teacher, Mr. Dietrich Wiebe.

Winter struck with a vengeance in November. Activity on the corner lot at Irtysh and Ermak streets slowed to a crawl. Still, Heinrich was pleased with what had been accomplished. The corrugated tin roof was fastened to the wooden rafters of the warehouse. Solid wooden doors were hung. Shutters were installed in the brick window wells and a strong floor of stout pine boards was laid.

The weather was far colder and snowier than any they had experienced in South Russia. The Rempels struggled with the cold, but it seemed to them that the firmer the grip of winter, the happier their Siberian neighbors became.

"This is the life; the best time of the year!" they happily declared. "The summer is all heat and wind and dust. Now you'll see what life in Siberia is really all about, when the roads are icy and the snow-banks are high!" Wearing their warm reindeer hide coats with the fur side out, they shouted gleefully, "Snow and cold make for the best sledging!" They urged their willing horses to pull their sledges ever faster along the snowy roads and over the ice-covered Irtysh, occasionally tipping over into the snow banks just for fun of it. Faces covered in snow, they would climb back on the sleighs laughing and coughing as the icy crystals stung their lungs. And then, with a shout at the blowing horses, off they went again.

The children at school taught Katarina and Henry how to make a *snegovik*, a snowman, by piling balls of snow atop each other. They decorated their *snegoviki* with hats and scarves. When their makers weren't looking, they raided each other's snow sculptures and, with excited shouts and gleeful laughter, happily destroyed them.

At home, Katy spent hours sewing and mending their hard-worn clothing. In the evenings Katarina helped and gradually became skilful with needle and thread. When the mending was complete, cross-stitching became a passion and their creations were proudly hung on the walls.

6

Katy and Heinrich also became friends with their neighbors, Yevgeni and Sveta Bartok. Sveta Bartok was very attractive with her blue eyes, blonde hair and high Slavic cheekbones. She was the mother of four very noisy children, who, whenever the weather allowed it, were sent outside to play in the snow with Katarina, Henry and Joanna. Sveta's bespectacled husband, Yevgeni, who always appeared disheveled no matter how much effort he put into dressing, worked in a bank in Omsk.

One day, while Heinrich and Yevgeni discussed business and politics, Sveta showed Katy how to make pelmeni, little dumplings loved by Siberians.

"They're just like our pirogies, only smaller," remarked Katy in delight.

Sveta and Katy rolled flavored ground beef into dozens of little balls and wrap them in thin slices of unleavened dough. It became a competition, with each seeing if she could make her pelmeni smaller than the other. Those that weren't used for that evening's meal were placed in glass jars and put outside to freeze. There they were left until pelmenyi was again on the menu.

During the winter, Heinrich poured over the pamphlets he had received from Deere and Company in America, deciding which implements he would order for his first inventory. He was especially impressed with what he learned about the new tractors. One, the Big Four "30" gas tractor produced an astounding twenty horsepower at the draw bar. The thought was astonishing: the equivalent of twenty horses all pulling together! He could hardly contain his excitement as he thought about all that power so easily and efficiently put to use! Farmers would be unable to resist harnessing such power as they looked for easier ways to plow their fields!

When he knew what he wanted to order, Henry made the sledge trip across the frozen Irtysh to make arrangements through the A. Gashin and Sons Trading Company on Lyubinsky Avenue across the street from the imposing two-storey baroque-style Moscow Shopping Arcade. He was dazzled by the beautiful architecture of the many buildings in the mercantile center bounded by Lyubinsky Avenue, the market-square, and Atamanskaya, Dvortsovaya, and Kaznakovskaya Streets that had earned Omsk the prestigious label of "The Chicago of Siberia."

Heinrich was disappointed to learn there were not enough tractors being built for them to be exported to Russia. Plows, though, were a different story. Deere and Company had an excellent reputation. Their plows were setting the standard for farming technology. He was promised that his order would be placed immediately and that delivery from the United States could be expected in several months, probably in late summer or, at the latest, early in the fall of 1914.

Heinrich returned home with the hope and expectation of good things to come. He gave himself to caring for his family and enjoying the interlude that the cold of winter brought him. On many days, he busied himself with the chores of chopping and piling the wood needed to keep the fire in the big Russian stove burning. He also carried from the well in the backyard the buckets of water that were required each day for drinking, cooking and washing.

When he wasn't busy with chores, Heinrich spent hours drawing blueprints for his house and planning the building to be undertaken in the coming spring. On some days he chafed at the forced inactivity and restlessly prowled about the dacha as he waited for the weather to moderate. He longed for the return of the days of green, and warm sunshine.

In a fit of boredom one January morning, when the icy temperature of minus sixty actually made going outdoors a truly dangerous proposition, Heinrich decided to try his hand at scrollwork. He had always marveled at the intricacy of the decorations on so many Siberian houses. After a visit at the Bartok's where he had commented on a beautifully made piece of scrollwork, Yevgeni had brought over a small jigsaw. Heinrich practiced for a few days on old scraps of wood and found that he enjoyed the work. He soon began by creating small compositions that contained leafy ornamentations.

When Henry was not at school, he loved to watch his father at his creative work. He pestered him for permission to give it a try himself. Henry had already drawn a simple design on his own thin board. Heinrich let his son use the saw on his own creation. He encouraged Henry and showed him how to hold the saw in order to make a perfect circular cut.

Afterward, Heinrich showed his son how to smooth the finished work by sanding with the grain, not against it.

"If you keep that up, you'll soon be better than me!" he proudly complimented his beaming son.

As Heinrich gained confidence, he moved on to make decorative cuts that included wise sayings. Over the course of the first week of February 1914, using a thin piece of dark walnut, he painstakingly sawed the motto,

Today is the tomorrow
we worried about yesterday
and all is well.

Making Friends

1

In March of the new year, Heinrich made a trip to the Borodin Company in Omsk and purchased the logs and other sawn lumber he would need for a summer kitchen. It would be a small, four-room log cabin with a large porch and easily accessible by a short walk from the future family home. Temperatures on the Kalunda Steppe often reached 40 degrees Celsius and higher in summer. As far as Katy was concerned a summer kitchen, which had been a necessity in the hot climate of South Russia, was a must for her new home in Siberia. It was imperative that the logs be delivered as soon as possible. If left too long and temperatures began to warm, a month of muddy roads would make heavy transport impossible and the project would be far behind schedule. Heinrich paid the grinning salesman a hefty premium in "tea money." He didn't like to think of it as a bribe. Still, a gift of rubles was always the best way to ensure prompt service.

The pine logs for the summer kitchen, loaded on low sleds drawn by powerful teams of straining horses, arrived while the snow-covered ground was still frozen solid as slate. Sweating men using long pike poles grunted and cursed with the effort of rolling the logs off the sledges. Meanwhile, the harnessed horses stood stamping their great hooves on the iron-earth and a fog enveloped them from the steam rising from their bulky, hot bodies.

As the grip of winter began to weaken, work began in earnest. Bundled in their sheepskin coats and hats, the hired men worked tirelessly with axe and saw, huffing clouds of steam all the while. On some days the cold was extreme and icicles formed on their mustaches and beards. They laughed at the sight of each other's faces and continued without giving a thought to the elements. They were tough men, bred and born in Siberia. They were used to the cold and snow. And anyway, a swallow or two of vodka helped to warm the body in ways sheepskin never could.

One day in April, Henry came home from school looking dejected and sad. Katy tried to get him to talk to her but he refused. That evening, at the supper table, Heinrich prodded him.

"Henry, you are very quiet tonight. Is anything the matter?"

Henry looked downcast. "The Tsar's birthday is in May. To celebrate, all the school children of Omsk are going to march in a huge parade in front of the Governor General. Our school is marching, too! But it's only for the older students. I can't be in the parade because I'm too little. Katarina gets to go, but I can't. It's not fair!"

Heinrich thought for a moment. "Well," said his father, "perhaps we can go as a family and watch the parade. Would you like that?"

So it was that on May 9, the day celebrating Tsar Nicholas II's birth, the Rempels took the crowded ferry from Kulomzino, across the Irtysh River, to Omsk. They joined throngs of people trudging to the square in front of the Nicholai Cathedral where the festivities would take place. Once there they soon found a place amongst the crowd of spectators.

The Rempels could hardly believe their eyes at what they saw. On a platform that had been erected in front of the onion domed cathedral sat all the city's dignitaries in their colorful, elaborate uniforms. Standing at attention in the square before the platform was a sea of soldiers. "Twenty thousand!" the people around them were saying. There were soldiers representing the cavalry, infantry, and artillery. Cadets from the Military Academy stood proudly in their rows. Each group was dressed in its distinctive uniforms. The men held their rifles stiffly on their shoulders. And off to one side, hundreds of students from all over Omsk stood at attention in their school groups.

Henry complained to his father that he couldn't see, so Heinrich hoisted him onto his shoulders. From this vantage point, Henry scanned the field until he found the students representing the Mennonite school. Their columns were small in number, but the students looked smart in their uniforms of dark grey pants and light yellow shirts. The shiny brass buckles on their belts gleamed brightly in the sunlight.

"There's Katyusha!" he exclaimed when he spotted his sister.

It seemed to take forever for the festivities to begin. Everyone waited in the growing heat of the day. A wind started to pick up. Small dust devils whirled here and there. Finally, the grey-bearded Archbishop of Omsk came forward and offered a prayer of blessing. Only those close by could hear him, but the crowd followed his hand motions and crossed themselves after he finished. Then, accompanied by the military bands, the entire assembly sang the Prayer for the Tsar, "We pray for the power of love." Hearing the untold thousands of voices singing for the beloved Tsar gave Henry shivers up and down his body, from the top of his head to the tips of his toes.

Next, the Tsar's representative, Governor Otto Karlovich Schmidt, stepped forward. Rows of medals decorated his broad chest and he held his golden Staff of Office. The Governor General walked off the platform onto the parade ground. He strolled along in front of each group of soldiers and students, greeted them, and thanked them for their participation. Each group made a short, loud, shout of response. When the Governor General had talked to every group, which seemed to Henry to take hours, he returned to the stage. The bands immediately started playing the National Hymn and all the people in the square joined in singing. As the song ended, a General on horseback rode out in front of the assembled throng. He swept a polished sword out of its scabbard and waved it high in the air above him shouting, "Three hurrahs for Tsar Nicholas!"

Everyone shouted, "Hurrah!" three times with great enthusiasm. They had barely finished when cannons boomed their loud praise to the Tsar of All the Russias in three great, ear-splitting volleys.

With that, the parade began. The officer cadets were in the lead as they marched passed the dignitaries. Men who had come from all over Russia to train at the Military Academy in Omsk smartly turned their faces toward the stage as they marched by. They lifted their legs high and stepped forward as one as they set the pace for the thousands who came behind. The impact of twenty thousand feet stamping the ground in time sent vibrations up the legs of the spectators.

The cadets were followed by soldiers from the infantry divisions. After the infantry came the cavalry, mounted on their snorting, high stepping mounts. Next the artillery paraded by, their mounted cannons pulled by straining horses. The wheels of the caissons carrying the cannons lifted clouds of dirt as they turned, which trailed off like smoke in the wind. There were more cannons than Henry could count. Finally, the children of Omsk marched by the grandstand, proudly parading in their school groupings for the officials seated there.

It wasn't until late in the afternoon that the festivities were finally over. There would be fireworks that evening, but for many the long trip home meant they would have to miss the colorful spectacle. Tired and hungry, the crowds dispersed. The Rempels wearily took the ferry home to Kolumzino.

When they arrived at the dacha, Heinrich was in a reflective mood.

"Henry," he said, "what do you think all those soldiers with their guns and horses and cannons are for?"

Henry had seen a few soldiers here and there, but never the armed multitude he had watched this day. He could think of no answer. The parade had been impressive, but parading could hardly be the reason for the existence of so many armed men.

"Their job, Henry, is to protect Russia. Their purpose is to kill Russia's enemies." He paused. "However, we do not believe in killing our enemies, do we?"

"No," replied Henry, "God will keep us safe."

"That is what we believe," affirmed his father.

Heinrich looked at Katy and remarked soberly, "It is ironic that we thousands stood together singing, 'We pray for the power of love,' at the top of our voices and then watched as the power of the gun was paraded before us."

3

All through the summer of 1914, Heinrich continued his routine of supervising the work on his property at the corner of Irtysh and Ermak. As soon as school had recessed for the summer break, Henry had also resumed his daily trips with his father.

On their walks to the lot, Heinrich strode purposefully and seldom looked to the right or left. Henry's eyes, on the other hand, were seldom still. Most houses were bordered by high wooden fences made of old weathered slats of wood. Many of the fences were in sorry states of disrepair, with boards missing or lying about ignored on the ground, and gates hanging askew. The large, gaping holes in the fences made convenient windows into the forbidden worlds beyond. Henry was always looking, searching to discover the secrets behind the fences. What did the houses look like inside? Who lived in them? What did the people look like? What were they doing? At one house, Henry sometimes caught glimpses of a barefoot boy with a mop of shaggy black hair on his head. The boy invariably was playing by himself or with a large black dog. Henry even made eye contact with him on a few occasions. However, being shy, it never occurred to Henry to shout out a greeting and the boy paid him little attention.

One day in July, when the glaring sun was beating with unrelenting violence out of a cloudless sky, as if trying to make up in twelve hours for its negligent absence during the frozen days of January, Henry was again sitting in the shade of the Siberian elm tree. The construction was happening on two sides of it, and when the family home would be built next year on the third spoke, the tree would form the hub around which the activity on the yard would rotate. Besides the shade from the tree, an intermittent breeze helped bring some relief from the heat of the afternoon, though the dust carried on the breeze created its own annoyance.

Henry was drawing a picture in his sketchbook of a small brown dog that belonged to the neighbor across the street. It lay panting in the shade of the elm a little off to his left. The sketchbook had been a gift from his teacher at the end of the school year as an acknowledgement of Henry's artistic ability. As Henry drew he became aware of a rustling sound, a passing shadow and then of the stares that came over his shoulder as someone sat down on the grass beside him. Henry was absorbed in his work and did not want to miss the chance of finishing his drawing while the dog lay still, so he chose not to acknowledge his visitor.

A puff of wind lifted the corner of the page. As he smoothed it down, Henry looked around at his visitor and recognition dawned on his face.

"I've seen you before, in the yard by the house down the road. You have a really big dog. Is it yours?"

While he talked, Henry erased a front leg on his drawing. It just didn't look right. How could he capture the perspective? He drew the leg again, using the side of the pencil to create shadow. He took a long slow breath and let it out.

When the boy remained silent, Henry introduced himself. "My name is Henry Rempel." He continued sketching, making sure that the dog's tongue in his picture looked as naturally limp as he could make it. "What's your name?"

"Anatoly Fyodorovich Lepinov. And Sasha isn't mine. He belongs to my dad."

Anatoly picked up some dirt and threw it at the sleeping dog. It landed on the dog's face. The dog sneezed and rubbed its eyes with its paws, first the right and then the left.

Henry looked at Anatoly in surprise. "Why'd you do that?"

"I dunno," Anatoly said with a grin. "Anyway, I like your picture. And you can call me Tolya. Everyone else does."

Henry showed Anatoly a few other pictures he'd done in the sketchbook. For a seven-year-old, he had a good sense of perspective and the use of shading to create areas of light and dark with a three dimensional feel. Anatoly looked at the pictures, making grunting noises in his amazement at Henry's talent.

Their visit was interrupted when Anatoly noticed Heinrich looking his way. He asked, "That guy in the fancy duds. Is that your dad?" Heinrich was in his three-piece suit and tie, as usual.

"Yes."

"Is he rich or somethin'?"

Henry was puzzled by the question and didn't know what to say.

"He looks rich," Anatoly muttered. "My dad says to watch out for kulaks and such, landowners and rich people who make sure the rest of us have barely enough bread to survive." He looked at Henry and smirked. "But he says not to worry, things are gonna change! And soon!" And without so much as a '*do svidaniya*, good-bye,' or even a backward glance, he quickly got up and left.

Later Henry asked his father if they were rich. Heinrich simply answered by saying that God had blessed them for their devotion and hard work. When Henry asked why the days of the rich were numbered, Heinrich only looked troubled and asked Henry where he had heard such rubbish. Henry suddenly got an uncomfortable feeling that he was somehow betraying a confidence. So he replied that he'd heard some men speaking in the street.

A few days later Anatoly was back. Henry was watching as a carpenter chiseled indentations for the door hinges into the pale, knotted pine board where the front door of the summer kitchen was soon to be fastened. The carpenter was an old Mennonite fellow named Nachtigal. Nachtigal had huge ears out of which hair grew in great clumps. Henry found it amusing to imagine tiny creatures creeping about in the bristly peaks and valleys of Nachtigal's ears and would giggle hilariously, much to Nachtigal's disgust, who knew he was being laughed at, but could never figure out why. Nachtigal was quite a skilled carpenter and Henry, for once, was engrossed in what he was doing.

"Hello, Henry," Anatoly said as he climbed the front steps and acted as if their previous conversation had never happened. He gazed intently at the log structure and watched as wood chips flew in all directions accompanied by the sharp percussion of hammer on chisel.

"Hi, Tolya. I thought you don't like rich people. What are you doing here? Anyway, my dad says we're not rich."

"Yeah, well," Anatoly's retort was noncommittal. "By the way, what is this building?" He had never seen a summer kitchen before. He gave Henry a peculiar look, narrowing his eyes and pursing his lips. "It looks pretty small for a house. Maybe it's a rich man's crapper you're building here. I betcha that's what it is."

Henry had almost had enough of this rude fellow. His face began to redden and he tightened his fists by his sides.

At that moment Heinrich noticed the two boys talking together. He could almost see the steam coming out of Henry's ears. Knowing his son, he wondered what could have happened to make him so angry.

He called out, "Come here, boys! Introduce me to your new friend, Henry."

Henry took a deep breath and unclenched his fists.

"He's not my friend. His name is Anatoly. He lives down the street."

Anatoly looked nervous and shifted his weight back and forth from one foot to the other as if he really wanted to be somewhere else and would leave at any second. Heinrich shook Anatoly's hand and smiled at him.

"How old are you Anatoly?"

"Nine."

"Well, I'm very pleased to make your acquaintance. I've seen you before, playing in your yard. Since we're going to be neighbors, I would really like to meet your father. What's his name?"

"My father is Fyodor Alexandrovich Lepinov. He works at the railway yard," Anatoly stated proudly. "He's a Bolshevik!"

Heinrich chose to ignore the last comment.

"Oh, and what does your father do when he is working at the rail yard?"

"I dunno. He's a machinist or a mechanic or somethin'. He fixes things. Engines, whatever's broken."

"And your mother? Does she know you are here? She must be worried that you are not at home."

"Oh no," Anatoly said off-handedly. "She keeps busy in the house and always tells me ta find something ta do so that I'm not botherin' her. She doesn't care where I am."

Anatoly didn't want to tell this nosey stranger that his mother was very fond of vodka and spent most days alone in the kitchen, working on her bottle.

Anatoly's reply brought a disapproving frown from Heinrich, for whom the parent's responsibility in caring for the child was of absolute importance. What could be more important than raising one's offspring? "Children are a gift from God!" he would often exclaim.

Heinrich came to a quick decision.

"Well then! I've got a job for the two of you that will give you something useful to do. Are you interested?"

Anatoly and Henry looked at each other doubtfully and shrugged their shoulders.

Heinrich was not to be deterred. The best way to end a conflict before it got out of hand is to have the combatants work to a common purpose, he thought.

"All right then. We've got a great big pile of sawdust and shavings from cutting the logs and scraping the bark off of them. There are also lots of chips lying about from making notches in the logs. Now listen. In the warehouse you will find some cloth sacks lying by the side door on the south end. Henry, how about if you get some sacks. Anatoly can find a shovel. There's one leaning on the wall close to where the bags are lying. One of you can shovel sawdust into a bag while the other holds it open. Keep the bark, chips and wood scraps separate in their own bags. You can carry the filled bags to the street and sell them to people who pass by. See how much money you can get for them. Everyone is always looking for good wood for fuel.

Anatoly looked at Heinrich suspiciously. "And what will I get for helpin' you? A pat on the head an' a kick in the behind and a, 'Off you go now, you're not needed anymore?' Bread isn't free and I'm hungry all the time. My dad says I'm developin' a hollow leg!"

Heinrich chuckled. This Anatoly might one day make a fine businessman! "What if I give the two of you half of the money you make to split between you. Do we have a deal?"

Anatoly thought about arguing. The deal sounded too good to be true. He had never had a kopeck of his own. He saw the look of excitement on Henry's face. The boys looked at each other and grinned. The thought of making a few kopecks for themselves was exciting! Neither had ever been given such an opportunity before. Without another word, they ran off and quickly got to work. The sawdust flew in all directions, ending up in their hair and down their shirts and pants where it stuck to their sweaty skin and itched horribly. But by the end of the day, the yard was relatively clean, twelve heavy sacks had been filled and stored in the warehouse, and their argument was long forgotten.

The next morning Henry and Anatoly set up shop right on the corner of Irtysh and Ermak. Any time someone passed by they shouted, "Good dry shavings for sale! Ten kopecks for one bag!" To an old woman who came along, they called out, "Grandmother, we have good kindling! Prepare for winter now!" They laughed at the thought of cold and snow when the hot sun was blazing down upon them.

Some customers tried to haggle with the boys. "You're robbing me blind!" they would bluster. "Your sawdust is mixed with dirt!" Or, "These bark shavings are green! They'll make nothing but smoke! I'll be rotting in my grave before this wood will be dry enough to burn! I'll give you five kopecks, not ten!" One customer tried to wear the boys down with his arguments: "These wood chips are junk! They're useless! Dry manure will burn better! That's what we've been using since Grandfather Adam anyway! No need to change now." And with a sly look, "Let me take this garbage off your hands. I'll do you a favor and throw it away, somewhere where it won't be a bother."

But the boys held their ground. They insisted that their shavings were clean and dry, going so far as to open sacks to prove their point. By the end of the day they had sold all of them. They proudly brought their earnings to Heinrich, who happily gave each boy their share of the day's take. They pocketed their kopecks and ran to sit under the elm tree and plan other ways of making money. Their street was a busy one. There must be other things to sell!

And so Henry and Anatoly became fast friends.

4

The third member of what was to become an inseparable childhood trio was met quite by accident two weeks later.

It was another one of those typically hot and windy summer afternoons in Kulomzino. The dust swirled in the currents caking the skin and clothes, and the sun baked the dirt-clouded steppe with ferocious intensity. The boys were playing in the shade, using sticks and discarded wood to build a small fortress behind the warehouse. They were using the warehouse as the fourth wall and were putting the finishing touches on a very precariously balanced roof.

The air was full of the smells of pinesap, sunburned grass and dust. Not far away to their right was a thick tangle of brambles. The bushes formed a hedge going perpendicular from the street toward the depths of the lot. It created a border of sorts between the Rempels and the neighbor's place on the other side. For whatever reason, no one ever seemed to be home at the neighbor's. So, naturally, the occupants of the house remained a mystery.

As they played, Henry noticed a large brown rabbit nibbling on a patch of grass that grew in and around the brambles. There were a few green shoots among the dry blades. The rabbit was carefully searching them out and eating them. Henry could see the rabbit's nose wiggle as it chewed. He nudged Anatoly.

"Look. A rabbit," he said quietly.

"Let's make a snare and catch it," whispered Tolya.

Henry was enthusiastic. "I'll get some twine," he said in hushed tones. "There's some in the warehouse."

He crept away as silently as he could. When he reached the corner of the building Henry hurriedly opened the side door and scrambled inside to retrieve the twine. Back outside, he closed the door as quietly as he could and hurried back to where Anatoly was keeping watch.

Of course, even though they stole up to the brambles to set their trap with all the stealth they could muster, the rabbit immediately hopped off under the bushes and hid. As it sped off, Henry could not help but think of the rabbit story Sergei had told him. He hoped they'd have more luck than the cocky farmer. Anatoly set the snare—he'd obviously done it before— and the boys returned to their spot behind the warehouse. They waited to see what would happen. They waited all afternoon, but didn't see the rabbit again.

When he returned to the lot the next morning, Henry immediately went to check the trap. It was empty.

Two days later, while Henry was helping his father with some cleanup in the yard, he suddenly heard a piercing shriek that sounded alarmingly like a baby in great distress. It came from the direction of the tangled bramble bushes. The sound set his spine tingling! Followed by his father, Henry ran over to the bushes. He was shocked to see a big brown rabbit—its eyes practically popping out of its head—frantically kicking and twisting at the end of a long cord. A cloud of dust swirled about the rabbit, stirred up by its dancing paws. He was certain it was the rabbit they had seen the other day. Later, as Henry thought about the terrifying episode, he remembered that the sunlight shone through the swirling dust in perfect rays creating a sunburst that highlighted every single mote of dust in the air, while the taut string around the agonized, jerking rabbit's neck hummed and held it firm.

As he watched the rabbit fighting for its life, tears began to blur Henry's vision and he realized that he had not wanted to capture it at all. It had been a game! He had not thought it through! Now it was deadly serious! Panic began to rise in

Henry. He felt faint and thought he might vomit. He began to jump up and down and waved his arms spastically so that, for a moment, it appeared that he and the rabbit were doing some sort of strange violent dance together. He screamed for his father to somehow rescue the rabbit.

Suddenly, Anatoly appeared and dove onto the rabbit. He grabbed it by its ears and held it up at arm's length to avoid being scratched by its flailing claws. He had a lopsided grin on his face stretching from ear to ear.

"I heard the noise and came as quick as I could! What a catch! We'll have it for dinner!" he shouted.

"No Tolya, you can't kill it!" Henry pleaded.

Anatoly was shocked at his friend's change in attitude. "Nonsense! What's the matter with you?" he demanded. "Rabbits are for eating! And this one is nice and fat!" He jabbed it with the index finger of his free hand.

"But it's alive!" cried Henry. "You can't kill it!"

At that moment, from the other side of the brambles, a girl of about the same age as Henry rushed over to where they stood. There was fear and fury mixed together in the expression on her dark face. She ran straight up to Anatoly and scolded him loudly.

"What do you think you're doing? That's my rabbit! It lives in our yard! It escaped from its pen! Untie it and give it to me! Be careful, you're going to hurt it, you idiot!"

Anatoly was quite taken aback by the girl's fiery onslaught, but he was not about to give up his prize.

His grin was determined. "You can't have it! It's mine. I caught it. Anyway, it's not on your property. It is on Henry's property, isn't it, Henry."

He looked to Henry for support, but quickly realized that none was forthcoming.

The girl became so agitated that it looked like she would attack Anatoly. Her fists were clenched and her furrowed forehead creased down over her teary eyes. Clearly, she intended to launch herself at Anatoly at any moment.

Heinrich, who had remained quiet during the heated exchange, decided it was time to intervene. He placed his hand on the agitated girl's shoulder.

"Everybody take a breath and calm down." He turned to the girl. "What's your name?"

The girl glared at him. "Sonia Ivanovna Sarkovskaya. I live right there on the other side of these bushes. That's our rabbit. My father raises rabbits."

"Hello, Sonia." Given the circumstances, formal introductions seemed a little ridiculous, but there was no way around it. "This is my son Henry and his friend Anatoly," he said tersely, pointing to each of the boys.

By now Anatoly had released the noose around the rabbit's neck and it had calmed somewhat.

"Sonia, are you sure this rabbit is yours and not a wild rabbit? I've seen it wandering about in the bushes before."

"Yes it's mine!" Sonia said firmly, wiping her teary eyes with the back of her hand. "It keeps getting out of the cage. Look, it has a white spot behind its left ear. It's mine, I tell you!"

Heinrich examined the rabbit's head while Anatoly kept a firm grip on it.

"Yes, I can see the spot. All right. It must be your rabbit. I'm sorry. I hope the boys haven't hurt it." He looked at Anatoly. "All right. Give the rabbit to Sonia, Tolya."

Anatoly tried to argue his case. But he knew, now that there was an adult involved, he couldn't win. In the end he reluctantly returned the struggling rabbit to Sonia who took it and, with a final glare directed in Tolya's direction, marched quickly around the brambles to her house. Anatoly, expecting a wallop over the head for his transgression, gave Henry a dark look and made good his escape in the opposite direction.

That evening, Heinrich and Katy discussed the day's events. They were distressed that their first encounter with the neighbor had seen their relationship start off on such a bad foot. Katy offered to bake a batch of pirozhki for Heinrich to present the next day to the Sarkovsky's as a kind of peace offering.

"I found some cherries at the market today. They're really plump and sweet."

Heinrich agreed immediately. Katy called Katerina to come help pit the cherries while she mixed the flour, milk, and eggs. After she rolled out the dough and cut it into small squares, they placed the cherries in the middle, added a little sugar, and folded each corner to the center. Meanwhile, Heinrich built up the fire in the stove so that the oven would be good and hot when the small square fruit pies were ready for baking.

Later, as the smell of fresh pirozhki filled the rooms of the dacha, Heinrich reflected on how blessed he was to have been given such a kind-hearted and talented woman as a life's partner. In bed that night, he showed his love in ways that left Katy feeling warm and glowing. As she lay with Heinrich snoring softly into her shoulder she hoped that the children had been asleep in the other bedroom.

It would be some years before Henry, tucked under his quilt, would understand the nature of the sounds he had heard coming from his parents' bed that night.

The next day Katy went along with Heinrich and Henry, leaving Katarina to look after Joanna. When they arrived at the lot, they went straight to the Sarkovsky's door. Katy was carrying a small wicker basket in which lay a dozen fresh pirozhki carefully wrapped in a white linen cloth. They climbed the steps onto the porch and knocked hesitantly. They waited and knocked again. After a while, the door was opened slowly by a woman of similar age to theirs. She had a swarthy complexion, with narrow eyes and high cheekbones, and her jet black hair was partially covered by a colorful kerchief.

"*Dobry den*, madam. Good morning," began Heinrich as he introduced himself, Katy and Henry.

"*Zdravstvujte*. How do you do?" she replied noncommittally. "I am Tatyana. My husband, Ivan, is not at home right now."

When Heinrich explained the situation Tatyana laughed and said, "*Nitchevo*! Don't worry about it!" and invited them to come in. "The rabbits breed like, well, rabbits. You know." She gave a wink. "There is never a shortage of babies." She laughed loudly. When Heinrich didn't move, she repeated her invitation. "*Pozhalusta*, please, come in." And then she called, "Sonia, come and see who is here! Our new neighbors!"

Katy knew immediately that she was going to like Tatyana Sarkovskaya.

Sonia was not at all pleased but came into the room nonetheless. She and Henry sat at the table on which rested a vase with an arrangement of delicate blue flowers. They stole glances at each other while the parents chatted. Fortunately, the samovar was still boiling, so tea was made. Sonia softened considerably as she tasted the delicious cherry pirozhki and sipped her tea.

Later, as the Rempels left, there were smiles and promises to visit again. Heinrich and Katy were happy to have made a first step in getting to know their neighbor, and Henry had a new friend.

5

Three weeks later the Sarkovskys invited the Rempels to share an evening meal. Ivan greeted them at the door and led them into the sitting room.

"It is a pleasure to finally meet our new neighbors!" he exclaimed. "Tatyana and Sonia told me all about your first meeting." He chuckled. "Sonia protects those rabbits like they were her own children one day, and the next day at supper she will practically devour half of one by herself. Yes, she loves her rabbits, don't you Sonia!"

Sonia blushed crimson. Henry, standing in a corner by the stove, found himself feeling suddenly shy. He glanced at Sonia whenever he thought she wasn't looking.

With the children underfoot, the mothers quickly got frustrated and sent them all outside to play in the yard until the meal was ready.

With wonderful smells coming from the kitchen, the men discussed Heinrich's business plans and the progress of construction. Ivan told Heinrich about his work in the office of the Trans-Siberian Railroad. They also talked about the growing unrest amongst the workers at the Kulomsino rail yards. This was not an isolated problem that was unique to their town. Rumors of unrest in factories and cities across Russia, and the strong-armed response of the Tsar who did not hesitate to use his Cossacks to dissuade malcontents, were rampant and very worrisome.

"Shooting unarmed protesters will never solve Russia's problems," lamented Ivan Sarkovsky. Heinrich was inclined to agree.

Finally, everyone was called to the table.

"I've been cooking this for three hours," Tatyana said, indicating the pot of aromatic broth she placed on the table. "You mustn't let it boil, though." A platter of tender meat she had scraped off bones from the pot followed.

To the Rempel's surprise, there were no forks or knives laid out. Each person was provided with a plate, a small bowl and a cloth napkin.

"I am a Kazakh," said Tatyana. "I grew up in the Kachiry area on the Irtysh River south of here. My father was a farmer. Once our people were nomads. We roamed the steppe freely with our herds. But our dear Tsar and his soldiers built their fortresses and put a stop to that. So we had to put down some roots and Kachiry is where we put them. Once I was old enough, I left home and came to Kulomzino looking for work." She shrugged. "Perhaps fled from home is better way of putting it. But that's another story. Instead of work, I found Ivan! Well, actually, Ivan found me. But I'm babbling. You are our guests! Eat! Eat!" She laughed at herself. "We don't put much stock on formalities here." She crossed herself in good Orthodox fashion and began to spoon ladles full of delicious smelling meat over the bed of noodles and potatoes on each one's plate. Then she poured some steaming meat broth into each one's bowl.

"This meal is called beshbarmak. Beshbarmak means 'five fingers,'" Tatyana explained. "We eat it with our fingers and sip the broth. That's why there is no cutlery. It is a traditional Kazakh meal made with some spices, onions, and kazi, which is what we call our spicy sausage. I hope you like it!" She didn't tell them that the kazi was made from horsemeat.

The Rempels had never eaten with their fingers before. They looked a little suspiciously at the food on their plates. There was some tentative picking and pushing of meat around the bowl. But when they had tasted it, the adults all agreed it was excellent. Just when he was beginning to really enjoy the meal, Sonia leaned over to Henry and whispered in his ear that there was horsemeat in the kazi. The thought of it made Henry blanch. He found himself doing everything in his power not to gag as he tried to swallow the meat he had been chewing before the announcement of its origin. Since the sausage refused to go down, Henry took to storing it in his cheeks. His father gave him a stern look and the meat went down, not without a gag or two, hidden behind his small hand. Sonia noticed his discomfort and giggled, much to Henry's embarrassment.

In the end, the flavor of the meal won its approval and most of what was on their plates was thoroughly enjoyed by all the Rempels. For dessert, shelpek was served. Also a traditional Kazakh delicacy, shelpek was made of sweet dough, plaited and cut into finger length pieces, and deep-fried in oil. These were served with tea and proved to be a big hit, especially with the children.

And so July gave way to August 1914.

A Change of Plans

1

History is inexorable in its flow. Nothing can resist the sweep of time and the consequences of the events that result from the decisions of those in positions of power. Heinrich would forever remember the day when the tsunami of history struck from out of the west, along the steel tracks of the Trans-Siberian Railway, and changed their lives forever.

The first hint of the trouble to come exploded along the human telegraph system, bouncing from ear to ear with shocked looks and whispers of disbelief. Quickly those tentative breaths were transformed into an excited clamor of patriotic fervor. War! Russia was at war!

The day was like many others, oppressively hot and dusty. The sky was clear, but a dirty haze covered the horizon. A strong wind hurtled itself out of the west. Heinrich was overseeing the installation of glass in the windows of the summer kitchen. He heard a commotion outside and went to investigate. A few agitated people were talking loudly in the street. Soon others joined them and they called out to each other, "Have you heard? It's war! We are at war!"

There was excitement but also great confusion for the official news traveled slowly across the vastness of Russia. In 1914, few in Siberia had access to electricity. Radios were almost unheard of. The telegraph with its thousands of kilometers of wire was the quickest link. However, today's news for the people of Omsk was often last week's headline in St. Petersburg. Rumor filled in the gap.

"When? When did this war begin?"

No one seemed to know. One thought it was yesterday, another, last week.

In the excitement of the moment, neighbors questioned each other and speculated, "With what country is Russia at war? Who are we fighting? Who is the enemy?"

Some, remembering the debacle that was the Russo-Japanese war, said, "Japan. It must be Japan! We are finally righting the wrongs done to us in that shambles of a war we fought against them a decade ago! We should never have allowed the Japanese to stay on Russian soil these ten long years!"

Others thought, "Turkey! We're at war with Turkey! We're probably fighting over the Crimea again! They beat us last time, but they had better watch out! We'll really give them a good thrashing this time around!"

And still others declared, "No, we're at war with England! You can never trust the English!"

It was only after days of speculation that the truth became known. Russia was at war with Germany!

For the peasant patriots of Russia, the reasons for the war were immaterial. Political disagreements were set aside. The streets were quickly filled with marching columns of enthusiastic young men singing the praises of Mother Russia and of Tsar Nicholas II, God's Appointed Autocrat of All the Russias. The Trans-Siberian Railroad began carrying trainloads of fresh-faced, smiling, hand-waving recruits from Kulomzino and its neighboring communities into the west, to do battle against the evil invader.

Overnight, Heinrich's hired help vanished. He was left to finish the summer kitchen on his own, using the skills he had learned by watching and helping the workers doing their jobs during the previous months. When he returned to the Borodin Company office in Omsk to order the timber he would need to build the family home during the final phase of construction, Heinrich was given vague promises. Timber was in short supply.

"*Nitchevo*," they would say. "Maybe tomorrow, maybe next month, whenever the wood becomes available, we'll let you know."

With growing unease, Heinrich walked the streets of Omsk to the Merchant's Mall on Lyubinsky Avenue and stopped by A. Gashin and Sons to find out what he could about the status of his farm implement order. He pushed open the heavy door and climbed the creaking wooden steps to the second floor office.

"What! You're expecting a shipment of plows?" The clerk actually laughed. "Don't you know there's a war on? All the trains have been diverted for military use! Vladivostok is one huge armory. I hear rumors that the warehouses can't contain all the guns and ammunition being shipped from America. Sorry, Mr. Rempel, but at the moment, no one has time to think about plows!"

Heinrich returned home greatly discouraged. He had been on the brink of opening his new business. But now, when plows were being beaten into bullets, his dream of owning a farm implement store would have to wait. As he rode the ferry back across the Irtysh, looking at the west bank toward home, Heinrich leaned on the railing and wearily contemplated the uncertain days ahead.

2

Heinrich looked out the window at the mountainous gray swells of the North Atlantic beyond. We were seated in a lounge sharing a cup of tea. Somewhere in the cloudy distance, a new land beckoned. The motion of the boat, as it rode the waves, left him with a constant feeling of being slightly nauseous.

"The first years of the war brought changes. There were some food shortages. But we had a big garden so we always had enough to eat. Of course, the shortage of labor made it impossible to finish building our home, even had we been able to get the bricks and lumber we required. Our shipment of Deere and Company plows never did arrive. There was always a very good reason given: the war explained everything.

"Soon after the war began, we moved into our cabin that was intended to be our summer kitchen. Given the times, it would have been imprudent to stay in our beautiful dacha. The cabin had been built with four rooms. The front rooms were used as a kitchen and living area. At night, Henry slept on the bench by the oven. The back rooms were used as tiny bedrooms. The girls, Katarina and Joanna, shared a small bed in one. Katy and I slept in the other. The rooms were small, but it was good to be home on our own property at last, even if we were 'camping in the little house,' as we all liked to think of it.

"Fortunately, we still had some income. We still had our share in the mill. Crops were good and the army bought all the flour and seed oil the mill could produce. And, at high prices! The war saw to that as well.

"We managed; we had each other, my Katy and I, we had our children. We had our faith. We derived much comfort from our association with our brothers and sisters in our church in Tchunayevka."

Heinrich smiled to himself as his thoughts took him to a pleasant, far-off place.

"Do you like music, Doctor? We used to have events at our churches called Saengerfests. They always took place in fall, after the harvest was completed. Choirs from village churches in our region would get together and compete. Each year the festival was hosted by a different community.

"Saengerfests were a good excuse for us Mennonites to get together and reacquaint ourselves with old friends and relatives who lived distances away. The days would be filled with singing and lots of eating! Oh did we eat: watermelon and rollkuchen, borscht, sausage and perogies, and such." A pained expression appeared on his face. "We did not appreciate then how good our lives were, how blessed we were.

"As I remember it, the last Saengerfest was held in the fall of 1917. We hosted it at our church in Tchunayevka. Katy could not attend because she was expecting to give birth at any time. I remember the singing that year was particularly glorious. For me, a tune is as slippery as a fish. I can never catch hold of it. But I can appreciate good music when I hear it! There was one choir, from Friedensruh, a few kilometers north of Isyl-Kul, a couple of hundred kilometers west by rail. It was wonderful! The choir's conductor, Jacob Funk, was deaf in one ear. He'd been kicked in the head by a horse as a young man. The Funks were farmers. The patriarch Peter Funk bought an estate, a chutor. Its previous owner had called it *Ljubimovka*, Village of Love. The family grew grain, and experimented with growing fruit trees in the harsh Siberian climate. Anyway, Funk really knew how to get the best from a choir. They sounded like the angels."

Heinrich's expression hardened.

"It became fashionable to hate anything and anyone German. We represented the enemy within. In 1914, soon after the war began the teachers and administrators of all German schools in Russia were to be replaced by Russians. The German language could no longer be used for instruction. Fortunately, we were far enough away from St. Petersburg that the Tsar's edict was only loosely enforced.

"For some, though, it was a bad time. People started disappearing. We made inquiries until we learned the truth. Anyone who had recently come to Siberia from Germany was arrested, on the sly of course, and quietly shipped to Tobolsk, east of Omsk, where a prison camp was established for them. We were spared, I suppose, because we had been in the country for so long. Goodness, we were born there. Was it not our country, too?

"At first, the news from the war was positive. Our armies made huge strides against the enemy. At least that is what was loudly reported. And, for a while, it was true. But it was not long before the incompetence of our leaders began to spell disaster. The truth could not remain hidden for long. Men by the trainload began returning from the front in the white hospital cars. They were wounded, many in horrible ways. As time passed, there were stories of more and more soldiers with gunshot wounds in a leg or hand. Some of these men quietly confessed they had shot themselves in order to be able to return home. Still others were even more desperate. They told of how they had shot their officers and deserted. Whole platoons, battalions even, all together, at one time. They simply had had enough.

"The returning soldiers told stories of their betrayal. Far more men enlisted than could be armed. Thousands were sent to battle carrying only wooden clubs! Can you believe it? Men were sent to fight sharing weapons, one rifle amongst two or three. The men spoke of the cold; most were not given the clothing needed to face the freezing temperatures of winter. Nor were they fed enough to sustain their strength. It was a catastrophe! Millions died of exposure and starvation. Millions more were captured by the enemy."

I listened to Heinrich without interrupting, wondering at the emotions roiling behind his eyes.

He looked down at his hands and clenched his fists. "What a beast is man!" he whispered.

Heinrich slowly shook his head, stood, and, without another word, left.

As one who lived through that war, I cannot say that I disagreed with his assessment.

3

With the war, inflation became a serious issue for the workers of Russia. Unrest grew as production fell. Mills were closed and workers lost their jobs. The rising price of food far outstripped the ability of the masses to pay for it. Worker strikes and job actions became commonplace across Russia, from St. Petersburg to Vladivostok. The Tsar's brutal response was to call out his Cossacks to suppress the revolts. The violence of this action only served to further incense the population.

Revolution was inevitable.

One cold evening in February 1917, Heinrich was visiting with his neighbor, Ivan Sarkovsky. They were seated at the kitchen table. The Russian oven was filling the room with a comfortable, warm heat. Katy had served a snack of fresh baked buns with jam made from last summer's raspberries sweetened with watermelon syrup. They had washed the buns down with strong tea, sipped out of saucers to cool it more quickly, with sugar cubes clenched between their front teeth.

While the icy wind outside buffeted the windows and door, Ivan, who prided himself on his advanced political thinking, was holding the floor indoors. He was a Socialist

Revolutionary. Henry, from his bench by the oven, overheard their heated conversation.

"What our country needs," argued Ivan, "is a complete rebuilding of society, right from the ground up. Our present system has failed completely. This war has been a complete disaster. To make matters worse, Russia's masses are unemployed and starving. Our problem is that the Tsar and the capitalists own everything and the proletariat masses own nothing.

"I'll tell you what needs to happen." Ivan looked meaningfully at Heinrich. "For one thing, the land must to be taken away from the rich! What does one man need with a thousand acres when his neighbor has none? The land must be distributed to the landless who can work it as tenant farmers of the state. Think of the mountains of grain that could be harvested if the landless were put to work on their own fields. Another thing. Our factories are lying idle! They must be put into the hands of the workers by whose sweat and labor they are run and who depend on them for their livelihood. The workers will soon get those factories up and running. They will work to provide the necessities of life for the families of Russia are living in poverty and destitution. We must create a communist state where wealth is shared by all.

"And furthermore," he didn't even pause for a breath, "we need a strong, democratically elected Duma to represent the people's wishes. A real democracy where everyone's voice is heard! That's what we need. No more being told what's what by the bourgeois elite. No more under the thumb of the Tsar and his capitalist minions. God tells us to look out for the poor. Let's create a country where all are equal and there are no poor!"

Ivan slammed the palm of his hand down on the table to emphasize his point.

Heinrich was not sure how to react to Ivan's comments. He agreed that his Christian duty was to feed the poor, but how was that even possible in a land awash in poverty? And he was inclined to laugh at some of Ivan's ideas that he considered to be quite ridiculous. Take the land away from the landlords? Give the factories to the workers? How impractical!

On the other hand, his friend's speech also left him feeling quite alarmed. Heinrich was not interested in politics in the least. He was a businessman. Aside from the farm implement business he hoped to establish, he had never discussed his business affairs with Ivan. Now he had an uncomfortable feeling that his neighbor was somehow implicating him in the grave ills that plagued his country. Was he, Heinrich, one of the hated capitalist bourgeoisie? He owned shares in a large mill. He was a boss of workers. Had the company been treating his workers poorly? He thought not. The workers received fair wages. What else could they expect?

"I certainly agree that we need to look out for the interests of the poor. That is our Christian obligation," Heinrich suggested. He didn't want to offend his friend.

"Yes, it is," pounced Ivan. "But the Church has failed in this duty and what the Church has neglected to do, or has been unable to do, we must do through a new Federal Russian Republic! The state will carry out what God has commanded. When people are properly organized, they are in the best position to take care of themselves and help others.

"But," Ivan hesitated before continuing, "we are in a dangerous time." He lowered his voice. "There are those in my party who believe that the only way to fully achieve our goals is by an armed uprising. They would even use terror as a weapon. They are not concerned for the welfare of the innocent. For them, everything must be destroyed before it can be made to fit their ideal of a true communist state. Even the family is no safe haven. As the Bible says, 'Brother will fight against brother.'"

Ivan nodded his head wearily, looking at the floor by his feet. "We are headed for some trying times, my friend."

Ivan looked up at Heinrich seated across from him. He leaned forward, resting his arms on the table.

"But it's those damned Bolsheviks that we will really need to keep our eyes on."

"What do you mean?"

Ivan paused. "There is an old tale my mother used to tell. This should help you understand. Once there was an old miser who had three sons. One cold night as he sat counting his money, the miser heard Death calling to him to come join him outside in the blizzard. The miser immediately began to eat all of his gold and silver rubles, so that no one, not even his sons, would have a share in his money when he was gone. By morning he was dead because of all the money he had swallowed. The miser's sons built a nice coffin. Their wives washed the body and placed it in the coffin. They took their dead father to the church so that he could lie below the icons and find his way to heaven. They asked the priest to say a prayer for the old man. That night, as the priest was praying, Death suddenly appeared. He grabbed the corpse and began to shake it up and down. The gold and silver rubles the miser had swallowed fell on the floor with many clinks and clanks. As he carried the corpse out the door, Death looked at the priest and said, 'You can have the money, but I want the bag!'"

Ivan sipped his tea. His chair scraped on the floor as he nudged it closer to Heinrich who felt confused as to the meaning of his friend's story.

"Let me tell you something," continued Ivan. "The Russian peasant is a miser. He squanders his money by pouring it down his throat in the form of his beloved vodka. That is all he cares for. But, now I want you to really listen, because Death, that's what this is really all about." He lowered his voice again. "The Bolsheviks, they are Death. Mark my words. When the Bolsheviks come, they will leave nothing behind. They'll take the bag and the money. They'll take everything! They say they're for the workers and the peasants, but they're not. Be warned. They're a bunch of thieving bandits. After they've dealt with the peasant lying before the icons, before they leave, they'll kill the priest, they'll steal the icons and they'll burn down the church. Death has far more respect for the peasant and the Church than the Bolshevik ever will. You see if I'm not right about this!"

On the afternoon of March 15, 1917, in response to widespread strikes and demonstrations protesting against his policies and his unpopular German wife, Tsar Nicholas II stepped down from his throne. The slippery descent to Bolshevik rule in Russia had begun in earnest.

4

I was walking on the promenade deck with Henry. The sun at long last was shining in a bright blue sky with a warmth that rejuvenated our sea-soaked spirits. The waves below had finally calmed to mounds instead of mountains.

Henry chuckled. "Agnessa likes to call herself a child of the revolution. Has she told you that yet? She brings it up quite often."

We stopped and leaned on the railing overlooking the water. The multiplicity of blue shifting in the sparkling seas below was mesmerizing. Small clouds in the sky added shifting patterns of gray and white here and there.

"She was born on Oct 24, 1917, the evening before the Bolshevik coup. While her mother was struggling in the labor of birthing, Vladimir Illich Lenin was arriving at the Bolshevik headquarters, what was formerly the Smolny Institute for Noble Maidens. The party of the proletariat was preparing for its final push to power."

5

Henry had not even known that his mother was pregnant.

Toward the end of September, Henry was instructed by his father to help his mother in every way possible. Katy was to do nothing without assistance. It seemed a strange arrangement, but Henry did not second-guess his parents. He became Katy's arms and feet.

Every day after school, Henry hurried home where he was at his mother's beck and call, helping her with all of her household tasks. As the days progressed into mid-October,

Henry found himself even helping Katy to rise out of her chair. It was when she began to need him to lean upon as she walked that Henry began to worry. What was wrong with his mother? Her color was good, but she moved slowly, ponderously, in her long flowing dresses and would stop frequently for rests. Was she was gravely ill with some mysterious ailment?

The family was sitting around the fire on the afternoon of October 24. It was already getting dark outside, though the time was barely four o'clock. A few candles were strategically placed on wall sconces and on the table so that there was light in the room. Katy was teaching Katarina to knit and thinking that it would soon be time to make supper. Henry and Joanna were seated at the table where he was amusing her by drawing funny faces on old pieces of paper. Heinrich was reading a favorite passage in his Bible aloud for his family to hear.

Suddenly, Katy grimaced. She clutched her belly. Katarina gave her a worried look, but Katy gave her a quick smile and continued with her instruction. No one else had noticed.

As the pain returned with increasing regularity, Katy knew what it meant. "Heinrich, it is time. It has begun," she said calmly.

Heinrich looked startled for a moment and in his confusion almost blurted, "What has begun?" but caught himself in time. Flustered and fearful he quickly composed himself. He looked at his children.

"Katushya, take your brother and sister to the Sarkovsky's house. Tell Mrs. Sarkovsky that it is time and that she is needed here. You and the girls are to stay at the Sarkovsky's until you are sent for. Do you understand?"

Katarina nodded vigorously.

"*Na ja* then. Go!" And then more impatiently, "*Schnell*, Katyusha! Hurry! Go!"

Henry, listening to all the instructions, wanted to say, "No, I don't understand at all! Time? What time? What's going on?" But from the look on his parents' faces he knew now was not the time for argument. He shivered and wondered if his fears were finally being realized. Was his mother dying?

The children got up quickly from the table. In his haste Henry knocked over the bench. The noise of the clatter increased the sense of urgency that permeated the room. Henry and Katarina shrugged into their coats and grabbed their hats that hung on pegs by the door. They helped Joanna get into her coat and boots.

With Katarina holding Joanna's hand and Henry close behind, the children hurried up the path to their neighbors' door. It was a cold night and snow crunched and squealed under their boots as they ran, echoing the fear that pounded in their hearts. The bright moon in the clear sky lighted their way as they ran through the break between the blackberry brambles that separated their property from the Sarkovskys'.

Henry bounded up the steps in front of the girls.

"Something's happening to mother!" he shouted when Tatyana Sarkovskaya opened the door.

Katarina breathlessly added, "Father says it is time and you are to come right away!"

Ivan Sarkovsky came to the door and stood beside Tatyana.

"What is the matter?" he asked his wife.

"The baby is coming, I must go and help," Tatyana replied brusquely. "Look after the children."

Katarina stood uncertainly on the stoop. "Baby?" she thought.

Tears swelled in Henry's eyes. His mother was dangerously ill. It was obvious. He became aware that his whole body was trembling. He held Joanna's hand tightly. She began to cry.

Without another word, Tatyana turned and rushed into a room at the back of the house. Henry brushed his own tears away with his sleeve as the children were ushered into the kitchen. While Ivan helped them take off their coats and boots, Tatyana appeared carrying a bag into which she was stuffing a few things she had collected. She hurried to the door to leave and for the first time saw the fear on the Rempel children's faces. Getting down on one knee she pulled Joanna close and gave her a hug. She looked reassuringly at Henry and Katarina.

"Come, come, children. There is nothing to be afraid of. This happens every day. Your mother is going to be just fine. She is only having a baby!"

Her announcement was met with looks of incredulity and surprise.

"Didn't you know?"

The next day, October 25, 1917, as the Rempel children joyfully were introduced to their new baby sister, Agnessa, the Bolsheviks' Red Guard, using the weapons given to them by an inept and shortsighted government, stormed the Winter Palace in St. Petersburg.

6

"The Officer Cadets at the Military Academy revolted!"

Anatoly listened as his father, Fyodor Alexandrovich, loudly repeated the news he had heard while at work at the Kulomzino railway station.

It was a month since the start of what Ivan liked to think of as the "Glorious Revolution." Many things had changed. Omsk was governed by an uneasy coalition of Bolsheviks, Mensheviks and Socialist Revolutionaries. Determined to work together, they tried to accommodate the plethora of perspectives coming from amateur politicians whose views differed on the vast spectrum from the far left of radical communism to the far right of radical socialism. With no compensation given, all land in the vicinity of Omsk had been taken from landlords, including the Tsar, the churches and monasteries, and placed into the hands of the peasants and working class. The homes of the rich had been confiscated and were rapidly being transformed into flophouses for the many refugees who roamed Omsk's streets, victims of the war in the west, or into offices for the new governing communist secretariats. Even the dachas along the Irtysh River were now the property of the people and were being used by party leaders for work and pleasure. Industry had also been confiscated, without compensation, and was now owned by the communist government.

Anatoly's mother looked at Fyodor through eyes bleary with alcohol fog. She was not feeling well, but her husband was too preoccupied to notice or to care. Fyodor laughed and slammed his fist on the table, making her empty bottle jump.

"The bastards refused to recognize the new socialist government of the people. Imagine that!" He laughed again. "Counter-revolutionaries! Bloody monarchists! They died like dogs in the street!"

7

Over the next months a great deal changed for Heinrich Rempel and his family. The Tsarist ruble was replaced by a Bolshevik ruble. The exchange rate had not been kind to Heinrich's savings. Inflation took the rest. More devastating, though, was the loss of the family's source of income. The mill in which Heinrich was a silent partner was 'liberated' by the communists. It was now being run by a committee of workers under the direction of a foreman named Gulich. The fact that Gulich was a political appointee who had no experience running a mill added insult to the injury. Heinrich had been warned by his friends not to set foot on the property. Few outside of the close Mennonite circle knew of his involvement there. His silent partnership was best kept secret lest those who sought to avenge themselves against the evil bourgeoisie should discover his identity.

It was in April 1918 that Heinrich was ordered to attend a meeting of the new *Zemstvo*, the town council. The paper delivered to his front door indicated that he was to answer to unspecified charges. Heinrich trembled at the prospect of the meeting for he had no idea of what to expect. What was the offence he had committed? Rumor had it that the council was harsh in its judgments, with no sympathy for those who were brought before its members. The world was being turned upside down and Heinrich was completely at loose ends.

When things were bothering him, for which he had no solution, Heinrich liked to go for a brisk walk around the block. In the past, the walk had had a soothing effect upon him, allowing him to quiet his thoughts, and perhaps to discern an acceptable course of action. But lately, increasingly, as his control over the events in his life was slipping through his fingers, on his walks Heinrich found himself being driven to prayer and cries to God to have mercy on his family.

On this day, as he walked and pondered his situation, Heinrich was aware of the many people on the street who seemed to have no reason to be there. These people did not live in the houses that lined the streets of his neighborhood. They were ragged and dirty, and carried small bundles of belongings slung over their stooped shoulders as they plodded slowly along. Over the last couple of years, more and more of these dispirited folk had appeared in Kulomzino. On his trips across the river, Heinrich had noticed that the streets of Omsk were also crowded with refugees. They came to the railway station, crammed in overcrowded cattle cars—railway coaches had disappeared with the coming of the Bolsheviks who said that all were equal so all would ride together in the same circumstances—and they brought with them stories of conflict in the west and the south of Russia. Occasionally one or another of the braver, or perhaps more desperate, vagrants would approach a resident and extend a hand in a plea for help. More often than not, they were met with an angry remonstrance, or an averted eye.

"We have our own problems. Leave us alone. Be off with you. You have no business here."

Heinrich was lost in his thoughts as he happened by the Lepinov's place. He was met at the gate by Fyodor Alexandrovich, who had just returned from work at the rail yard. Even though he had put in a long day, Fyodor was full of energy and was all smiles as he greeted Heinrich. Fyodor stood in Heinrich's way on the side of the road and beckoned him to come into his house.

Lepinov was a tall, powerfully built man. His beard was black and grew in wild, thick curly tufts from his neck to his cheekbones. His shirt, which once had been bright red, was grimy brown as were his once-grey pants, filthy with the grease and oil stains from the equipment he repaired. Any exposed skin was as dirty as his clothing.

Heinrich was a bit reticent about joining his neighbor whom he had never formally met and about whom he'd heard several alarming stories. But Fyodor was not to be deterred, nor did he look like the kind of person one could refuse.

"Comrade Rempel, my good neighbor, I see ya out on the street but you've never been my guest. Let me offer ya a drink, some vodka. A drink to our health."

He laughed, slapped Heinrich on the back and steered him up the walkway.

"Thank you, no," Heinrich responded, hesitantly, nervously. "I, uh, I don't drink vodka." Not wanting to offend Fyodor's hospitality, Heinrich added, "I'll have tea, though, if the samovar is hot." He forced a weak smile.

As they entered the front door, Lepinov hollered for his wife to bring tea and vodka.

"Olga! Where is she, the useless woman," he fumed. "I love her y'know, how could I not, we've been married these fifteen years! But she's a sot, she is. There's no denyin' it. Olga!"

When there was no response, Fyodor muttered to himself, something about doing everything himself. He poured tea from the samovar and brought it to Heinrich. It was lukewarm. Fyodor poured himself a drink out of a bottle half full of clear liquid, raised his glass toward Heinrich and said, "To your health, comrade." He looked meaningfully at Heinrich and downed the vodka in one gulp.

Fyodor put the glass down with a bang and again looked hard at Heinrich.

"Like I already said, I don't know ya real well, comrade. You're a Mennonite, right? German. Imagine drinking one's health with a cup of lukewarm tea. I don't get it. It ain't natural."

He seemed to be talking to himself for a moment, but then focused back onto Heinrich, who was sitting on a bench deciding what to do with the wretched tea.

"Well anyway, what I do know is that we live in different worlds, you and me. I work at the railroad, swinging a wrench and fixing what's broke. You, I'm not so sure about. I've watched ya with your building on the property down the street and you appear to be decent enough folk. Where ya get the rubles to do all that work, I don't know. It probably ain't my business, though some would argue that point." And as an afterthought he added, "Certainly my boy, Tolya, thinks highly of your boy. You too, for that matter. That counts for somethin'!"

These sentiments surprised Heinrich. From what he'd observed, Russian men didn't seem to care two kopecks about their children. But Lepinov didn't give Heinrich a chance to respond. He plowed on with what he had in mind.

"Now, I am gonna give you some advice."

Heinrich stiffened at the thought that this common laborer should think he had anything to say to him.

Seeing his neighbor's reluctance to hear what he had to say, Lepinov raised his hand. "No, ya listen ta me. I have a good friend on the Zemstvo. I don't mind telling ya, there are those who've been asking about ya. After all, ya are my neighbor. They want to know things. There are no secrets in our new communist society," he said proudly. "Everything is shared!"

A chill ran down Heinrich's back as he heard Lepinov's words that the council was asking about him. A look of alarm appeared on his face. He was about to speak, but Lepinov put up his hand. He would not be interrupted.

"Now, here's the problem. They tell me that ya haven't applied for a labor book. That may not seem like such a big deal, but do ya realize ya could be sent to prison for not havin' one? Everyone must have a labor book. It's the new law! Don't ya read the information postings?"

When Heinrich returned his stare with a blank look, Fyodor shook his head.

"I didn't think so. Now listen ta me, comrade. Ya don't seem ta have a clue about how the world works, so I'm goin' ta give ya a bit of a heads up. The *Zemstvo* wants to talk to ya about why ya don't have a labor book. Ya gotta stand before the council and explain things."

"But I know nothing of such things! What can I say?"

"Now, calm yerself. I'm doin' ya a favor here. When ya stand before the council, make sure ya tell them straight up what ya do for work. No lies. They'll catch ya up quick if ya do. And then there's nothin' for it. There's no helpin' ya. Apologize for not getting yer labor book when ya were supposed ta and maybe it'll go good for ya. The comrades on the council, they're all good sorts. They're just looking out for the interests of the people, ya know."

Lepinov checked to make sure Heinrich was getting all of this.

"I've put in a good word for you, comrade neighbor." He smiled reassuringly. "Ain't nobody goin' to hurt ya. Ya"ll be all right," he added with more confidence than he felt.

Not knowing what to think, Heinrich thanked Fyodor for his advice. He left Lepinov's house wondering at this turn of events. He was nervous about the prospect of being called before the town council. Since the revolution, the old council had been replaced by a group of strong communist sympathizers. Some were Bolshevik. Others were Socialist Revolutionaries. But Fyodor Alexandrovich's words gave him some hope. As he walked along the road Heinrich began to formulate in his mind what he would say to the council. He began to calm down. Things would work out; he had faith that God would protect him.

8

The building to which Heinrich had been summoned was across Prince Alexander Street from the Trans-Siberian Railway Station. It sat amongst a hodge-podge of buildings in the industrial district of Kulomzino that had once been factories and repair shops. With the war and now the revolution, everything seemed to have come to a standstill and the buildings were mostly empty and abandoned. This particular building had been a small shop in which repairs had been made on the upholstery of the first class coaches. The coaches had been removed from the trains and were now sitting idle and derelict on sidings in the yard. The building had been commandeered for other, more important, government purposes and now the local Zemstvo, or soviet, as the new town council liked to call itself, was using it as their meeting hall.

The room into which Heinrich was directed was dimly lit. What little light emanated from the small flickering electric light bulb hanging on a long cord from the high ceiling was discouraged from doing its job by the haze of cigarette smoke that floated in the air around it. Nevertheless, Heinrich stole a glance at the light. Electric lights were few and far between in Kulomzino. He looked about the room and noticed old equipment and bolts of fabric were stacked aimlessly in one corner. Papers were strewn on the floor. Boards had been nailed over a window that had once looked into the street. Shards of glass lay on the floor beneath it.

The five members of the council stared at Heinrich. They were seated behind a rectangular table on which rested a ubiquitous bottle of vodka. Glasses were scattered about. In his three-piece suit Heinrich felt very out of place. He stood facing the councilors, holding his bowler hat between his hands and nervously clutching it to his chest. Now that he was face to face with the council, the light in the room made its members look sinister and his resolve was rapidly evaporating.

"Citizen Rempel."

The chairman, Commissar Grigory Uspensky, was a large, muscular man who had been a blacksmith before being elected to his present political position. He had addressed Heinrich without looking at him. Commissar Uspensky was seated to Heinrich's right, at the end of the table. He was shuffling through a pile of papers. The chairman paused to take a sip from his glass. The sound of the glass striking the table when he put it down startled Heinrich; it seemed amplified, much too loud for such a small cup. Finally, the commissar looked at Heinrich.

"I do not call you 'Comrade' because I do not know your political leanings. I would like you to tell me, but I think I already know." He paused again. "But that is not what we are here for today. We will leave that discussion for another time."

Heinrich tried to keep his composure. His hands were sweating and he felt a trickle of liquid under an armpit. He wanted to blow his nose; he could feel it begin to run.

The Commissar seemed to come to a decision and got right down to business.

"Citizen Rempel," he began gruffly, "you have not applied for a labor book. You cannot work without one. Did you know that everyone is required to have a labor book?"

Heinrich's heart skipped a beat. "No, I'm sorry, your Honor."

Commissar Uspensky interrupted harshly.

"Don't call me that. We are all equals here. I will not be addressed by that old monarchist claptrap!"

"Yes, sir," Heinrich responded nervously. "I was not aware that I was required to carry a labor book. I had not read the council's announcement postings."

"Your ignorance is no excuse. It is your duty to inform yourself, Citizen Rempel. The will of the people must be obeyed by all."

There was a pause.

"What work do you do, Citizen Rempel?"

"Comrade Chairman," Heinrich began, remembering Lepinov's advice. He had prepared his words carefully. "I am preparing to open a business that will supply plows for the farmers of Omsk. We need to grow as much food as possible on the fertile steppes of our region to feed the workers, the women and the children who live in our city and the rest of Siberia. The plows I want to import have a revolutionary new design. With these plows the work of the farmers will be made so much more efficient. I have ordered the plows from Deere and Company. They are coming from America. I have built a warehouse where I can store and sell them."

Heinrich felt some pride in his plan and was sure the council would see the benefit to the people of what he was proposing.

The Commissar and a couple of others at the table laughed.

"Plows. From America!" they scoffed.

"Yes, sir. These plows can revolutionize farming. They actually lay the earth over in a perfect furrow behind the plow. It makes the farmer's work so much easier." He shifted his feet nervously, knowing from the look on the faces before him that his words were not having the desired effect.

A man seated beside the Commissar scowled, "The workers of Russia will make their own plows. Our comrade farmers do not need plows from America."

"Forget about selling plows, Citizen Rempel," Commissar Uspenski growled. "There is no room in the new, Soviet Russia for private enterprise." The last two words were spoken, distastefully, as if they held the portent of evil. "All goods are now being distributed through the consumer communes. Find something else that is useful to do."

A low voice at the table to Heinrich's left spoke up.

"You say you have an empty warehouse. Have you seen all the refugees in the streets? They need roofs over their heads. Do something that will benefit the workers' revolution. Build apartments in your warehouse. Help us get some of these people off the street."

Thoughts swirled in Heinrich's head. Denied permission to open his store! Forget about selling farm implements? Turn the warehouse into apartments?

Commissar Uspenksy glared at Heinrich.

"An inspector will be around to make sure you comply. Comrade Dernov has the labor books."

Just then they were interrupted by a man who threw open the door. He rushed into the room and crouched down beside the Commissar. He whispered animatedly in his ear. Uspensky started in surprise and jumped to his feet.

"Get out. We're done with you for now." He spat the words in Heinrich's direction.

As Heinrich hurried out, the door was slammed behind him. He heard loud, excited talking coming from within the room. He did not stop to consider what the fuss was about, but hurried into the street. Once outside, Heinrich found himself holding a new labor book. He could not remember exactly how it came to be in his hands; he had a vague impression of someone giving it to him as he left. As he stood in the street, Heinrich realized that all around him, men were coming out of doorways, shouting and running across the street toward the railway station. For a moment he thought they were coming for him, but they all passed him by. Everything felt surreal. He could hardly focus his thoughts. It did not occur to him to wonder what the commotion was about.

Heinrich hurried home.

That night Heinrich and Katy had a quiet conversation. The children were all in bed. He was seated at the table staring at his hands, at nothing. Katy was finishing cleaning up the supper dishes. He told her the bad news: no plows, no business, the order to build apartments. He began to weep. Katy came to him and hugged his head to her breast.

"What are we going to do?" he cried through his tears. "We have no choice. The council will allow no argument. These men are ruthless."

He wept for his lost dream and the helplessness he felt.

Katy took a breath. "You know," she said, "I've been thinking recently that the little house is getting too tight for us. Don't you agree? Now that we have four children, there is simply not enough room in here. We're constantly stumbling over each other. Why don't we move into the apartment in the warehouse? We would have more room and then we could rent out the little house, too. What do you think?"

Heinrich looked up, unconvinced. Katy used her apron to dry his wet eyes.

Meanwhile, as Heinrich and Katy lamented and discussed their future in the imagined safety of their little house, the former Tsar of All the Russias, Nicholas II, together with members of his family and personal household, were being detained and held captive on a train at the Kulomzino Station by a detachment of Red Guards.

The day was April 28, 1918. Heinrich would learn of the details from his neighbor, Ivan.

"I was walking in the rail yard, when the train arrived. Like everyone else in the area I went to see what was going on. For days, we'd heard rumors that the Royal family was to be moved from Tobolsk, where they had been imprisoned since the abdication, to Moscow. No one really knew why they were being moved. Some said the Tsar was to be put on trial. Another rumor had it that he was going to be directed to sign a peace treaty with Germany at Brest-Litovsk to give it more weight in the eyes of the world. One rumor even suggested the monarchy was going to be reinstated, with certain conditions limiting its power, of course.

"But it was very obvious they were going nowhere, at least for the moment. When the train arrived at the station, the Red Guard was there to greet it. The train had to stop for a refill of water and wood. It was a simple matter to block it. There certainly were enough guns about. Later they moved the cars onto a siding. They removed the engine and the Red Guards surrounded the cars containing the Royal family. A crowd gathered, like flies on a sausage they were. Some stood quietly, thinking God only knows what. Others shouted to bring the Tsar out so he could experience some real Siberian justice. There were some pretty nasty things being said, I can tell you. But the Zemstvo and the Guards were in complete control. A few harsh words and the people behaved themselves. This was not going to be allowed to become a lynch mob.

"People came and went from the train car. Apparently there was a special commissar from Moscow, named Yakovlev, who was escorting the Royals. He brought them to Kulomzino because he was trying to avoid Ekaterinburg, where the Bolsheviks insisted they would stop the train and detain the prisoners. But he misjudged the Siberian Soviets; they were not about to give up their prize. The Ekaterinburg Soviet got wind of Yakovlev's plan, telegraphed the Omsk Soviet, and here we are. What I didn't see for myself, I was told by people I trust. It's all true.

"And you know," Ivan added as an afterthought, "now that it's done, I'm not sure how I feel about it. He was the Tsar after all."

The Romanovs were held captive at the Kulomzino station for two days. On the evening of April 29, Yakovlev lost his struggle to control his prisoners' fate. He was ordered by his superiors in Moscow to proceed to Ekaterinburg. The train carrying the royal family traveled through the darkness into the west, toward Ekaterinburg where it arrived the next day, where the Tsar and his family were given up to the Bolsheviks, and where they were soon to be murdered in the basement of a nondescript country house.

Two

Foreign Intervention

1

I arrived in Omsk, Siberia on a cold day in October 1918.

After enduring eighteen months as a prisoner of war, my time at the detention centre in Doeberitz, Germany, came to an abrupt end one drizzly day in April 1916. There was a particularly severe outbreak of a virulent form of influenza circulating amongst the Russian prisoners and as a result I had been spending all of my waking hours at the camp hospital. I was examining a patient suffering from double pneumonia, as surely a death sentence for the poor fellow as any firing squad, when two guards entered the room with a summons to appear before the Commandant. As I was marched across the compound, I could not for the life of me come up with a good reason for such a meeting. The guards occasionally could be prodded into conversing with us, but that day my escort was tight-lipped.

I was ushered into Colonel Bogen's office. The Commandant was a small man. He wore a pair of wire-rimmed spectacles resting on a flat nose that leaned toward his right cheek, evidence of a break that had healed poorly. The colonel looked rumpled and tired as he hunched over his desk with his face buried in a pile of papers. As I waited, standing at attention, a large fly buzzed spastically against the cloudy windowpane in a futile effort to escape to the outdoors. The Commandant finally put down his pen and looked up. He picked up a swatter and, after two misses, managed to kill the fly.

He got right to business.

"Good morning, Captain Benny. You will be pleased to learn that you are being repatriated. Report to the parade ground at 14:00. From there you will be transported to the station where you will board a train that will take you to a ship in Rotterdam bound for England. Do you have any questions?"

Repatriated? I knew that I should have some questions, but could think of nothing to say. My mind was blank with the shock of his announcement.

"Well then." He rose from his chair and saluted. "Thank you for your efforts on behalf of the patients at the hospital. Your services will be missed. Good bye."

Just like that. I was going home!

During what has euphemistically been called the Great War, the Germans and the Brits had a policy of exchanging POWs, especially officers, for repatriation. Why? Perhaps it was a last remaining vestige of the old days of chivalry between enemies. Honor among thieves, as it were. I have my own theory that the motivation was simply pragmatic: warm bodies were needed to replace losses on both sides of the trenches. Whatever the reason, I considered myself fortunate to be one of those chosen.

And it happened just as he said it would.

After a period of rest and recuperation, I was assigned to serve in a POW hospital. The irony of the posting didn't escape me. It was the Belmont Prisoner of War Hospital, in Sutton, Surrey; the obvious difference being, this time the prisoners were German. The Belmont Hospital was a large, uninviting barracks of a place standing on land between the Brighton Road and the Sutton By-Pass, slightly to the north of the Belmont Railway Station. It was surprisingly well supplied and outfitted. We managed to provide quality health care to men we would otherwise have gladly tried to kill, given other circumstances. That irony, too, did not fail to escape me.

2

In December 1917, at a meeting of the Allied Supreme War Council comprised of representatives from Britain, France, the US and their allies, the decision was taken to intervene in Russia. With the October Bolshevik revolution, the political situation in Russia that autumn had become extremely unstable. Winston Churchill was the British Secretary of War at the time. He was a passionate hater of the Bolsheviks whom he regarded as terrorists. Churchill was one of those who pushed hard to bring assistance to any organization of Russians who wished to dismantle the Reds' hold on political power. To make matters worse, in March 1918, Lenin signed a peace treaty with Germany at Brest-Litovsk effectively taking Russia out of the war. As a result, the German armies tied up in the east were now being redeployed to the western front. That, of course, was putting tremendous pressure on Allied forces. Intervention in Russia and the reestablishment of a second front became a high priority.

Ambitious plans were soon in place to send expeditionary forces into Russia. By the summer of 1918, bases of operation were set up, with little initial opposition, at Murmansk and Archangel in the north. To reach into the heart of Russia through its back door at Vladivostok, a mission to Siberia was also set in motion.

3

Late in January 1918, I was transferred from the Belmont Hospital and attached to the Twenty-fifth Middlesex Battalion. Its commander was Colonel John Ward, who was also a Labor MP in the British Parliament. The Middlesex wore the grand nickname, the "Die-Hards," because of a gallant action during the Peninsular Wars against Napoleon. But this incarnation of the Die-Hards was far from being a front-line unit. In military terms, they were what was known as B one-ers. They were a reserve battalion doing garrison duty in Hong Kong.

Frankly, I was very unhappy with my new assignment. At the time, it made no sense to me whatever. Though I could hardly have thought of myself as assisting the war effort while stationed in a hospital dedicated to catering to the needs of former enemy combatants, I was still doing work that was important and helpful in the cause of serving the needs of my fellow man. Being assigned to a secondary battalion, in Hong Kong of all places, far from the action in France and the urgent needs at home and with no indication of the purpose for the posting, seemed utterly nonsensical.

With no choice in the matter I reluctantly left my duties at Belmont. With many an "*Auf wiedersehn*" spoken by patients with whom I had developed bonds of friendship, I again went to sea.

After a long and arduous journey that took me by ship to Persia, overland by train to India, and then again by sea, I finally arrived in Hong Kong in April. It was the beginning of the rainy season and I remember the day as being particularly frustrating. No one seemed to be expecting me. Nor, of course, did they have any idea why I had been sent. But a doctor is always a welcome addition to a military unit and I was immediately posted to the infirmary where the largest complaint among the soldiers seemed to be the huge boils they suffered as a result of the prickly heat that covered the island with a muggy, relentless ennui. I did my duty, but I grumbled along with the rest of the men in the sweltering afternoons. When there was nothing to do, which was often, we would sit on the veranda of the infirmary complaining about the heat and the pelting rain while fondly reciting memories of home.

All that changed in the last week of June.

I remember we had just finished breakfast when we were abruptly ordered to make preparations to ship out. Our ears perked up when it was added that we should ready ourselves for cold weather. Though we weren't told where we were going, it didn't take much imagination to predict our destination. The battalion gossip network soon had us all informed; a planned mission to Siberia, scrubbed in January, was being remounted. Sailors from allied ships in the harbor had just seized control of a Russian port city in the Sea of Japan, Vladivostok. That's where we were headed.

At last I was able to find some sense in where the Fates had brought me. Someone in the upper echelons of The Powers-That-Be, I supposed, had taken note of my fluency in Russian and decided I might be of some use on a mission to Siberia. I found reassurance in the thought, but little comfort.

On a Saturday in July we went to sea aboard a refitted, rusty cargo vessel, the Ping Suie, headed northeast for Vladivostok. It was only later, after we arrived, that we would be given our orders. They were, and I quote, "to assist the orderly elements of Russian Society to reorganize themselves under a national government and to resurrect and reconstruct the Russian Front." Quite a task for 800 officers and men! In fairness, though we were the first Allied army battalion to arrive, we were a fairly small fish in what would soon become a very large pond. It wasn't long before we were joined on our assignment by battalions from Canada, France, Japan, and the United States, though, as it turned out, the Americans refused to venture any further west into Siberia than Irkutsk.

We arrived in Vladivostok on the third of August 1918. Aside from sailing through a typhoon in the Sea of Japan that left us all terrified and seasick, the voyage was uneventful. Needless to say, we were all grateful when at last we saw in the distance the rocky slopes of Russian Island and realized we would soon be setting our feet once more on solid ground.

As we sailed north with Russian Island on our starboard side, we could see a line of dark scars on its hills. They marked a series of fortresses that were part of the defenses of what was the most heavily guarded port on the eastern Pacific, the home of the Russian Pacific Fleet. We entered Golden Horn Bay with the Egersheld Peninsula to port, and there was Vladivostok. Grandly named Rule of the East, its dirt streets and low brick buildings hugged small hills that clustered around and fled together up toward the highest peak, Mt. Kholodilnik.

We were the first Allied army troops to arrive. An air of celebration greeted us in the harbor as the many ships lying at anchor were merrily decorated with colorful flags in their masts and rigging. The blasts of the ships' horns echoed discordantly off the surrounding hills. It was a fine welcome that made us all feel proud. Standing by the deck rail of the Ping Suie while she was piloted to her berth at the pier, we gawked and pointed like cheerful tourists on vacation.

An honor guard from the armored cruiser HMS Suffolk presented arms and stood at attention as we disembarked. When we were gathered in formation on the wharf, various international and local bigwigs regaled us with their speeches: fanciful words about supporting our Russian Allies and working together for the common good of all against the scourge of the Bolshevik terrorists. The sentiments were worthy, but you'll forgive my impertinence for I have long since become weary and distrustful of men in positions of political power.

Though it was August, the day was quite chilly. Glad to be ashore, we made a fine sight as we marched smartly along Svetlanskaya Street to the town square. We were led by a Czech army band and a contingent of sailors from the Suffolk, resplendent in their sparkling whites. Everyone greeted us with salutes and cheers; everyone, that is, except for the Japanese soldiers who, as we would later learn, looked upon us with scorn as inferior beings and therefore gave us no acknowledgement whatsoever.

After a lot of foofaraw, we finally reached our destination, a ramshackle collection of buildings on a hill just outside the town at a place called Niloy-ugal. As we wearily set down our packs our high spirits sank into our boots. We were told that attempts had been made to clean up the place in preparation for our arrival, but our barracks were dirty and unsanitary. We got to work and did what we could to make them habitable.

In the not too distant future many of us would come to appreciate those barracks most heartily. For within the week, half of the battalion would be digging trenches in which to sleep and fight in the marshy wetlands along the Ussuri River. There they would show their mettle and earn the right to carry their nickname, the Die-Hards, in a fiercely fought battle that would, for a time, break organized Bolshevik resistance in eastern Siberia.

For the rest of us, another important task lay at hand. To assist Russia in its struggle against Germany, the Allies had sought to provide the Tsar's armies with the munitions and supplies it so desperately needed. Now, by some estimates almost six hundred and fifty thousand tons of war materiel was lying stockpiled in the fortresses surrounding the port town of Vladivostok. There it sat, a tremendously tempting treasure trove in a country where anarchy had replaced the rule of law. Our first job, along with some American sailors and a sizeable contingent of Japanese infantry, was to keep those shiny guns, cannons and all other manner of paraphernalia needed to fight a war from falling into the wrong hands. After the Brest-Litovsk peace treaty, hundreds of thousands of German, Austrian and Hungarian prisoners of war had been released from prison camps all over Siberia. They were now running free, and though many had been able to board trains heading west toward home, many others had banded together in impromptu partisan units and were wreaking havoc in the countryside. Some had joined the Bolsheviks and, in the guise of pushing forward the ideals of the communist revolution, were terrorizing everyone who had the misfortune of meeting them. Any one of these groups would have dearly loved to get their hands on the stores lying idle in Vladivostok.

4

I very quickly learned that for every group of educated Russians you had an equivalent number of ideologies. Oppressed for generations by Tsarist rule, they were finally free to express their thoughts. And express them they did, going off in all political directions at once. That was why it was so difficult to unite them. They couldn't agree on a common philosophy.

The two largest groups, the Socialist Revolutionaries and the Bolsheviks could never see eye to eye when it came to remaking the Russian social and political landscape. The Socialist Revolutionaries were most popular in rural Russia. They considered Russia's peasants to be the revolutionary class and wanted to socialize the land by putting it into the hands of the peasants. The Bolsheviks were popular in the cities. They considered the proletariat, the industrial workers, to be the revolutionary class and wanted to nationalize the land. The Bolsheviks wanted the land to be controlled by the state in order to serve the needs of the proletariat. With such extreme differences in ideology, there was no room for compromise.

So you can understand why, on June 29, 1918, the Socialist Revolutionaries in Omsk decided to take a stand against Bolshevik communism. They dissolved the elected government in Tomsk and formed the Provisional Government of Siberia, with Omsk as its capital.

One of their first moves was to return to their owners the industries confiscated by the Bolsheviks.

5

In September 1918, the Middlesex battalion was ordered to proceed to Omsk. We were loaded into old converted cattle-trucks for the eight thousand kilometer journey. Each wagon was outfitted with an iron stove in the middle. Two tiers of wooden bunks were built along the walls and on the ends so that each car could hold about twenty men. The center of the car on both sides opened with a sliding door, so we were able to enjoy plenty of fresh air on days when the temperatures became hot. All told, there were three trains traveling together to accommodate all eight hundred of us, our supplies and the battalion's stable of horses.

The trip took weeks to complete. It was filled with stark contrasts, from traveling days on end passed fields of unharvested corn lying black and wasted on the ground, to endless expanses of sand dunes, followed by green forests, and marshy steppes. Blackened and devastated villages along the track gave testimony to the ravages of anarchy.

The journey was made slower because every few days we had to stop for a rest day to exercise the horses, not to mention our own stiff limbs. When we stopped, ragged and starving refugees would mob our trains, hands outstretched in a silent appeal for food. We were only too happy to share what we had from our rations.

Our progress through Siberia was also hampered by the disorganization of the railway. This was caused, in large part, by the chaos that followed the eviction of the ruling Bolsheviks from towns along the way by citizens emboldened by rumors of help to come, sometimes only hours before our arrival.

On one occasion we arrived in a small town expecting to be met by a replacement engine and its driver. The station however was entirely deserted. A patrol was sent out to investigate. The poor man was soon found trapped in the mechanic's shed with a gun pointed at his head. The Bolsheviks who were trying to dissuade him from helping us made a run for it and disappeared into the forest. A squad of men gave chase but soon returned without having been able to find the cowards.

The Bolshevik flag was still flying on the town's flagpole. I accompanied a group of soldiers whose job it was to remove the red rag and hoist our own Union Jack. Our experience in most towns was that the Russian people generally welcomed such a gesture with relief and gladness. Our presence represented a return to stable government and security.

On this particular occasion, however, an old woman in the small group of observers who were watching us seemed to be quite upset by what we were doing. Her matted hair protruded at odd angles from underneath a tattered kerchief. Her dark coat was in ruins and her bare feet were wrapped in dirty rags that held the memory of color beneath their grime. She muttered to herself and shook her head, becoming more agitated by the minute.

Thinking I would like to find out the reason for her distress, I made my way over to where the woman stood. She started in surprise when I spoke to her.

"What troubles you, Mother?" I asked in polite Russian.

Her surprise quickly gave way to anger. She glared at me and waved her arms about while shouting, "Go back where you come from! Get out of here! You've no business here! Be gone with you!"

I had seen the anarchy and destruction that followed the Bolsheviks wherever they went so I was rather taken aback by her attitude. I asked her why.

She looked me in the eyes and after a moment shrugged. "Well, it really doesn't matter. Our men will soon find enough earth to bury every last one of you! And that will be the end of it."

She spat upon the road and disappeared among the shacks that lined the street. A mangy black dog ran after her, its nose close to the ground as it followed an invisible trail in the dirt.

When I translated her words for the men in the squad, they shuddered. It seemed to them the old hag had put a curse upon us.

As we marched back to the train, another woman came up to us and kissed our hands as if we were the Messiah returned in the flesh. "*Spasibo, spasibo*! Thank you, thank you for coming!" she wept. "We would all be dead if not for you!"

She pressed an icon into my hands. "God go with you. God protect you."

6

Omsk welcomed us with open exuberance and unbridled joy.

We arrived there on the afternoon of October 18. The railroad station and the newly constructed Trans-Siberian Railway Administration Building next to it were bedecked with a colorful display of the flags of many nations. The new Russian flag proudly flew at the center of the display. Representatives of the new Provisional Government met us and spoke excited words of welcome. Russian women came forward and presented us with the age-old symbols of Tartar welcome: a loaf of bread and a handful of salt handed on a wooden platter on which was painted the image of the grand Administration Building before which we were standing.

With the welcoming ceremonies taken care of, the battalion marched to the Cadet School where the men would be fed and entertained. The officers were invited to the Officer's Club. Along with many of the wealthy and important members of Omsk society who were in attendance, we were treated to a royal feast. The mood was entirely festive. Cheer and good will splashed about the hall like water in a fountain. After a meal fit for a king we watched as Russian officers in sparkling white uniforms danced with coiffed matrons and young blushing women in low-cut evening gowns of pastel-colored silks. And all the while waiters carrying trays of baked delicacies tried their best to keep us eating. Champagne in fluted crystal glasses tickled our throats and for those with less particular tastes, Russian beer flowed freely. Laughter echoed throughout the hall accompanying the string sounds of the quintet playing on the dais.

I wondered if I was the only one who felt uncomfortable with the opulence we were enjoying while the memories of the miserable living conditions we had so recently observed in the majority of the towns and villages along the Trans-Siberian Railway were still fresh in our minds. Russia was plainly a land of great contrast.

Our appearance in Omsk opened a floodgate of relief. I was sitting at a corner table, trying to remain unobtrusive in a room where many wanted to be noticed. During the festivities I had noticed a woman draped in jewelry and white silk dancing on the arm of a Russian officer. Noticing me, she took it upon herself to come over for introductions.

She talked of the fear she had lived with during the past months and I could see the truth of it in her eyes. She told me the Socialist Revolutionaries who controlled the government were targeting officers for imprisonment and execution, vilifying them as one of the main enemies of the new Russia. Every morning, the bodies of officers who had been murdered in the streets were gathered up in wagons and carried off for burial. As an officer, her husband was automatically on the blacklist. She said she would finally be able to sleep the night through, now that the British army was in Omsk.

Another woman later spoke to me of her teenage son, a cadet, who had slept with a loaded rifle at his bedside since the

Bolshevik revolt had begun. Every night he trembled in his bed, expecting a knock on the door as they came for him. His loyalty was to the Tsar. He had participated in the cadet mutiny in the first days of the revolution and had escaped the slaughter. It would only be a matter of time before his name was known and his home discovered. Now she had convinced her son to relinquish his weapon. The streets were being patrolled by the English, the "*Angliyskiye soldaty.*"

In the days that followed, everywhere we went the gentry of Omsk greeted us with open arms and invitations to tea. Had we not had our duties, we would have been happily occupied all the waking hours of the day visiting in the homes of these kind and grateful folk.

7

On November 11, 1918, a truce was signed ending hostilities in Europe. The war was over! For the Middlesex and the other Allied forces in Siberia, though, the end of the war in Europe changed nothing. Our fight was in support of those who struggled to wrest Russia out of the grip of Bolshevism and that struggle was barely begun.

On the night of November 17, a group of army officers and Cossacks arrested the four Socialist Revolutionaries who were part of the Directorate of Five who comprised the Provisional Government of Siberia. The next day a Russian patriot and polar explorer, Admiral Alexandr Kolchak, appointed himself the Supreme Ruler of the Provisional All-Russian Government. Kolchak's first order of business was to move into a palatial residence on the banks of the Irtysh River from where, backed by royalist generals and Cossack troops loyal to the Tsar and supported by the allied armies of the West, he embarked on a campaign of war against the Bolsheviks and their Red Army.

An Oasis of Peace

1

Fyodor Alexandrovich Lepinov was not a happy man. In fact, most days his emotions were in turmoil, alternating between dark depression and barely suppressed, impotent fury.

At work in the Kulomzino rail yards, Lepinov fretted and fumed in the company of his fellow workers. What was to be done? The glorious revolution they had rejoiced to be a part of, the great workers' movement that was to usher Mother Russia into a new age of equality and prosperity for all, which had begun with so much promise, was stalled as surely as a steam engine in an avalanche. Ever since the Socialist Revolutionaries had removed the Bolsheviks from power in Omsk, Lepinov's dream of a true communist state had been shattered. In his opinion, Socialist Revolutionaries knew nothing about what was best for the Russian people!

And now there had been another coup. This one saw the rise to power of a Tsarist Admiral and things were taking a disastrous turn. All power and authority was now concentrated in this one man, this dictator, this Kolchak who was committed to utterly defeating the revolution Lepinov and his comrades had worked so hard to achieve.

"This monarchist bunch is worst of all!" he argued. "At least the SR's, ignorant buggers though they are, want some sort of change. But this bunch!" Lepinov groaned in exasperation. "They trot about in their white Tsarist uniforms with their Cossack lapdogs by their side and all they want ta do is get things to where they used ta be. Well, we're done with the monarchy! It's the workers who're gonna make the decisions from now on."

Someone interjected, unheard, under his breath, "Those Cossack lapdogs pack a big bite!"

"You're right, Lepinov," mused a comrade, ignoring the Cossack comment. "They want their precious monarchy back. They want to put us, the industrial workers of Russia, back in our place under their heel where we've always been, with no rights, no work and no food."

"They think they can set back the clock," someone else added.

Even more infuriating for the revolutionaries, though, was the presence in Omsk of thousands of foreign soldiers from Britain, France, Canada, Japan, and who knew how many other countries.

"It's as plain ta see as the whiskers on a rat's nose," Lepinov rued, "the only reason these foreigners are in Omsk is ta help Kolchak's White counter-revolutionary government stay in power and fight its war against the working class."

These discussions were repeated almost daily and the level of frustration and desperation grew daily as well.

Something must be done! But what?

2

Anatoly Lepinov did not go to school. His father was loud in his denunciation of the formal, public education delivered by the Russian Orthodox Church nor could he afford the fees they demanded, so in his childhood years Anatoly had spent his days playing by himself or roaming the streets and byways of Kulomzino. But since his twelfth birthday, Lepinov had begun taking Anatoly to the Trans-Siberian Railway yard to help in the machine shop. He intended for his son to follow in his footsteps as a machinist. Anatoly watched how Lepinov repaired damaged and worn out parts on the train wagons and engines. He fetched tools for his father and did other simple odd jobs.

However, Anatoly had little interest in grease, heavy wrenches, or broken machinery. When his father became distracted, Anatoly would flee the workshop and wander about the yards. The revolution had left rows of abandoned railway cars on unused tracks. These wagons had been broken into and vandalized, and then were transformed into homes for many refugees who had fled the fighting in the west and had traveled the rails to Kulomzino in search of safety. Anatoly even saw families camped underneath wagons, using whatever scraps of tin and wood they could find to provide some protection from the weather. In the warm days of spring and summer, these makeshift homes provided adequate shelter. But now, in the deepening cold of winter, the people living in these makeshift hovels clung desperately to the fragile strings of life as they huddled together around smoky fires inside and under the wagons, seeking some protection from the snow and icy wind.

In the evenings or on days when his friends were not in school and when their chores had been completed, Anatoly spent the hours playing with Henry and Sonia. The children stayed outdoors as much as they could, enjoying as only children can the bright sunshine reflecting off the white frozen landscape.

When the friends became chilled, they would huddle up against the brick walls of the warehouse. The rays of the weakening sun collected in the brick of the south-facing wall and the children would bask in the smidgen of warmth that radiated onto their backs in the frosty cold.

A favorite game was wrestling. Sonia was quick and wiry and gave Henry all the trouble he could handle when they tussled and tried to throw each other into the soft banks of snow. When the boys struggled and grunted to see who could best the other, Anatoly always came out on top. In fact, Anatoly was regularly able to defeat any boy who challenged him to a wrestling match.

Most of the time the matches ended with smiles and handshakes. One day, though, the wrestling ended badly. A neighborhood boy named Vlad lost his temper after he again found himself face down on the frozen ground. He shouted in anger as he picked himself up and his buddies who had stood by to watch piled onto Anatoly, knocking him over. The mittens came off and soon there were bruised eyes and battered noses that left droplets of red blood-sprayed abstract designs in the white trampled snow.

Heinrich was working at some chore or other when he heard the commotion. He went outside to investigate and discovered a collection of various neighbors and curious passers-by encouraging the boys in their melee. The spectators were being treated to a spontaneous recreation and were finding it quite amusing! They were even attempting to help matters along, with many a call of, "Watch your back! Look to the left! Mind his right arm!" And groans of, "Whoa, that was a good hit!"

Heinrich ignored the ring of spectators and waded directly into the melee. First he grabbed his son by the arm and pulled him out of the fray. This elicited a few boos and whistles from the gallery, but had the effect of causing the rest of the combatants to slowly lose their zeal for the fight. They broke off, staring bewilderedly about and wiping their bloody noses on their grubby jacket sleeves. As quickly as it had begun, the fight was over. Some of the boys turned tail and ran, scattering in several directions.

The spectators were not pleased that their entertainment had been ended. More than a couple of them grumbled as they shuffled on their way.

"Poor sport. He should have let them finish it. How's a boy ta learn ta look after 'imself if he don't knock a few heads about when 'e's a kid?"

Heinrich ignored them. He looked Henry over. One of his eyes was swelling, but other than that, he seemed no worse for the wear. Heinrich next summoned Anatoly to his side. He seemed unfazed by the pummeling he had received.

"Are you all right, Tolya?" he asked.

When Anatoly assured him that he was, Heinrich added, "Come into our house with us. I want to talk to you." It was a command, not an invitation. "You, too, Sonia," he added to the girl who was looking solemnly at Henry's puffy eye.

When everyone was cleaned up and comfortable, and Katy had given them all a cup of tea to warm their bellies, Heinrich looked sternly at each of the children: Henry, Anatoly, and Sonia. Katarina and Joanna were seated beside them as well.

Addressing his own children, Heinrich scolded, "Children, have I not taught you that it is wrong to fight?"

Henry, Katarina and Joanna all nodded their heads in agreement. Though he was not being addressed, Anatoly managed to look sheepish. He was not sure where all this was going. He'd been fighting ever since he could remember. Everyone fought. How else were they to hold their own out on the street?

"But Mr. Rempel," said Anatoly quietly. "People are always fighting. My dad tells me I must fight if I'm ta survive. He even shows me how."

Heinrich looked hard at Anatoly. "What has fighting ever gained?"

Anatoly smiled and replied, "Well, if I'm fast enough, the other guy gets to have the bloody nose!"

Joanna brought her hand to her mouth to suppress a giggle.

"Yes, but what will that have accomplished?" her father replied. "What happens the next time you meet your enemy? Aren't you afraid the fight will start all over again?"

Anatoly was thoughtful. "Sometimes it does. Sometimes I just walk on the other side of the street. And sometimes they never bother me again."

"What would happen if you tried to do something good for your enemy? Would it be possible to settle your differences that way?"

Anatoly shook his head and laughed. "He'd think I'm crazy! Imagine doing something good for your enemy!"

3

For Lepinov and the rest of the workers at the Kulomzino railway yards, the civil war being waged by Kolchak's White forces against the Bolsheviks became personal when, one day in November two armored trains crossed the Irtysh River and stopped at the Kulomzino station to take on wood and water. There was something unusual about these broneviki. The two trains were carrying British sailors and were armed with huge cannons from a British warship.

It was soon discovered that the British armored trains had come from Vladivostok. They were mounted with long-barreled cannons taken from the armored cruiser, HMS Suffolk, and were speeding westward to assist in a fierce battle being waged in and around the city of Perm. The Red Army was struggling to hold its own against tough opposition from a White army aided by soldiers from a Czech army and its broneviki. In the end, the workers later learned, with the help of those British guns, the Red Army had been badly defeated and forced to retreat.

"What are we gonna do about all these bloody foreign interventionists?" demanded Lepinov in frustration.

A group of six or eight machinists, welders, and mechanics was sitting on old boxes and blocks of wood in the shed, sharing bottles of kvass and smoking. Most of them were big men, and dressed in their heavy, brown leather aprons, with grimy hands and dirty bearded faces they looked like a congregation of disgruntled trolls. Very little work was being done these days. The workers, almost to a man, were strong Bolsheviks and they were very discouraged.

Vershinsky was the exception. He was a cheerful man who liked to say that he was not convinced by the arguments of any side —Monarchist, Socialist Revolutionary or Bolshevik. He was keeping his options open, he would say with a smile, and would make his decision on whom to support when the time came.

Vershinksy's happy demeanor did little to lift the low morale in the machine shop, for the men were in a very awkward situation. They were proud of their ability to repair and maintain the railway's steam engines and rolling stock. But now, any work they did aided the efforts of those who were waging war against their comrades in the Red Army. The Whites were in control of the railroad and the engines they repaired were being used to pull soldiers and armaments to the western front. Yet, if the workers in the machine shops wanted to eat, they had to obey their new masters.

Lepinov was leaning forward, resting his chin on cupped hands with his elbows on his knees. He dragged his fingers over his cheeks and rubbed his forehead as he sat up. He growled and continued talking.

"We're cut off from our comrades in the east and we're cut off from our comrades in the west."

He paused, thinking. Someone handed him a bottle. He took a big swallow of kvass and passed the bottle to his comrade to the left. He looked around the circle.

"We're trapped on a tiny island surrounded by a river polluted with stinking foreign interventionists and counter-revolutionaries."

He felt hopeless and looked to his comrades for a solution to their problem. No one spoke until they heard a voice that up until that moment had been silent.

"Well then," mumbled Gorshkov, a welder who peered at his comrades with a perpetual squint.

Gorshkov's eyesight had been badly damaged when one day in a fit of impatience he had spent an afternoon welding with a crack in his protective goggles. He had damaged them and there was no spare pair of tinted glasses to be found in the shop. Gorshkov had boasted, "I don't need those goggles anyway. I've been doing this so long I can weld with my eyes shut." But, of course, Gorshkov had had to look. Now he was plagued by an annoying dark spot directly in the centre of his field of vision. Whether from pride or fear of losing his position, Gorshkov had admitted his problem to no one. His mates all knew the truth. He needn't have worried. His secret was safe with them. The boss never found out. And though the quality of his work suffered for a while, Gorshkov's comrades covered for him until he learned to compensate for his handicap. For their kindness, Gorshkov was deeply grateful.

"Well then," Gorshkov said again, throwing the smoldering stub of his cigarette in the direction of the corner where it narrowly missed landing in a pile of oily rags. "I think what we're going to have to do is dam the river, if you take my meaning."

"What do you mean, comrade?" asked Ovechkin, a huge boilermaker who was never quick to understand the subtleties of language. He needed things spelled out clear and simple. "Don't speak in riddles, man!"

Lepinov sat up straight and for the first time in a long while felt a tinge of hope. Dam the river! Perhaps there was something they could do, after all.

Gorshkov looked purposefully at Ovechkin. "What do you think I mean? It's obvious, comrade."

Ovechkin frowned. As well as not being very bright, he was also fond of vodka. Kvass was not for him. What was the point of drinking something that made you only a little drunk? He had been tipping a bottle of vodka for most of the morning.

"The railroad is the river, see. The bridge over the Irtysh is its weak spot. No bridge, no river. No more trains going to reinforce the Whites," said Gorshkov with more patience than he felt.

A hesitant smile creased Ovechkin's dull face. Just as quickly the frown returned.

"But comrade," he slurred. "There *is* a bridge across the Irtysh, a long iron bridge. What do you mean, 'no bridge, no river?'"

Some of the workers who had remained silent up to this point shook their heads. Others chuckled.

"Good grief man, do I need to spell it out for you?" asked Goshkov in exasperation.

Lepinov, who had understood Gorshkov's meaning immediately, rose to his feet. He could barely contain his excitement.

"Comrades," Lepinov said in a hushed voice, "We are gonna need one hell of a lot of dynamite!"

4

If you had asked Heinrich Johann Rempel what his political leanings were, he would have told you that, as a Mennonite, he would always be grateful for the invitation of the Tsarina Catherine the Great that brought the Mennonites into Russia, a land of opportunity in which his family had prospered since 1789. Aside from that, he would say that as a

Christian he was more concerned with the Kingdom of Heaven than with kingdoms of this Earth; so as long as the current rulers allowed him to practice his faith and earn a decent living, they were of no concern to him.

And strangely enough, in that regard Heinrich was not so different from his Bolshevik neighbor, Fyodor Alexandrovich Lepinov, whose utopian dream for his family and the families of his comrades was driven by a desire to have a leak-proof roof to sleep under, plenty of good bread to fill the empty stomach, and honest work to bring dignity to a man's soul. Unlike Heinrich, though, who had no use for alcohol, Lepinov would also have added the desire for a steady supply of vodka to warm the blood into the deal. Lepinov was not interested in empire, only in the fair distribution of wealth and a decent standard of living.

In the months before Lepinov decided to take the radical step of conspiring to become a saboteur in support of the revolution, the Rempel family's concerns were more mundanely centered around the simple but challenging need to keep food on the table. With each change in government there followed a change in currency. Soon after the October 1917 revolution the new Provisional Government had issued "Kerensky rubles", the Kerenki, to replace old Tsarist rubles. Then the Bolsheviks had introduced their own ruble notes to replace the Kerenki. Whatever money was being used at the moment always seemed to be worth less than the currency it replaced. Corruption was rampant; the black market was flourishing. Prices for food staples continued to increase. It all added up to the need to make do with less.

Aside from their personal woes, though, the Rempels were distracted and distressed by the hordes of vagrants wandering the streets of Kulomzino. The quiet of their community had been broken by the massive influx of refugees. Wherever the family went they met dirty, desperate people searching for food and a safe place to sleep. Some of the children and adults held out their caps in mute appeals for alms. Many didn't have the energy to beg, but simply trudged along without taking their eyes from the ground before their feet. Katy's heart broke when she saw them.

One day in the spring of 1918, a few weeks after Heinrich's fateful meeting before the town council, as the Rempels entered their little house Katy burst into tears. She and Heinrich had just returned home from the market. They had managed to find some precious flour and salt. With the other supplies she still had, Katy had been looking forward to baking fresh bread for her family. However, baking bread was now the furthest thing from her mind.

As Heinrich and Katy had been about to open the gate of the walkway to their house they had been stopped by a dejected and impoverished family: a frail-looking woman with a collection of large bundles at her feet, a sturdily built man stooped under the weight of a trunk he was carrying, and two small weary-looking children. The children were sitting on the ground with their backs leaning on the Rempel's picket fence. They seemed to be intently picking at the new shoots of soft, green grass and were eating any they happened to find. The expression on the faces of the parents told that they had come to the end of their road. They were exhausted. The look of hunger and desperation in their eyes pierced Katy's soul.

The woman held out her hand. "Some kopeks for the children, kind ma'am? It's been days since they've eaten anything to speak of."

Heinrich guided Katy around the vagrants.

"No, sorry, we have little enough for ourselves," he said, though he felt shame as he spoke.

"It's not much we're askin' for, sir," tried the woman again, pleading.

The man did not speak, but slipped his trunk to the ground with a thump. He groaned, bent over, and sat wearily on the trunk.

Katy stood indecisively. What should she do? She had seen so many people in need. Somehow she felt herself unable to turn her back on this family whose road had ended at her gate. It was obvious they were in a very bad way! They were starving; anyone could see that.

Beside her, Heinrich, with the groceries held firmly in one arm, pushed the gate open and beckoned Katy to follow.

"Come Katy, there is nothing we can do."

And with that he led her to their door and into the house. It was then that Katy had burst into tears.

"But Heinrich, we must help! It is too much! All these people. How do they survive? We must do something!"

"They are not our concern," recited Heinrich with less conviction.

But Katy would not put up with her husband's apathy. Something needed to be done. The refugees had found their way to her door and she would not deny them.

"Those people are obviously exhausted. If we leave them there, who knows what will happen! They may die right on our doorstep. I will not have their deaths on my conscience. You would not want that, would you?"

She was getting angry.

Heinrich was ashamed. "Of course not."

"Then do something for these poor folks!"

She paused for a moment. The beginning of an idea was taking shape in her mind.

"Listen, we have the warehouse. We have been talking about moving into the apartment that was to be used for the hired help. We need the space, you said so yourself. The council ordered you to split the warehouse into apartments. These people could live in one of them."

Heinrich looked doubtful.

Katy pushed on.

"And we've got this huge yard. The soil is good; we have our garden and the rest goes to weeds and dust. The families could put in their own gardens. They could grow their own food. You must see the sense in that!"

Heinrich had to agree.

"OK, we'll do it. But, where will they stay until the apartments are built?"

"They can live in the little house. We'll move into the warehouse apartment tomorrow."

Heinrich laughed. "You've thought of everything, haven't you! Go and invite them in."

Katy hurried down the walk to the road. The family was still there. They hadn't moved, although the woman was now lying awkwardly beside her collection of bundles.

"Would you like to come into our house?" she asked. "I'm sure I can find something for you to eat. We will heat the samovar and make some tea."

That is how the Rempels met the Goshorevs.

5

Aleksey Alekseyevich Goshorev, his wife Ludmila Viktorovna and their children Petr and Lyuda were from Rostov, a city on the Don River. In December, Rostov had been attacked and captured by Cossacks loyal to the Tsar. The family fled the chaos and after months of searching for a safe haven, the Trans-Siberian railway deposited them in Kulomzino. When the Goshorevs found themselves on the ground at the gate of the small log house on Irtysh Street, they had literally come to the end of their energy and their resources.

As it turned out, Goshorev was a skilled carpenter. In the trunk he had lugged from their home in South Russia, Aleksey had carried the tools of his trade. Many were the times he had been tempted to dump his burden by the wayside. The possibility of practicing his trade had seemed dim as the chaos of Rostov had seemed to follow them through town after hostile town.

That first afternoon of their meeting, as the Goshorevs sipped hot tea and ate slices of warm bread fresh from the oven, Ludmila overheard Katy and Heinrich in the kitchen pondering how to go about transforming the warehouse into suites. The Goshorevs were resting on the porch. A bench and chairs were permanently arranged there because when the weather was pleasant the Rempels enjoyed sitting outside and watching the sun go down. They would often sing together until the darkness and cool of the evening sent them indoors.

Ludmila Viktorovna nudged her husband. "Alyosha, you're a carpenter," she whispered. "Tell them." She gestured toward the door. "You could help."

Aleksey, feeling small rays of hope returning with the warmth of the tea and the delicious bread, cleared his throat. Despite the kindness of this family, he was still cautious. Over the last months, he had been rebuffed too many times.

"Sir?" His voice was hesitant. "Excellency?" He was not sure what appellation to use in these confusing times of change. "Uh, Mr. Rempel?"

Heinrich came to the door.

"Sir, I am a carpenter. I have tools. Here, in my trunk," he said, gesturing toward it. "If you need a carpenter, I could do the work. If you wished."

"Really!" said Heinrich, astonished.

And so, Aleksey Goshorev and Heinrich Rempel set about dividing the warehouse space into three new apartments.

Since the existing suite took up one quarter of the warehouse and the other three quarters was a bare shell, it simply required that they construct a ceiling along its length and add two dividing walls to form the three apartments. The front wall of the warehouse already had four windows. The large double door in the center would need to be removed and replaced by a wall containing two smaller doors for the middle units. The end unit could use the door already placed on the end wall, just as the Rempels did in their new apartment. The other big job would be to construct a brick Russian stove to heat each unit, with a chimney climbing through the ceiling and out of the roof.

Because the Goshorevs were to live in one of the units—they moved into the first one that was completed—Aleksey worked for next to nothing. His wages paid for some of the food the Rempels shared with his family and little else. But he was content. His family had a home; he had work. The future, once so dark, was brighter. They would survive.

A couple of weeks into the renovations, who should arrive on the Rempels' yard but old Sergei. With him was a weary, crumpled-looking, grey-haired woman whom he introduced as his mother, Vera Chulkipova.

Sergei ruefully apologized for appearing on the Rempel's doorstep with no invitation.

"We have no place ta go, ya see."

When Heinrich asked him what he meant Sergei's eyes became misty.

"Our village. It ain't there no more."

Katy, who had been working in the garden, wiped her dirty hands on her apron and joined Heinrich at the door.

Heinrich urged Sergei to explain.

"Please go on, Sergei. What do you mean, your village is no longer there?"

"First it were the war. Most of the boys got all excited and took off. Joined the Tsar's army, so they did. Wanted ta fight the Germans. They hated the Germans." Sergei shook his head mournfully. "Begging yer pardon, Your Honor. But yer the only German I ever met and yer a good man, so ya are.

"But then came the bloody Bolsheviks. One day the militia rode into the village on their shaggy Siberian ponies and waving their big guns about. They was looking fer recruits. But like I said, there weren't no young men for them ta force into joining 'em. Like I said, they'd all gone off ta war and not a one of 'em came back all these years since."

Sergei took a slow breath.

"There were a few old men in the village. They took 'em to a barn and strung 'em up by their arms. Tormented 'em an' then shot 'em all. Just like that, and that's a fact!"

He was crying now. His words came tumbling out as the pitch of his voice rose in his grief.

"They set fire ta the whole village. There warn't nothing left of the place. Cinders and coals was all we found. My mother, she hid in the bushes. An' she ain't said a word since. I warn't in the village at the time. Otherwise I'd probably be dead like the rest of 'em."

Sergei blew his nose into a rag from his pocket. He pulled his mother to him in a hug. "It's okay Mother. Yer safe here."

An audience had gathered as Sergei recited his tragic story. Everyone was silent.

Someone muttered, "What is this evil that is loose in our land?"

Sergei looked pleadingly at Heinrich.

"I don't know why I came here, Yer Honor. I only know as you was always a kind and a fair man ta me. And me an' my mother jus' didn' know where else we could go."

It was Katy who spoke up.

"Heinrich, why don't they stay in one of the apartments? There are two empty."

"But I was hoping to rent out the other apartments. We need the income."

"What will you do, turn them away?"

"No, I couldn't do that. But . . ."

"Then it's settled."

Katy took Vera Chulkipova by the arm and guided her into the apartment next to the Goshorevs.

"There is no stove, yet," she said as they entered the bare room, "but we are sharing mine until the others can be built." Vera wearily looked about her. Seeing her look Katy added, "Don't worry, the men will build some furniture for you. You will feel at home in no time."

Sergei's coming turned out to be a godsend for Heinrich and Alexey. Neither had been looking forward to the tricky task of building the brick Russian stoves. Neither had any experience with constructing such things as flues or the labyrinthine chimneys that allowed the oven to double as such an effective heating system. Sergei had been building Russian ovens since he was a boy apprentice with his father.

Sergei smiled broadly when Heinrich told him there was a job that required his skill. He straightened his back and rotated his shoulders. Heinrich heard the joints crackle. The burdens Sergei had been carrying seemed to melt from his appearance.

By mid-summer the apartments were completed. The units were spartan; a large single room with a Russian oven furnished with a table, chairs or bench, and a bed. But nothing could lessen the joy of the families who were fortunate to occupy them and each soon transformed their space into a home.

7

Finding a family to occupy the fourth apartment proved simple.

One day while walking in the town, Aleksey met an acquaintance on the street.

"Dr. Ulyanov, how are you?"

They greeted each other warmly, as only people who have been thrown together in the hardest of times will. Aleksey and Ludmila had run into Maxim Ulyanov and his wife Nadezhda Avanskaya a number of times on the road from the west. The Ulyanovs were also fleeing the devastation in Rostov. At one town, Goshorev could not remember its name, his son, Petr, had become violently ill. Dr. Ulyanov had appeared, seemingly from nowhere, and had somehow coaxed Petr back to health. For that kindness, Aleksey would be forever in Dr. Ulyanov's debt.

In their conversation, Aleksey learned that, upon arriving in Kulomzino, Dr. Ulyanov was offered work in the railroad hospital, a small facility that had once looked after the health of the railway workers and its passengers, but was now open to anyone. He was very happy to be employed and received a small remuneration. However, Nadezhda Avanskaya was very unhappy with their living arrangement. With the glut of refugees in the town, the Ulyanovs were being forced to share a small cottage with two other families.

"You're in luck!" exclaimed Aleksey cheerfully.

"What do you mean?"

"We only just completed an apartment in a building where my family and I live. It's owned by a fellow named Rempel. German, but a fine chap. It's empty. I'm sure they'd put you and your wife up."

The next day Dr. Ulyanov and his wife came to meet the Rempels. The decision to welcome them into the growing community that lived at the corner of Ermak and Irtysh was an easy one. And to Heinrich's delight, the Ulyanovs agreed to pay a small monthly rental fee!

8

One day in August Fyodor Lepinov strode purposefully into the Rempel's yard. He walked up to the doorstep and rapped loudly on the door.

Heinrich opened the door.

Without an introduction Lepinov burst out, "Well neighbor, I see that you have become quite the communist! We should all take an example from you!"

Heinrich was quite taken aback but was given no chance to respond, even had he thought of one.

"Yes, Comrade Rempel, with all the people livin' on yer property, ya've shown us all what it means ta level the classes and provide for the Russian worker.

Flustered, Heinrich replied, "Well, we are only doing our Christian duty. That doesn't make me a communist."

"Well, Comrade Rempel, in my books, that's what ya are. But don't let it disturb ya."

Heinrich thought he smelled alcohol on Lepinov's breath. Fyodor only smiled and plunged on.

"I see that yer little house is empty. It's a bleedin' shame when there are so many who haven't a place to stay. I have a cousin, name's Melzhin. Man's got a wife and a small kid. He works at the rail yard. Whaddaya think? Could they live in yer little house?"

Overwhelmed by his boisterous neighbor and feeling obliged because of the help Lepinov had given when faced with the summons before the *Zemstvo*, Heinrich could only nod his assent.

So, the little house was rented out to Vladimir Melzhin, his wife, Natasha, and their baby of nine months, Oleg. Melzhin was a vocal Bolshevik who occasionally accosted Heinrich with his views. Strangely, he didn't consider Heinrich a landlord – someone to be despised. Rather, he looked upon him as a man who needed only a little convincing to become a convert to the cause of revolution.

For his part, Heinrich would politely nod at Melzhin's admonitions, but afterward he would shake his head at the radical ramblings of his tenant.

With the income from the rent paid by the Ulyanovs, the financial strain on the Rempel household began to ease a little. Furthermore, aside from the radical Vladimir, who was tolerated by everyone, the families got along well, visiting together in the evenings, sharing food and stories. The parents drank tea, or kvass depending on the preference, while the children played out in the yard in the gathering dusk.

While the turmoil continued to build outside of its gates, the community at Ermak and Irtysh was an oasis of peace.

Death Pays a Visit

1

From out of the east an icy gale shook the frozen steppe. Birds and animals caught unawares sought refuge from its ruthless blast in whatever protective nooks and crannies could be found along streams and gullies on the wind-wracked plain. The storm rattled gates and ripped shutters from walls as it careened through the deserted streets of Omsk. The bare branches of the bush willows on the riverbank bent and thrashed wildly about as the winter wind blew across the ice-entombed Irtysh.

The storm attacked the unsuspecting, sleeping village of Kulomzino. Along its relentless path, knife-edged ice crystals skimmed the snow-crusted ground, fleeing, ever fleeing never resting, whirling and twisting between fence posts, around buildings, along alleys and roads, forgetting from whence they had come, not giving a thought to where they were going. The fierce wind pushed and tugged at the darkened homes of the sleeping villagers as if urging them to flee before it. The houses moaned sorrowfully in reply.

Refugees in their flimsy shelters constructed against buildings, under derelict railcars and in the covered hollows they had laboriously dug into the ground desperately held on to each other in vain attempts to anchor themselves to the frozen earth while about them pieces of their makeshift walls and roofs broke away and fled helter-skelter, blindly, frantically flying only to crash headlong with sharp bangings into immovable obstacles standing in their way. No escaping for them, for unlike the snow which was formless and could shift and change with the currents, they were solid and clumsy.

The moon shone with clear brilliance out of a sky scudded here and there with clouds like torn rags. Between the clouds, the stars hovered above the roofs and watched as, at the stroke of midnight, the night-shift workers at the Kulomzino Trans-Siberian Railway Station quietly took up their appointed positions. They checked to make sure their weapons were in good firing order, that extra ammunition was close at hand, and then they shuffled their feet, and rubbed their gloved hands together, huffing on them to stay warm.

Somewhere a dog sniffed the frigid air, sensed the magnitude and the wonder, and began barking. Its call wove into the fabric of the storm and rose above it in a staccato of alarm. From the lanes and alleyways of Kulomzino a hundred other dogs joined in its beckoning clamor. The chorus was loud and raucous for a time, but after a while the singers lost the song. They paced, guard dog alert, silently restless.

Only the wind continued its eerie, mournful howl sweeping by windows and doors up and down the streets of the town.

Elsewhere in Kulomzino, carefully chosen members of the 20th Siberian Regiment who were sympathetic to the cause left their fires and went to take their turn at the watch-posts on the roadways and in front of important buildings. Some tucked themselves behind the sandbag walls of the bunkers on either side of the track at the foot of the long iron-spanned bridge across the Irtysh River. Muttering greetings or laughing softly at some quiet joke, they prepared for what was to come at the same time as they braced themselves against the cold. They waited for the morning and the challenge that would surely be theirs. Some nervously crossed themselves, praying for God's blessing and protection. Others peered about with fire in their eyes sure of the nobility of their purpose. Released from their duties after a long day in the trench, their grateful, sleepy comrades retreated to the warmth of the barracks and the security of their thick wool blankets.

Across the river in Omsk, the tired horses of General Ivanov-Rinov's Siberian Cossacks stood in their stalls, resting after the long, swift ride that had followed a quick summons to the city. And while the horses blew and stamped and searched for edible morsels in their mangers, their eager Cossack riders honed the edges of their sabres, their beloved *shashkas*. Painstakingly, they sharpened their lances and cleaned their rifles, looking forward to the action they knew would mark the dawn.

It was the night of December 23, 1918 and Death was coming to Kulomzino.

2

The Rempel children had spent the entire day indoors because of the fierce wind that had lashed the town since dawn. It was far too cold to go outside. Their skin would freeze in seconds. Henry had stuck his nose outside for a moment. He'd let fly a wad of spit and was amused to see it freeze solid with a sharp snap a moment after it left his mouth. His mother had scolded him and told him to shut the door; they would all catch the death of themselves if he let any more frigid air in.

Little Agnessa had fussed all day. She seemed to have a touch of fever, just enough to make her skin slightly warmer to the touch than one would expect. She was cranky. Her whimpering too often turned to wailing. Katy, with the memory of two other infants who had succumbed to fever, watched over Agnessa with all the motherly care she possessed. Occasionally Katarina and Joanna took turns helping their mother. They had tried to humor Nessa, as they called her, with comic faces and laughter. They had carried her and cuddled her, but their efforts had only led to louder wails. It had been left to Katy to spend the day catering to the needs of the unhappy infant. The only time the baby would relax was when her mother held her, gently rocking while softly singing the lullabies of her own childhood.

With nothing else to do, the children had practiced their parts for the Christmas pageant that was to be held on Christmas Eve at the school. Each had a recitation to learn. They took turns standing in front of the Russian oven, arms by their sides, looking their siblings in the eye to gather courage for the larger audience to come, and rehearsed their lines. By evening they all knew their parts by heart.

As the children lay in bed that night and waited for sleep to come, they listened to the wind's shrieks as it battered against the front door and the window beside it. However, the storm was not the only reason sleep evaded them. Earlier in the evening, Katarina had overheard her father speak a forbidden word. Family rules against swearing were strictly enforced. The children heard rude and foul language spoken often and loudly on the street or when playing in the yard with friends, but they wouldn't have dreamed of uttering it themselves.

Papa's word was law; one good spanking was all the encouragement one needed to obey. Henry would always remember the day when he had taken it into his head to defy his father. It had occurred soon after they moved into the dacha by the river. Henry had thrown a spoon on the floor and had been told to pick it up. For some reason he could not remember, he had refused. Papa had said, "Henry, pick up the spoon." Unsurprised by the audacity of it, Henry had replied without hesitation, "No." His father patiently repeated, "Henry, pick up the spoon." "No," came the quick, calm reply. Papa had put Henry over his knee and given his bum a couple of firm swats. The command was repeated, as was the refusal, as were the swats. This had continued three or four more times until, overcome, not by the pain of the swats—Henry couldn't remember that they had hurt at all—but by the implacable will of his father, Henry had finally obeyed.

And now Papa had sinned; he had said a bad word, one of the worst, right there in Mama's kitchen! The children lay under their covers as Katarina whispered the moment of his offence, Katy's quick scolding, and Papa's cheeks flushed with embarrassment. Joanna giggled nervously.

It had happened this way.

After his daily chores were done, Heinrich had spent his time preparing for his own Christmas presentation. As chairman of the committee that oversaw the running of the Kulomzino Mennonite School, he had been asked to say a few words. He took his responsibility very seriously.

Heinrich had pondered carefully the words he penned on the page, wanting to bring hope to his listeners after what seemed like endless years of trouble: first the war, then the revolution, unemployment, high prices, the town glutted with hungry refugees bringing with them disease, crime and unrest. His thoughts kept returning to the birth of the Christ-child being celebrated at Christmas. God had come into the world as a human baby to bring peace on earth and good will to men. Well, women, too, and children, he reminded himself, though, he had to admit, it was the men who did the most fighting and so were most in need of God's peace and good will. The vast majority of the refugees were women and children; the men conscripted into the army, or killed, or run off to join the militias. Why always the need to fight? On the other hand, the women and children, without their fathers and husbands were at loose ends and having a terrible time of it, just trying to survive. Yes, God's peace and good will was certainly a blessing that everyone needed in these hard times.

Heinrich wanted to somehow reconcile for his audience the presence of God's peace in the world with the terrible conflict that had raged in Europe and continued to rage in Russia. His thoughts kept returning to the refugees. He could not imagine the heartache and sorrow the hundreds of thousands who had passed through Kulomzino station in the last years had experienced. Many of them had stayed, desperately seeking some semblance of security in his village and in Omsk across the river. There were so many that housing them against the cold of winter had been an urgent concern, lest they all freeze to death. Many were being housed in office buildings and factories, sleeping wherever space could be found on and under desks, benches, and tables, in hallways and on floors. Each morning they wrapped their meager belongings into bundles and vacated for the day so the workers could get on with their tasks, going forth to wander the streets in search of food or, better still, work. Some found food, waiting in the long lines at the American Red Cross stations, but few found any work. Many other refugees, who were unable to find shelter in buildings, were living in the most primitive conditions imaginable. Their makeshift hovels could be seen everywhere. Thousands were even living in holes dug into the hard earth and covered with sheets of corrugated tin or whatever other materials could be found. How could people survive in such conditions? It was unfathomable. And where might they find God's peace?

Heinrich shook his head. How had it come about that so much misery had found its way to their small village?

And, of course, there was also the unstable political situation. First there had been the Reds with their Bolshevik agenda, taking away private ownership of all businesses. For him that had meant losing the income from the mill; worse, it had meant he could not pursue his dream of starting a farm implement supply store. Now the Whites were in power. At least they had returned the factories and mills to their rightful owners. But, with all the foreign soldiers around, what was next? Every time he crossed the river to Omsk there seemed to be more of them.

What did it mean? It all seemed too much for Heinrich to put together. But the Christmas Eve service celebrating the birth of the Prince of Peace was just around the corner. So he persevered.

Heinrich was writing with his favorite fountain pen and he dipped the nib carefully into his inkwell after every few words. The inkwell was made of clear glass. It was about the same width as the palm of his hand and stood, perhaps, about two finger widths high. It had a thick, wide base and the well above the base looked like a large bubble with a flat bottom. The inkwell had belonged to his great-grandfather and Heinrich treasured it as a family heirloom. He always regarded it with affection for it reminded him of his family, all of whom lived so very far away.

At some point in the evening, the stopper on the inkwell had broken off. It had been held in place by a thin ring of brass attached to a spring-loaded hinge that was itself attached to a brass band affixed to the glass lip at the top of the well. Without warning, the stopper had fallen off. The brass ring had broken just by the hinge. Fortunately, it had come off in his hand and not landed on his pants, or worse yet, his white shirt. The ink had stained his skin black.

Despite himself, Heinrich had uttered, perhaps more loudly than he intended, "*Scheisse*! Shit!" the moment the cork landed in his palm.

Katy overheard him and scolded, "Heinrich, your language! The children will hear you!"

She hid her smile of amusement. Despite everything that was happening outside the door of their little house, theirs was a happy home. But, rules were rules!

Heinrich was contrite and quickly apologized. He looked to see if any of the children had noticed. They all seemed to be concentrating on their tasks.

But Katarina had heard, and she took delight in recounting her father's transgression until sleep finally carried the children to places of warmth and quiet.

Getting up from his chair at the table, Heinrich went to the kindling box by the stove and looked through the sticks of wood until he found a suitable piece. He took his jack-knife, gave it a few swipes on the whetstone, and began to carve a new stopper for the inkwell. He would have to do an exact job, for the new cork would not be attached to the frame of the ink well as the old one had been. It would have to fit snuggly.

The stopper was a small one, so carving it required patience as well as skill. First he shaped the wood until it resembled the tip of his index finger. The tough part, after flaring the top, was to cut the stopper off from the rest of the stick and then smoothing all the jagged edges on the small piece. Heinrich was not aware of the time as it passed; only that Katy had followed the children to bed some time ago. He was almost done and wanted to have the new stopper finished before he retired.

The candle on the table guttered as a draft passed by.

As Heinrich concentrated on his work, he became aware of loud barking. The dog across the street was making a horrible racket. Heinrich put his knife and unfinished stopper on the table. He got up and crossed the room to look out the window. It was a dark night; he could barely make out the fence marking his property line by the road. He heard the wind that still buffeted his house. He saw nothing of concern.

Heinrich returned to his work. After a few more minutes of careful whittling, the stopper was finished. It fit cleanly and firmly into the mouth of the inkwell. If it were somehow jostled, the well would not leak.

Happy with the result, Heinrich quietly undressed and got into bed. Katy was asleep. She was lying on her side so he snuggled up and formed his body to fit hers. He wrapped his arm around her waist. Heinrich was content as he listened to her breathing. He felt her warmth down the length of his body and again reminded himself of how much he loved this woman.

3

It was early in the morning. Heinrich could have looked at his gold pocket watch, but simply feeling the chill in the room told him the night was old, for the fire in the Russian stove was reduced to embers. The temperature in the room was close to freezing. Something had woken him. He was not sure what it was that had disturbed his sleep. He listened for a while, but heard nothing except for some gusts of wind.

Sleep was just taking Heinrich back into its cotton ball embrace when sounds in the distance caused him to come fully awake. It sounded at first, faintly, like the explosive cracks one hears in the forest when in the deep cold of winter the tree sap freezes and pops the bark away from the trunk. He had experienced that alarming sound more than once while traveling through wooded areas in the dead of winter. But Heinrich quickly realized there was more to these sounds than frozen sap. As the popping noise continued, Heinrich gradually realized they could be, in fact, he was sure of it, they were shots from a gun. Or, hearing the increasing intensity, from many guns! Some were faint, obviously coming from afar. Other shots, alarmingly, sounded like they were much closer.

There was no question of sleeping now. More and more shots could be heard. Katy woke and asked Heinrich what was happening. A few minutes passed as they listened to the cacophony growing outside. Suddenly, they heard the sounds of what could only have been explosions! Two, three, now a fourth! The last explosion actually rattled the windows of their house. A picture fell from the wall and hit the floor; its glass shattered. The explosions sounded like they were coming from the direction of the railway station. What was happening?

Now the children were awake. First the girls appeared at the heavy curtain that formed the wall of their parents' bedroom, shivering with the morning cold. Henry was only a moment behind them. Katy beckoned them all to come and they tumbled gratefully onto her bed. She threw open the covers. The children scrambled beneath the quilt.

Cozy in her cradle, Agnessa sucked her thumb and breathed a soft whimper in her sleep.

Heinrich got up and threw some wood onto the embers in the Russian stove. When Henry made to follow him, he scowled and told him to stay with his mother. Feeling a mixture of insult and relief, Henry quickly climbed back under the warm quilt.

Cautiously Heinrich crept over to the small front window. He peered out at the shadowy street through the crack between the window frame and the lace curtains. Aside from some tentative wisps of smoke struggling to escape a chimney across the street, there was no sign of any movement. Even the tree branches were finally still.

Katy and the children huddled together in the bed, hugging each other close, hardly daring to imagine what could possibly be happening in the streets of their small community. Another explosion rattled the house. Fear spilled over the family like rain leaking through holes in the roof, first dripping here and there then falling with more persistence until they were all becoming soaked with it.

By the window Heinrich stood trembling. He began to pray, "Our Father in heaven, hallowed be your name. Your kingdom come, your will be done, on earth as it is in heaven. Preserve us in this time of trial and deliver us from evil. For yours is the power and the glory."

As their part in the plot to remove Admiral Kolchak and the Whites from power, Gorshkov and Fyodor Lepinov were assigned the job of assisting a group of men whose task it was to blow a span out of the Irtysh River railway bridge. The decision had been made to blow up the bridge in order to cut off communication between the British headquarters in Omsk and the armored trains carrying cannons from the HMS Suffolk that were fighting in the west, as well as from the naval taskforce at Ufa. Of course, at the same time it would also cripple the movement of the dreaded Czech armored trains.

"We'll kill all three birds with one stick," chuckled Lepinov.

Surprisingly, the jovial Vershinsky, until this night the noncommittal one, was there. No one commented on his presence and he gave no explanation. It was simply accepted that he had finally come to a decision and was acting upon it, as were they all. His support was cheerfully welcomed.

"Comrade Vershinsky, finally you are one of us!" someone said, pounding him on the back.

Vershinsky only ducked his head in acknowledgement and smiled.

Everyone had arrived at the appointed meeting place shortly after midnight. Most of them tried to appear like what they were doing was nothing out of the ordinary, but it was obvious, no matter how nonchalantly they tried to behave, that they were all very nervous. For most of them, ordinary machinists, mechanics and electricians that they were, this was their first foray into the life of the revolutionary saboteur.

The problem was, the group had only been provided with a few sticks of dynamite. They had looked at the pitiful pile and had shaken their heads in disappointment.

"How are we ta blow all that steel ta kingdom come with that pathetic bit of dynamite?" Fyodor voiced all of their concerns.

It was soon decided that more explosives were required to make a decent job of it. Someone was immediately sent to find more. For the past few hours they had anxiously waited for his return.

The storm that had been plaguing Kulomzino since the previous day seemed to be abating, but its gusts still frostbit exposed flesh in less than a minute. For protection from the elements, the conspirators were sitting on the lee side of a shed overlooking the river. Even there, though, the wind sometimes ambushed them and plucked at their sleeves. The cold seeped through the folds of their sheepskin coats and chilled their bones. Small icicles formed in their mustaches and the tears froze in the corners of their eyes. But these were hardened men, used to the winter freeze. They ignored the discomfort. Some smoked and talked quietly, guarding their cigarettes in the palms of their gloved hands. Others sat wrapped in their own thoughts. A bottle of vodka passed from gloved hand to gloved hand. It brought welcome warmth to their innards.

It had been agreed that, when the time came for the explosion, the soldiers guarding the bridge were to be warned. After all, they were fellow revolutionaries playing their role in the destruction of the White filth and their interventionist allies.

"No sense sending good comrades to meet their Maker ahead of their time!" someone in the group had joked. "They'd fly up, and when they'd reach the Pearly Gates His Supreme Holiness might not be ready for 'em and send 'em right back down again."

He'd laughed at his witty remark. "Or, maybe that other one, old Lucifer," and here he'd paused and spit into the snow by his side while making the sign against the evil eye, "maybe old Death himself would take one look at 'em as they came down and maybe he wouldn't want 'em either. 'If'n you're gonna join us down here,' he'd say all red in the face because of his fiery temper, 'we ain't acceptin' nothin' but the whole package. We don't want bits of bone and pieces of gristle down 'ere. We want all o' ya or none o' ya! Get back up there, and when ya've found the rest of yerselves, then ya can come on down an' give us another try!'"

"Hah, hah, hah," he'd chuckled. "Then where would we be? With nowhere to go, those boys'd come after us an' give us hell for blowing up their sorry Russian backsides." And he'd laughed uproariously until someone had shushed him.

When the joker paused for a breath, Gorshkov had interjected, "Comrade, you'd best save your breath. Trust me, you're going to need it." He spoke firmly but quietly, in his calm, sure way. "Death is a fisherman who casts a wide net. When he makes his throw, you just make sure you're not in the way. For once he starts to tighten those lines, unless you're very fast on your feet, your time on this earth is done."

Hearing Gorshkov's somber warning, several of the men crossed themselves. More than one regretted not having brought an icon. It didn't hurt to cover all the bases when danger was afoot. There was no more joking. This was serious business.

After that they'd sat in silence for a while. Finally the reality of their situation began to chafe.

"How're we supposed ta blow a bridge with a few measly sticks o' dynamite?" Lepinov, with his chin tucked into his sheepskin collar, complained bitterly.

"Comrade Cheshkov is bringing more, don't worry," assured a small man with wire-rimmed glasses, named Zhukin.

"I don't like it. He should have been here by now. The night's gettin' on," fretted Lepinov.

Gorshkov was gnawing on a small *rybka*, a salt-cured fish like a sardine that Siberians were fond of.

"Don't twist yourself in a knot, old man!"

He spat a bit of bone into the snow.

But Cheshkov did not come and as the night grew old it began to look increasingly like they were not going to be able to carry out their mission. The men began to quietly discuss their options.

"I say we give it up for a lost cause," one of the conspirators put in morosely. "We haven't enough dynamite to blow up an old shithouse."

"I'll throw you down the crapper if you keep that up!" snarled Lepinov.

"Now don't get all excited," someone murmured. "Keep your voices down, comrades, or you'll bring trouble on us. I heard last evening there's Cossacks across the river. A new battalion just came into town. Reinforcements."

The light of dawn was beginning to reveal the buildings about them and the bushes on the river bank when Gorshkov, who always seemed to be one step ahead of everyone else in his thinking—perhaps because he had consumed less vodka—stood up, gathered the sticks of dynamite together and crept in the direction of the bridge. Over his shoulder he said, "I don't know about you comrades, but I'm not leaving until I get done something of what we set out to accomplish. It will soon be daylight. If we can't blow up the bridge, the least we can do is blow up the track. Anybody with me?"

Vershinksy, Zhukin and Lepinov got up to follow. The rest muttered things like, "What's the use?" and "It's already too light out. You'll be seen." They shifted and shuffled in indecision until the first decided to abandon the scheme. The rest quickly followed his lead. They disappeared down the lane heading away from the river into town.

"Cowards," hissed Lepinov.

In the muted light that heralded the wintry dawn, the four conspirators crept cautiously toward the bridge. They had been told the soldiers guarding the approach to the bridge would be sympathetic. Being unsure though, they took no chances. They scrabbled along the embankment, out of sight, until the time came when they were forced to leave the cover. Then they carefully crawled onto the railroad bed.

Crouching on the track, feeling exposed for any eyes to see, the saboteurs quickly scooped out three small holes in the gravel between the wooden ties and beneath the iron rail. The sticks of dynamite were gingerly placed into the holes.

Each charge of dynamite had a fuse about a meter long. Because of the gusty winds, lighting them proved to be a bigger challenge than expected for no sooner had their matches flared than they were snuffed out.

"D'you hear that?" whispered Zhukin. He was fumbling with his third match.

Borne faintly on the wind, a rustling noise could be heard. The men paused in their work. They crouched lower to the ground and listened intently. From far away, there came a shout. It did not sound like a shout of alarm. All four saboteurs realized it at the same time. The shout sounded like a command being given to a large group.

In the distance, they heard a horse neigh.

"Quickly! Trouble's coming!" Lepinov's heart was suddenly in his throat.

With Gorshkov trying to create a small windbreak—he'd quickly realized that his vision would not permit him to touch the flickering match to the small end of the fuse—the other three men each had his own fuse to light. They tried to synchronize their clumsy attempts so that all the fuses would be lit at the same moment, but haste and relighting matches quickly left their attempts to coordinate their actions in a shambles. If only the wind would die for a moment!

Now they heard a rumbling sound echoing on the ice at the base of the bank below them. It was being carried in waves from out on the frozen river. The groans and rumbles in the ice were gradually getting louder.

Gorshkov glanced back over his shoulder. Coming across the river in the dim morning light he saw a sight that instantly made his blood freeze.

"Cossacks!" he shouted.

Looking out over the ice, they could see a long line of horsemen trotting side by side toward the western shore. They were not yet in full gallop, so there was still time.

Lepinov's fingers trembled as he made one last try. He struck his match. It flared. He cupped it in his hands to protect it from the wind. Carefully, he held it to the fuse. The fuse erupted with a sudden bright sparking that slowly began to travel down the length of the cord.

In the distance they heard another shouted command from the Cossack commander. With a sound like the gasping whisper of Death's breath, the brigade drew their swords and broke into a gallop. Shots erupted from the bunkers on either side of the bridge deck as the soldiers of the 20th Siberian

Regiment made a futile attempt to hold off the charging horsemen.

Taking a quick last look at the burning fuse, Lepinov roared, "Run!"

The earth began to tremble and the saboteurs hadn't taken a score of strides before the Cossacks were upon them. They were overtaken by a chaos of hoof-beats, shouts and screams, the whistling sound of sabres being swung through the air, and the blasts of gunshots. From the corner of his eye Lepinov glimpsed a Cossack slash his sabre across Vershinsky's neck and down his back. Vershinsky gave a short gurgling cry and fell into the soft snow on the riverbank.

Lepinov could hear a horseman bearing down on him from behind. As he ran, he ducked and swerved. Fyodor heard the whoosh of a sabre and before he could react he felt a stinging cut open on his head. He ran on, feeling the warm blood run down his neck. Pounding his legs, he willed his burning lungs to give him the strength to move another step. He did not give a thought as to why the Cossack who had swung at him was no longer there. He was beyond thought or reason; his actions were guided by instinct and the desire to survive the hell in which he found himself.

In front of him, Lepinov saw Gorshkov stop and turn. From his waistband Gorshkov pulled out a pistol. He quickly aimed it at a Cossack pursuing him and pulled the trigger. Instead of the Cossack, the bullet hit his mount. As though they had been turned instantly to water, the legs of the Cossack's stallion gave out from under it. The horse with its rider crashed to the ground, ramming into Gorshkov and careening over his limp, ragdoll body.

Zhukin was nowhere to be seen.

A blinding flash followed immediately by a thunderous explosion tore the air about him. Lepinov felt as though his head and his chest would split apart. He willed his body to run but his legs and arms flailed in thin air as he was lifted up by the blast. Another explosion rent the earth and the air about Fyodor. A sudden blackness took him and the swirling snow accepted his broken body into its icy white embrace.

Mayhem

1

With the breaking of day the winds assailing Kolumzino died, but in the town the storm raged on.

As the light grew stronger, Heinrich could hear the sounds of shots and explosions coming from the direction of the railway station becoming less frequent. More alarming, though, were the shouts, cries, and gunshots he now heard coming, it seemed, from all directions at once. It was a terrifying clamor, as if the whole town was in a terrible turmoil.

Behind the blanket-partition, Katy and the children, still huddled in the bed, were also hearing the fearful racket. She was trying to comfort her children and occupy their minds by telling Bible stories, but was having little success.

"Remember Daniel in the lions' den? I'm sure the lions must have been crouching all around him. They roared and slobbered and showed their fierce fangs. They swiped their big paws at him, trying to get him with their long sharp claws. They leaped toward him and tried to attack him. But, do you think Daniel was frightened?"

Joanna's small voice whispered, "Yes."

"Well, he might have been," conceded Katy, "but God was with Daniel and protected him. He will protect us just like he protected Daniel."

"Are there lions outside?" Joanna asked fearfully.

Henry spoke more bravely than he felt. "Don't be silly, Joanna. There are no lions in Siberia!"

"Shush, Henry, you're not helping. No, Joanna, there are no lions outside," Katy said, as calmly as she could.

But Katy was also having a hard time containing herself. Finally she called to her husband, "Heinrich, what is happening? I'm frightened! The children are frightened! What is happening?"

Heinrich looked through the window craning his neck every which way, but he saw nothing remarkable.

"I don't know, my love. I can't see anything. Perhaps I should go out to the street and look."

"No!" the response came quickly. "Stay inside. Don't leave us."

With that, Heinrich suddenly saw riders on horseback come galloping down the street. They were dressed in green tunics with red shoulder straps and green pants with a red strip down the leg. They were the Ivanov-Rinov Cossacks come to Kulomzino to quell the Bolshevik uprising. Some were waving their sabres about their heads while others gripped long lances. Still others were firing carbines into the air and at random targets.

Heinrich's attention was drawn to a scene playing itself out up the street across from the Sarkovsky's.

A man ran out of the house and onto the road. His shirt was torn and even from this distance Heinrich could see that it was red with blood. Two Cossacks emerged from the house. Lazily they sauntered to their horses and took the reins from their comrade who held them. With light springs the Cossacks mounted. With laughter in their voices they paused a moment to watch as the man frantically ran along the street. In his panic he tripped, fell, and scrambled back onto his feet. As his neighbor—Heinrich could now clearly see blood flowing from a wound on his head—ran desperately alongside the Rempels' yard, one of the Cossacks urged his horse forward. It swiftly sprang into a gallop. The Cossack, sitting confidently astride his galloping horse, with the greatest of ease, almost gently, lowered the tip of his lance, striking the running man in the center of his back. The Cossack let go of the lance as the man tumbled to the ground with the lance crazily waving back and forth like a sapling in a fierce wind. The man struggled for a few moments, then lay still, his face turned toward the Rempel's yard, his eyes open but seeing nothing, looking past the snow drifts piled against the picket fence at the brick building with its tidy row of windows and doors and the empty sky beyond.

It had happened in the time it took to blow onto a cup of hot tea to cool its surface and then take a sip or two.

The Cossack pulled his horse to a skidding stop. Foam covered its lips; it champed its bit and snorted. The Cossack turned his mount and trotted back to his prize. He leaned over and pulled the lance free with a firm jerking motion. He examined the bloodied point and wiped it clean on his trousers.

In his house, Heinrich stood dumbstruck. He didn't realize that tears were running down his cheeks and that he was trembling all over.

The Cossack straightened up in his saddle. He turned his head and looked toward the Rempel's home. He glimpsed Heinrich watching behind the glass. The Cossack's eyes met Heinrich's and held them. Heinrich saw his wide dark face and long black moustache. The Cossack smiled.

Heinrich gasped in horror and pulled himself away from the window. Panic struck him.

'Should I bar the door?' he thought. 'What if he comes here? What will I do? God help us!' He was shaking.

"What is happening?" Again the anxious voice came from the bedroom.

Heinrich hastily wiped the tears from his cheeks. "Not now, Katy. Keep the children in the bedroom. They must not come into the front room."

Though he tried to sound calm, his words came out breathlessly. Katy heard the tremor in his voice.

Heinrich dared to peer quickly through the window. For the moment all was quiet on the street. The Cossacks weren't to be seen. The body lay on the icy road. Streaks of blood had frozen where it had flowed; the man's face was pale as the snow that swirled about him. The falling snow was beginning to cover him, creating a temporary translucent shroud.

A door slammed close by. Heinrich saw Dr. Ulyanov hurry down the walkway toward the road.

Without thinking, Heinrich pulled on his overcoat, boots and hat. He called out, "I'll be right back," and went outside.

When Heinrich got to the road, Dr. Ulyanov was kneeling beside the fallen man.

"He's dead," Dr. Ulyanov said, looking up at Heinrich.

Heinrich stared in stricken fascination at the gaping, black hole in the man's back. He could not help but notice within it a timid white line of exposed rib-bone. His eyes moved to the white face with its dark red coating of frozen blood and its light dusting of snow, and to the calloused hands splayed out on either side. He had met this neighbor a few times, but was having difficulty remembering his name.

"Filipovich," he said to himself. "That's it."

"What's that?" asked Dr. Ulyanov.

"His name; it is Filipovich."

From up the road Dr. Ulyanov and Heinrich Rempel heard a hoarse shout and the muted sounds of a horse's hooves on the hard packed snow on the road. It was trotting toward them.

They stood and looked at the Cossack who was coming their way. He was the same man who had killed Filipovich.

"Hey, you there!" he shouted as he approached. "This ain't none a' yer concern. Get back into yer houses. We'll take care a' things out here."

The Cossack reined back his horse and stopped in front of the two men. When neither Dr. Ulyanov nor Heinrich made a move to obey, the Cossack made a threatening gesture with his lance.

"Are yuh boys deaf? Get back to yer homes."

Heinrich found some courage.

"But what about this man?" Heinrich demanded. "He's dead!" He almost added, 'You killed him,' but held his tongue. He remembered the look the Cossack had given when their eyes had met before. Heinrich had a feeling the man had enjoyed killing Filipovich. What kind of person was it that sat on this horse before him?

Heinrich's resolve began to crumble. With less conviction than he had thought to muster he added, "He can't be left lying out in the street like a dog."

"'E can an' 'e will."

The words erupted out of the ice fog of the Cossack's breath.

"Now listen here," put in Dr. Ulyanov, "I'm a doctor and I demand that this man be treated with respect." Maxim was angry. He had seen too many senseless deaths in the last few years. "What was his crime that he should be run down in the street and killed without any chance to defend himself?"

The Cossack looked uncertain for a moment, not because he questioned his actions in killing Filipovich, but because he was being addressed by a doctor. Here was a man from a privileged class. A millennium of class distinctions had conditioned him to defer to his betters.

After a moment he growled, "He's a bloody Bolshevik, if ya wanna know. An' my orders are to kill Bolsheviks."

Heinrich and Dr. Ulyanov were shocked at the Cossack's casual manner. Suddenly a thought struck Heinrich like a blow. He remembered Fyodor Lepinov, his neighbor, and his tenant, Vladimir Melzhin. They were both Bolsheviks. Were they in danger?

Two more Cossacks rode up and halted by their comrade. The dark look on their faces made Heinrich shiver.

The Cossack interrupted Heinrich's thoughts. He nodded toward the Rempel's yard.

"Now, 'nless ya wanna join 'im, which, I'm thinkin', I can quite easily oblige." He had spoken in a quiet, threatening voice that drifted into silence. He was getting impatient. "Ya'd best be gettin' off this road an' back ta yer families where ya b'long."

Which, of course, they did.

2

When Heinrich closed the door, he began to shake. He had not dressed fully for the temperature outside and was chilled to the bone. But that was not why he was trembling. What he had seen and what he had just experienced on the road left him shaken to the core.

Katy heard the door and came into the front room, pulling a shawl over her shoulders. She immediately saw the condition her husband was in and guided him to a chair.

154

"What is happening, Heinrich? What did you see?"

Heinrich didn't respond. He sat slumped in the chair, his head bowed, looking down at his hands, at the floor, at nothing at all.

The children emerged from the bedroom. They looked shyly at their father. They had never seen him like this. Joanna began to cry. She pulled herself onto Heinrich's lap and gently put her arms around his neck. He slowly raised his head. There were tears in his eyes. He put his arms around Joanna and returned her embrace.

In the other room, Agnessa began to cry.

"Katyusha," said Katy. "Nessa probably needs changing. Could you do it and then bring her to me?"

Relieved to have something to do, Katarina hurried to obey, grabbing a clean flannel and making the two necessary folds before untying Nessa's soiled one. Nessa immediately relaxed and began to burble in the glow of her sister's attentiveness.

Katy, meanwhile, put some hot coals into its center tube, and then filled the samovar with water. A good cup of tea would help to calm everyone's nerves.

"Henry," she commanded, "put more wood on the fire. It's freezing in here! Can't you see your father is shivering?"

Katarina brought Agnessa to her mother. Katy sat in a chair and prepared to feed her. Katy treasured the intimacy of her infant sucking milk from her breast. Today, however, the milk would not flow freely. Katy tried to relax realizing that the anxiety she was feeling was probably the reason. Agnessa fussed in frustration at the slow response, but after a time the milk came and she was satisfied.

When the coals in the samovar had heated the water Katarina opened the spigot and filled the teapot. She added some tea leaves.

"Joanie, bring the toasted zweibacks to the table," she ordered.

While Joanna got the zweibacks, Katarina poured tea for everyone. Then she put a daub of raspberry jam on each one's plate.

At the head of the table, Heinrich folded his hands and bowed his head in silence. When no prayer came from his lips, the children opened their eyes to take a peak in their father's direction. His prayers were always spoken clearly, with confidence. But when Heinrich closed his eyes to offer a prayer of thanks for the meal, he was startled by an onrush of thoughts and images that had nothing to do with food. In his mind's eye he suddenly saw the piercing look of the Cossack after he had pulled his lance free of Filipovich's body, and the enigmatic smile that had suggested complicity to Heinrich, complicity in Filipovich's death. Heinrich knew it was absurd to think that he, standing in his house, played any part in what had happened to his unfortunate neighbor. But the irrational thought stayed with him and he would ponder it for days afterward.

His thoughts tumbled. 'Could I have done something to save him? What could I have done? Nothing, there was nothing I could have done.'

Heinrich found himself whispering, "O God, forgive us our sins as we forgive those who sin against us. Amen," he concluded softly.

Katy looked at Heinrich with concern in her eyes.

The mood slowly lightened as the family shared breakfast. Soon the sipping of tea sweetened with jam could be heard. Heinrich put the jam in his mouth and sipped the tea while Katy and the children mixed a spoonful of jam into their tea. Toasted buns were dunked in the hot tea to soften them. Everyone ate in silence, relishing the food, letting the events of the morning slip out of their consciousness. The routine and pleasure of the meal calmed the family's nerves. It brought back some sense of sanity and the familiar routine of everyday life.

Outside in the cold of the Siberian morning, a shout of anger and the flat crack of a gunshot told a far different story. And everywhere the dogs once again lifted their voices in a chorus of despair.

The family had finished breakfast and had cleared up the table. Katy had assigned each of the children a chore to keep them occupied. Heinrich was again standing by the window, looking out to the road.

The air was completely still. It was snowing lightly. Heinrich could make out a small mound on the street. Filipovich's body was shrouded by a layer of white.

There was a scratching sound followed by an insistent tapping on a small window high in the back wall of the Rempels' apartment. Henry got a chair and placed it by the wall. He blew on the window and scraped at the frosty coating so he could see outside. Through the small hole in the ice, Henry looked out. To his surprise he saw Anatoly in the morning light with a terrified look on his face.

"It's Tolya! He's outside!"

Henry motioned with his hand for Anatoly to go around to the door. With a quick nod, Anatoly disappeared from view as he jumped off of whatever he had propped against the wall in order to reach the high window.

Heinrich opened the door and Anatoly burst in. Though it was brutally cold out, he had no mittens on. Nor was he wearing his sheepskin hat. He had on his sheepskin coat and felt boots, but it obvious he had left home in a hurry. He was shaking. His face was red. There were small white spots on his cheeks and ears.

"Tolya, what has happened? Why are you out in the cold without your gloves and hat?" asked Katy.

She noticed the early signs of frostbite on his cheeks and ears.

"Come by the oven." Katy tried to keep her voice calm. She didn't want to alarm Anatoly. "You must be very cold. We must warm you up!"

As Katy guided Anatoly to a chair in front of the Russian oven, she glanced at Katarina.

"Katyusha, bring a blanket to wrap around Tolya. Take the one at the foot of my bed. And Henry," she continued, "bring Tolya a cup of tea. It's still hot enough to warm him on the inside."

Soon Anatoly was huddled before the warm oven with a blanket wrapped around him so that, if you hadn't looked too closely, you might have mistaken him for an old babushka with a shawl draped over her head, sitting motionless, staring at the flickering flames. He sipped the tea gratefully while warming his hands on the porcelain cup. Katy allowed Henry to sit with Anatoly for company, but sent the girls to take care of Agnessa, who was in a mood to play. And all the while, Anatoly said not a word, neither in response to their questions, nor in friendly conversation. As he sat, he seemed to sink deeper and deeper into himself, unable to escape whatever misery tormented him.

Katy went behind the bedroom curtain and beckoned Heinrich to join her.

"We have to do something," she whispered. "Something terrible must have happened. This isn't like Tolya at all." She paused and peeked around the curtain. "Look at him, the poor boy."

Heinrich didn't need to look. He'd already concluded that something was terribly amiss at the Lepinovs. It was clearly written all over Anatoly's face and in the fact that he had arrived at their door in his present state.

"You have to go over there. To his house. We must find out what has happened."

Heinrich felt a burning in the pit of his stomach. He knew he must act but, after what he had already experienced, he wasn't sure he had the nerve.

"Take Dr. Ulyanov with you." Katy was persistent. "Find out if Tolya's parents are well. Or, perhaps they need help. Dr. Ulyanov will go with you. I'm sure of it."

Reluctantly, Heinrich went to the door and once more dressed to go out into the cold.

4

When Heinrich and Dr. Ulyanov ventured out onto the road it had begun to snow heavily. Glancing to where

Filipovich lay, they saw only what would have passed as a drift of snow, formed by the vagaries of the swirling wind.

Cloaked in the curtain of the falling snow they hurried along the road to the Lepinov's place. They walked warily, furtively glancing this way and that, hoping not to draw attention to themselves. Twice they saw the dim figures of Cossacks on horseback riding down the street in the distance and each time Heinrich's stomach leaped into his throat. Once, when they thought a Cossack might be coming their way, they crouched behind a fence. But they went unnoticed and were not challenged. On more than one occasion they heard shouting coming from a house they passed. Two houses on the street were engulfed in flames. The fires crackled and snapped. The leaping flames colored the sky orange. Black smoke spewed upward from the flames coming through broken windows and clashed with the swirling white snowflakes that fell into the ruddy canopy. No sign of life could be seen at either home.

At another house the front door was wide open. Two Cossack horses stood listlessly blowing puffs of smoky breath by the gate to its yard and nuzzled the snow in search of blades of grass to nibble. The men heard a loud scream and the crash of breaking glass. A woman's voice keened in sorrow and fear, then slowly rose into another piercing scream. Abruptly there was silence.

What horrors were being visited on that house, Heinrich could not imagine. His heart beat like a wild thing in his chest and he gasped for breath. He wanted to go and help the woman; he wanted to run home to safety. His mind seemed to come loose and his thoughts raced. Terror gripped him and he feared what might be happening to Katy and the children while he was out on this foolish errand. As Heinrich and Dr. Ulyanov hurried passed by, they struggled to make sense of the anarchy that surrounded them. They felt as if they had descended into a nightmare of hell.

Finally they came to the Lepinov's gate. Looking into the yard, Heinrich's heart sank. There, lying partially covered in snow, was Fyodor's dog. Its head had been almost completely severed from its body. Fresh snow covered the red blood that had pooled about its neck. In its mouth was still clamped a torn piece of green serge.

"Cossacks," hissed Dr. Ulyanov.

The gate into the yard had been torn off its hinges and partially blocked the entrance. Heinrich shoved it aside. The men gingerly stepped past the dead dog. They brushed against a bush blanketed with snow. The snow on its branches fell in clumps into the snow below creating a multitude of bumps and indentations like white teacups and saucers strewn around.

Dr. Ulyanov climbed the steps to the front door. It was open. He knocked on the door jam and quietly called out, "Hello? Is anybody here?" After waiting a moment, he called again, "Hello?"

In response they heard a faint moan coming from inside the house. Dr. Ulyanov hurried into the house toward where he thought the sound had come from. Heinrich quickly followed, closing the door behind him. Though embers smoked in the Russian stove, it was freezing cold in the house. Heinrich busied himself putting logs onto the fire to build it up. With the door closed, the flames slowly beat back the cold.

Dr. Ulyanov, meanwhile, had found Mrs. Lepinov. She was lying on a bed, partially covered by a blanket. Her dress had a large tear in it. She was shivering violently. Dr. Ulyanov did a quick examination to see if she had any serious injuries beyond the obvious ones. Finding none he gently wrapped Mrs. Lepinov in a blanket.

"May I clean your wounds?" he asked quietly as he looked more closely at her face. Her eyes were nearly swollen shut. There was dried blood from a cut on her cheek. Her lower lip was split and swollen.

She gave a faint nod.

"Heinrich, see if there's any hot water."

Fortunately, the samovar was hot and soon Dr. Ulyanov was dressing Mrs. Lepinov's injuries.

"Tolya." The word was a breath from Mrs. Lepinov's lips. "Anatoly," she repeated. "Where is my Tolya?"

"Mrs. Lepinov. Anatoly is safe. He is at the Rempels' home."

Mrs. Lepinov looked wide-eyed at Heinrich.

"It is true?"

For the first time, Heinrich spoke.

"Mrs. Lepinov. Your son is at my house. He is safe. My wife is with him. He was drinking tea when we left."

"Anatoly is safe," she confirmed to herself in a hoarse whisper.

Heinrich noticed there were bruises on her neck. He felt anger deep in his belly at the men who had abused Mrs. Lepinov.

"Mrs. Lepinov, where is your husband? Where is Fyodor?"

"I don't know. He doesn't tell me where he goes."

Mrs. Lepinov slowly shook her head. She looked from Heinrich to Dr. Ulyanov. Suddenly she seemed to gain strength. Her face turned into a grimace of fear and hate.

"Get out!" she shouted. "Both of you. Get out! You men are all the same! Get out!" she screamed and then shudders of grief shook her body as she wept more words of abuse at Heinrich and Dr. Ulyanov. When Dr. Ulyanov made a move to help her, she pushed his arm away roughly and screamed again, "Leave me alone! Get out!"

5

Heinrich Rempel had just returned home from the Lepinov's and had only begun to tell Anatoly that his mother was all right—he didn't want to alarm the boy with the whole truth of her situation—when there was a loud knocking of metal on their door. The girls were in the back room amusing Agnessa. Anatoly was still warming himself in front of the Russian oven where Henry kept him company. Katy was helping Heinrich out of his coat. Everyone froze. They could hear similar knocks, though fainter, on their neighbors' doors.

Suddenly the door was flung open and three Cossacks stormed in. Their sabres were drawn and they pointed them menacingly about. When they had taken in the scene of the frightened family, the Cossacks visibly relaxed.

"We are lookin' for Fyodor Lepinov, a notorious Bolshevik who lives down the road. Have you seen him?" demanded the leader harshly.

Anatoly's heart began to pound. Images of what he had seen in his house swirled in his head. He felt that he would faint.

"Also his son. We're lookin' for his son, Anatoly. Do you know where he is?"

Dread took hold of Anatoly. He began to shiver. "I must escape!" he thought frantically. Could he dash past the Cossacks and make it out the door?

Just as Anatoly was gathering the courage to make a run for it, Heinrich stepped forward.

"We have not seen either of the people you are looking for," he said firmly. "As you can see, it is only my family here in this room. You can search the other room if you like. You see my two sons by the stove." The lie, when it escaped his lips, had come surprisingly easy. "And there are my two daughters and the baby."

Katarina, carrying Agnessa, and Joanna had just entered from the back room. Katy hurried to where they stood fearfully staring at the armed men and hugged them to her protectively.

The leader of the Cossacks nodded his head and his two comrades went into the back room of the apartment. It only took a moment before they came back, shaking their heads to indicate they had found nothing.

As one of the Cossacks passed Katy he leered at her and patted her on the cheek.

"Aren't you a pretty one," he sniggered in a low husky voice. His breath close to her face smelled of cabbage. Two of his front teeth were missing.

Katy said nothing, but turned away, hugging her daughters even closer.

The Cossack leader walked over to the Russian oven and looked closely at the two boys. He grabbed Anatoly's chin and forced him to look up at him.

"This one doesn't look so much like the others."

"He takes after his grandfather," Heinrich put in quickly. "His name is Peter. My other son's name is Henry."

The Cossack looked doubtful.

"Well, all right then," he finally said.

He let go of Anatoly's chin and turned to go out the door. Just as he was about to leave, the leader turned to Heinrich and said, "Don't go anywhere. Yer gonna be needed later."

The chill in the house from the outside air that had invaded the room through the open door was gradually overcome as the big Russian oven warmed the kitchen. But the chill in the hearts of the family deepened as the day wore on and they worried about the Cossack's departing words.

"Thank you for saving me," Anatoly murmured with tears in his eyes.

He was safe, yet he could not stop thinking about his mother alone in their house. And, where was his father? What had become of him?

6

The next day was Christmas Eve. It was not until that morning that the Cossacks returned. This time Heinrich saw them coming into the front yard on their horses. Thinking to keep them out of his home, he put on his coat, fur-lined cap, gloves and boots and stepped out of the door.

"What can this be about?" Heinrich thought, perplexed and frightened.

"Get yer shovel. And a pick, if ya have one," the Cossack Lieutenant commanded. When Heinrich was slow to respond, the Cossack shouted "Hurry, old man! We haven't got all day!"

Heinrich left to find his shovel. When he was out of sight, Henry, who had been watching his father being bullied, suddenly rushed out of the house and ran toward the horseman.

"Leave my father alone!" Henry yelled.

The Cossack looked momentarily stunned at the boy's audacity. Then he laughed.

"I have no time for this, ya little imp," he said casually. He struck Henry on the head with the butt of his carbine. Blood welled into Henry's hair as he fell to the ground.

"Stay inside, girls!" Katy commanded as she ran to help Henry.

When Heinrich returned he saw his wife bending over his son who was struggling to stand up. Heinrich cried out in alarm.

The Cossack pointed his rifle at him.

"Let's do this peacefully," he said quietly.

"I'm okay, Dad," said Henry as Katy led him into the house.

Heinrich joined Dr. Ulyanov, Aleksey Goshorev, and Sergei. They had gathered in the front yard. Each was holding a pick or shovel.

"May I take a look at the boy?" asked Dr. Ulyanov. "I'm a doctor."

"No time," said the Cossack. "Follow me."

He turned his horse onto the road and the men had no choice but to march after him. Another Cossack followed in the rear.

Heinrich spoke to the doctor in a hushed voice.

"On a day like this, aren't you needed at the hospital?"

"I was turned back before I could get there. The sentries wouldn't listen to reason," Dr. Ulyanov replied bitterly.

As they rounded the corner onto Ermak Street, Heinrich looked into his back yard and was surprised to see that Cossacks had occupied the little house. He could see horses inside it. He thought of the Melzhins and wondered what terrible things might have happened to them. In fact, no one could later say what the fate of the Melzhins had been on that chaotic day in December; only that they had disappeared and were never heard from again.

The Cossacks, on the other hand, made the little house into a permanent barrack, at least until events turned against them months later. They used the house as a stable and slept with their horses in two of its small rooms. It would become a common sight, galling to the Rempels, to see them parading their mounts up and down its steps and in and out of their little house's front door.

All this was to come later, though, and at the moment Heinrich and his neighbors were being marched down Ermak Street. Every so often a few more men were herded in to join their group. As they walked past the Lepinov's house, Heinrich stole a glance over his left shoulder. There was a candle flickering and smoke was rising from the chimney. Good, Mrs. Lepinov must be doing better, he thought with some relief.

Finally they reached their destination. It was a bare plot of land next to the banks of the Irtysh River. In the distance, around a bend, the men could see the bridge spanning the river. A train was idling on it, clouds of white smoke spewing upward from its stack. From the flags flying on its engine, they could tell that it was a Czech armored train. On the roofs of its wagons, like tiny toy soldiers, Heinrich could see Czech soldiers manning their machine guns. His eyes moved to his left, to the northwest, in the direction of the railway station and the industrial district. Black smoke was billowing up from several locations.

Heinrich's attention was drawn away from the horizon to the field in which he stood. He noticed horse-drawn carts were coming and going. Men stood behind the carts and pulled the cargo off the back end. Some stood on top of the loads and threw the large bundles over the sides and onto the ground. Even from a distance it was obvious what was being unloaded. A chill ran down Heinrich's back. He realized it was human bodies he was seeing. Some wore the uniforms of soldiers. Others were dressed in plain clothes and were obviously civilians. Most were men, but he noticed a few women were among the dead. Regardless of who they had once been, they were frozen solid in the grotesque shapes in which death had claimed them and now they were being thrown onto piles on the snowy field.

It was only then too, that Heinrich realized that Filipovich's body had no longer been lying in the middle of the street in front of their house when their march had begun this morning. "Maybe he is here," Heinrich thought fearfully, and suddenly he found himself searching the faces of the bodies lying nearby.

The Cossacks arranged their work detail into groups and the men began the bone-jarring work of breaking through the iron-solid crust of earth and digging large trenches, creating mass graves for the bodies being deposited on the site. It seemed a hopeless task, so many were the corpses and so hard the work. Heinrich had no idea how many there were. There were more than he could count. To his relief, he found that he didn't know any of the victims he encountered, but as each corpse was roughly thrown into the ditch he had helped dig, he saw their horrible wounds and their frozen death masks. Heinrich's heart cried out to God for mercy, for these poor unfortunate souls, for his town, Kulomzino, for his country, Russia, for himself. With each falling corpse he felt himself falling ever deeper into a pit of numb despair.

The day wore on. There was no rest and no food. Heinrich ate snow to quench his thirst. It was in the afternoon when suddenly he heard the Cossacks talking amongst themselves.

"*Angliyskiye soldaty*! English soldiers!"

The exhausted workmen watched, some wearily leaning on their shovels while others collapsed onto the snow, as a group of eight English soldiers on horseback rode briskly onto the field. They were dressed in long black sheepskin coats, brown peaked sheepskin hats and huge fur boots. The Cossack Lieutenant greeted them. One of the Englishmen dismounted and immediately began talking with the large Cossack. Soon their voices rose and it sounded like they were arguing. The English soldier's face wore a look of disgust as his gaze took in the scene before him on the field. The Cossack laughed at him.

"What could the English be wanting here, on this field of death?" Dr. Ulyanov wondered aloud.

It wasn't long before the English officer remounted his horse. As the horsemen rode off, they passed next to where Heinrich and Dr. Ulyanov stood.

Heinrich had paid little attention to the visitors. He was too exhausted and heartsick to give them much notice. He had taken off his frayed gloves and was looking at his bleeding hands. Blisters had formed and torn away; his soft hands were not used to such strenuous physical labor.

Heinrich was aware that a horseman had stopped beside him. He could smell the horse's sweat. The leather saddle creaked as the rider shifted his weight. Heinrich looked up and was surprised to hear the English soldier speak to him in Russian.

"You'd best put some ointment and bandages on those hands of yours, Brother. And wrap them in some clean bandages. You don't want them to become infected."

The soldier dug a small tin of ointment and a strip of white cotton cloth out of his saddlebag and handed them down to Heinrich.

"Here, take this."

Heinrich wondered at the thoughtfulness of the Englishman. Somehow it was completely out of place on this field of horror, for darkness never welcomes light into its realm. But with that small act, Heinrich felt himself being drawn ever so slightly out of the abyss into which his emotions had tumbled.

Perhaps there was some small hope after all, because kindness did still exist.

Synchronicity

1

On the eve of the Bolshevik conspiracy to retake control of Omsk, I had been summoned to consult with Russian doctors at the residence of the Supreme Ruler, Admiral Kolchak. He was suffering from a severe lung infection with a fever and a hard, hacking cough. We kept him on bed rest and treated him with aspirin, a wonderful drug only recently become available, and with oil of cinnamon in milk to reduce the fever.

It was some time after two in the morning when pandemonium broke loose in the streets. We heard gunfire from many directions in the city. There were sporadic explosions. The sounds of fighting continued through the night. Closer to morning, huge blasts coming from across the river rattled the mansion's windows.

Kolchak's bedroom swiftly became a command post. Frantic messengers flew in and left just as quickly. Sick though he was, the Admiral attempted to exert some leadership and gain some measure of control over the chaotic situation.

Slowly details of the uprising became clear. Soldiers in the new Russian army were mutinying in the city. The Omsk prison, a large fortress-like complex, had been captured by Bolshevik rebels and a massacre of Socialist Revolutionary prisoners had taken place there. The Kulomzino train station and industrial area had become a war zone as Bolshevik railway workers joined forces with members of the 20th Siberian Regiment and waged a fierce battle against General Ivanov-Rinov's Siberian Cossacks. Some conspirators had been discovered trying to destroy the Irtysh Bridge, but had been killed or run off. The Czech Legion had sent an armored train to secure the bridge.

Later I learned that the Supreme Ruler had not been taken unawares. Through his network of spies, he had been forewarned of the uprising and had arrested the leaders of the rebellion at midnight, before their plans could be put into effect. They were all shot dead. News of their leaders' arrests did not filter down to the rebels so the uprising went ahead as planned. Kolchak had also called in Ivanov-Rinov's Siberian Cossacks to deal with the rebels. Once let loose, the Cossacks were uncontrollable. Thousands of rebels and innocents, both soldiers and civilians, were killed or wounded.

Our contribution to the suppression of the uprising was to occupy the Staffka, the Russian Army Headquarters, to prevent a full-scale coup. Colonel Ward marched into the headquarters with a squad of soldiers. He met no resistance. Apparently the appearance of a few "*Angliyskiye soldaty*" was enough to convince the General Staff that loyalty to their Supreme Ruler was the best course of action. After securing the Staffka, Colonel Ward led a detachment of soldiers to Kolchak's residence to ensure the protection of the Supreme Ruler. The rest of the battalion lay snug in their barracks while anarchy swept through the city. Our orders were to not interfere in "internal Russian affairs."

2

Christmas Eve. Quiet had returned to Omsk. It had snowed during the night, covering over the brutal stains that had marred the beautiful city. The morning air seemed not quite as cold. Dull grey clouds hung low in the sky threatening more snow to come.

Admiral Kolchak was still ill though feeling somewhat better. The Russian doctors felt my services were no longer required. A troika was sent to take me to the Russian Staffka where I was to report to Colonel Ward. The bells on the troika jingled with each prancing step as the trio of horses pulled the sleigh and broke the deathly quiet that permeated the streets after the previous night's cacophony of conflict. The only persons out of doors were soldiers bundled in their greatcoats who nervously guarded checkpoints at strategic buildings and roadways. They held their weapons at the ready and watched my troika with suspicion as it carried me toward them. They only relaxed when they realized I was an English soldier, after which they would wave and shout cheerful greetings.

I made my report to Colonel Ward who was relieved to hear of Admiral Kolchak's improved condition. Colonel Ward immediately assigned me to accompany a squad of soldiers that was being sent to Kulomzino to make an assessment of the situation there. Ominous rumors were rife of a slaughter that had occurred amongst the civilian population in the western suburb of Omsk.

And so, later that day I found myself on a field by the west bank of the Irtysh River. A group of exhausted Russian civilians had created a large trench-work into which hundreds of bodies were being dumped and buried. I felt my blood boil as I observed the barbarity of the scene being played out on that plot of ground. I also felt a deep sense of shame, for while the Middlesex battalion had stood idly by the town and citizens of Kulomzino had been cruelly savaged by the very forces we had been sent to support.

As we talked, Heinrich Rempel and I were standing by a large lounge window, watching the grey waves of the North Atlantic heave in the distance. Slowly he turned and looked at me as realization dawned in his dark, watery eyes.

"You were there!" he said softly. "The English soldiers on horses who came to the field. You were one of them?"

"Yes."

"It was you who gave me the ointment and bandages for my hands."

"Yes."

He wept at the memory of my simple act of kindness and the wonder of our meeting on this ship.

We embraced like brothers.

Feeding the Enemy

1

Christmas, 1919, brought with it a dangerous dilemma.

"The Bolsheviks have announced that it is strictly forbidden to hold a religious meeting in the school," pointed out Olga Hiebert, a teacher at our Kulomzino Mennonite School. "We could be arrested. Or, at least, I could be arrested," she added hesitantly.

A few parents, together with Miss Hiebert, were standing on the steps of the school and discussing the traditional Christmas Eve program that was supposed to take place in one week. Now, with the new government edict, they were not sure what they should do.

A parent, Isaac Peters spoke ruefully. "But we missed our celebration last year. Then it was for fear of the White Cossacks. Are we also going to allow these Red thugs to stop us from celebrating our Savior's birth this year?"

There were some nods of agreement. The discussion went back and forth.

"It is ridiculous," muttered Heinrich Rempel.

The group stood in silence. No one seemed to know what to say.

After a moment Heinrich spoke firmly, "We cannot allow the Bolsheviks to bully us in matters of worship."

"But it is Olga who is taking the greatest risk," Katy Rempel gently drew everyone's attention to the crux of the matter. "She should have the final say."

The group stood in silence as they realized the risk they were asking their teacher to make. Their breath rose around them in the chill air creating a vapor of unspoken prayers. Everyone looked at Miss Hiebert.

"I am willing to go ahead with the program," said the teacher cautiously. "It is important for the children to celebrate the Christ-child's birth."

"Then I shall help you," added Katy. "I can bring some Christmas baking for the children."

Heinrich looked at his wife sharply. On the off chance there was going to be trouble, he wasn't sure it was a good idea for her to be involved in organizing the event. But what could he say? His had been one of the loudest voices calling for the civil disobedience.

2

Last Christmas had come and gone without any public celebrations. Families had marked the day quietly in private, keeping to their homes for fear of the Cossack soldiers who were patrolling the streets of Kulomzino. The ill-fated Bolshevik rebellion had been put down mercilessly and no one wanted to test the good will of the triumphant Cossacks who swaggered proudly about on their prancing horses.

Much had happened in the year since those terrible days. Anatoly had lived with the Rempel family for a month. He had not dared to show himself outside for fear of being recognized and betrayed to the Cossacks. But as the days turned into weeks, interest in the whereabouts of the missing conspirators slowly vanished. Though his body was never found, rumor had it that Fyodor Lepinov had died in an explosion on the Irtysh Bridge. Anatoly refused to believe the rumor, steadfastly clinging to the hope that his father was alive and well.

"He's in hiding. One day he'll come home. You'll see," Anatoly solemnly avowed any time the fate of his father was brought up.

Finally, when it was deemed safe, Anatoly returned home to live with his mother.

The soldiers living in the little house were a constant threat and bother. They demanded food from their neighbors and harried them if it was not prepared fast enough. Fortunately, the large garden Katy and the children had planted in late spring and carefully tended through the hot days of summer had provided a rich crop. There had been rows of raspberries, white and black currants, cabbages, peas, carrots, and potatoes among other things. In the fall, these had all been harvested and put up for winter. The shelves in the cold cellar were lined with jars of canned fruits and vegetables. One wall was piled high with sacks of potatoes. In a corner stood a barrel of pickled cucumbers. So, no one went hungry. More than their constant demand for food, though, it grated on Heinrich, when he looked over at his beloved little house, to see the Cossacks pulling their horses up its steps and through the hand-crafted door and use it as a stable.

For a time there had been great optimism in Omsk as the White government announced glorious victories in its battle against the Red Army far to the west. This optimism had even led Heinrich to make a couple of trips into Omsk to discuss possible business plans with his banker. Perhaps there was hope yet that his farm implement order would come from America. When he was in the city he noticed it teemed with foreign soldiers. He saw French soldiers riding in automobiles, wearing thick fur coats with their red and grey kepis on their heads. British Tommies in their black fur coats, boots and hats marched briskly along the roadways. He passed Japanese soldiers who disdained the comfort of fur and braved the cold in khaki trench coats. Italian soldiers were bundled in their furs and he even saw a few Americans. It was odd to see so many foreign soldiers roaming the streets of Omsk, mixed in with the Omskovites who were trying to go about their daily business while also coping with the crush of refugees that seemed to grow in size every day.

One day when Heinrich was walking over the frozen Irtysh on his way home from the city he noticed a large crowd of Siberians gathered around a place on the river where the wind-swept snow had been cleared away to make an ice rink. Heinrich made his way over to see what was happening and discovered that Canadian soldiers in their striking fur coats and hats had attached blades to their white fur boots. They were speeding about on the ice doing figure eights and all sorts of other fancy maneuvers. Their audience was spellbound. The Siberians had never seen such a display before.

By summer the news from the front became less encouraging. The July 1 parades and speeches celebrating the first anniversary of the new Russia governed by Admiral Kolchak were overshadowed by rumors that the White armies were in disarray and the Red Army was pouring through the Ural Mountains onto the Siberian steppes. By October the reports from the front were downright alarming; by the beginning of November the evacuation of Omsk had begun.

Heinrich Rempel had forbidden his family from going anywhere near the Kulomzino Railway Station or the areas around it. Thousands of soldiers were being housed in every available building there and in the city of Omsk. They were suffering from an epidemic of typhus.

The family remained close to home and had no way of knowing that, despite the many patriotic cries to defend Omsk to the death, despite the posters that blanketed the town and urged men to join the White resistance by showing a grotesque Chinese man in a Red Army uniform marching along with a Russian baby skewered on the tip of his bayonet, and despite all the artillery batteries that were strategically placed about the city, one morning early in November the Kolchak government abandoned Omsk in a convoy of trains headed east and guarded by the Czech Legion. The Rempel's only hint of the dramatic change that was coming lay on the day the Cossack horsemen occupying the little house suddenly packed up their belongings and vanished.

The Allied armies that had paraded so gallantly in the streets of Omsk for more than a year had already taken the trains eastward past Irkutsk to Vladivostok where ships waited to take them homeward. After all, this had never been their fight.

That year the river was slow to freeze over, so the tens of thousands of refugees who were unable to flee by train were forced to wait until the last minute before leaving their hovels and places of refuge. Finally the day came when the ice would bear their weight and they crossed the frozen river in a mass of misery and trudged eastward in the cold and snow to an uncertain destination and end.

The Red Army entered Omsk unopposed on the 15th of November 1919. Fires had been lit in warehouses in the industrial district of Kulomzino to deny the invading army the stores of British supplies that had been meant for the White armies but had instead been hoarded by corrupt officials for sale on the black market. The fires served only as a bright beacon to welcome the Bolshevik horde whose gleaming eyes faced ever eastward toward the man, Admiral Alexandr Kolchak, and the ragged remnants of his armies that had dared to oppose their revolution.

Heinrich and his son Henry Rempel were standing in their front yard. They could see the bright glow of the fires of the burning warehouses as it reflected off the low ceiling of cloud cloaking the evening sky to the north. As they watched and wondered about what was happening, a group of ragged soldiers, some with red stars on their caps, appeared on their street and marched wearily along it. As the soldiers approached, Heinrich saw that some were entering houses along the street. A few came to his neighbors, the Sarkovskys, and climbed the steps onto the veranda, at which point Heinrich and Henry hurried into their own home.

It wasn't long before four dirty, bedraggled men armed with rifles slung over their stooped shoulders were walking up the Rempels' pathway. They dragged their feet in the snow as if they had walked all the way from the Urals without stopping. They did not look like conquering heroes. Rather, they looked very much like the many refugees who had walked that same street and whose footsteps they were retracing.

"Hurry children," urged Katy, while Heinrich prepared to open the door. There was no thought of denying the soldiers entry. "Go into the back room. Stay there. Do not come into the kitchen for any reason. And don't make any noise." She looked at her oldest daughter with anxious eyes. "Katyusha, please make sure Nessa is quiet."

When all the children were in the back room, Katy gave one last peek, putting her finger to her lips. "Now, shhhh." She looked at each child pleadingly.

As Katy came away from the bedroom there was a loud knocking on the door outside. Nervously, Heinrich pulled the door open. Without waiting for an invitation, the soldiers barged their way in. They went straight to the kitchen table. Four chairs scraped on the floor as the soldiers heavily sat down.

"Feed us," demanded one of them.

As the soldiers sprawled about the table their rifles clattered onto the floor. The soldiers paid no attention. They seemed exhausted. Their beards and the hair that sprouted from under their caps were matted with filth. Their skin was weathered and dirty. Their eyes were dull and weary. The soldiers seemed to have little interest in what or who was in the room. One of them laid his head on his arms on the table and immediately fell asleep.

Katy happened to have some thin borscht in a pot on the stove and this was soon heated and served. The men slurped the soup down as if they hadn't eaten in a week and kept eating until the large pot was empty. With their bellies full and wrapped in the warmth of the house, all four of the soldiers soon nodded off, sitting in their chairs at the table.

Katy and Heinrich looked at each other. The soldiers were wearing the jackets of uniforms the British had given to the Whites. Obviously they had been looted from some supply of stores that had been captured along the way.

As the soldiers snored, Katy slipped into the back room to reassure the children. Heinrich watched her go and then looked at the rifles on the floor. He quickly found himself in a quandary.

"Should I pick the rifles up?" he wondered. "They're all asleep. I could do it. I could disarm them, show them the door, get them out of my house."

A deep feeling of bitterness and anger welled up in Heinrich as he contemplated the ragged intruders. First it was the Whites, now the Reds. They were all the same: desperate men with guns who would not think twice about harming you if you didn't give them what they wanted. Where was justice?

"My God, where are you? Have you forsaken us?" Heinrich cried in his heart.

Heinrich knew it was irrational to think he could take on these men from the Red Army, but his eyes would not stray away from the firearms lying on the floor. He had never owned a gun or even shot one. He had seen it done, once on a farm, when a bull had refused to go down under the hammer. The shot had startled him, even though he was expecting it. What would he do once he held one of those rifles in his hands? He tried to imagine himself pointing a gun at the men and ordering them out of his house. What would he do if they resisted? And what if they left without an argument? Would they not come back? Of course they'd come back! And there'd be more of them next time. And then he would pay for his foolishness. His family would never be safe.

He remembered Psalm 23. "Even though I walk through the valley of the shadow of death, I will fear no evil." "But I do fear evil," Heinrich thought. "It has filled our town and our country and right now it slumbers here at my table." He recalled the next verse, "I will fear no evil, for you are with me." Again his heart cried out, "God, I believe. Help me in my unbelief."

Heinrich took another look at the faces of the sleeping men and wondered what tormented dreams they must be having. He saw their desperation and their idealism and realized that, but for the grace of God, he was not one such as them, sleeping the sleep of the dead at some stranger's table before going out and committing acts which Heinrich found difficult even to imagine.

As these thoughts roiled in his head, Heinrich was interrupted by a sharp banging sound. Realizing someone was at the door he quickly opened it. A soldier standing there looked in and shouted loudly to his comrades at the table. The sleeping soldiers woke begrudgingly and wearily picked up their rifles. They stood and lumbered out of the house without a backward glance; except for one, the one who appeared to be the youngest.

He looked back at Katy and with a weary, crooked smile mouthed, "*Spasibo*. Thank you."

4

It was Christmas Eve. The schoolroom was packed with proud parents and happy children excited to present their Christmas recitations. A Christmas tree stood in the corner, alight with small thin candles burning like bright stars in its fragrant pine branches. When Henry squinted his eyes while looking at the tree he imagined a whole Milky Way of sparkling magic lighting the room.

The program began with carols, sung with joyful tears in the eyes of more than a few of the adults who were grateful for this reverent celebration. Next, one by one the children stood before the audience and recited their Christmas poems. Olga Hiebert proudly stayed in the background, directing the children and helping those who miscued.

It was Katarina's turn. She calmly took her place in front of the small audience. Looking at her parents, she began reciting in a firm voice the poem she had written.

"The Christmas season announces the bright glow of the lights, and with all this comes joy and jubilation."

As she spoke, there was a commotion at the back of the room. Katarina tried to ignore it.

"With precious gifts I am blessed," Katarina recited, "more than I can imagine my happy eye observes! Our parents' love and goodness is what makes us glad, the cares that never end, you always have time for your children. These are the gifts I gladly bring forth, the joy that I have, so lovingly contemplated."

Katarina paused in her recitation long enough to look at her parents' proud faces. "How am I to repay what you have done for me? Oh Lord of the world, take my request. Bless my parents with good fortune on their life's journey! This is my prayer! Amen."

Her poem complete, Katarina lowered her eyes and rejoined her classmates on the bench at the front of the room. As he watched his daughter be seated, Heinrich felt an anxious hand tap his shoulder. Warm breath brushed his ear.

"Heinrich," whispered the voice of Isaac Peters. "Soldiers are looking in through the window. We must do something."

A burning pain struck Heinrich in the pit of his stomach. Quickly, fearfully, he stood and moved toward the door, his mind raced as he frantically tried to think of a way of dealing with the situation. Katy saw the ashen pallor of her husband's face as he left his seat. She watched with alarm as he put on his coat and walked toward the door.

Nervously, not knowing what to expect, Heinrich and Isaac went outside. Their first breaths of frigid night air caught in their lungs and made them cough. Heinrich pulled the collar of his winter coat closer about his throat as he and Isaac walked toward the unwelcome visitors.

Standing in the pale light of the window, their faces close to the glass as they peered at the proceedings inside the brightly lit schoolroom, were two Red Army soldiers. They had set their rifles on the ground in the snow and leaned the barrels against the wall. Fur caps were pulled down low over their ears against the freezing temperature. Their hands were hidden deep inside their thick winter coats. One soldier used his coat sleeve to wipe away the frost their breath had created on the windowpane.

Noticing the men coming toward them, the soldiers eyed Heinrich and Isaac suspiciously. They stooped, picked up their rifles and held them at the ready.

"So, comrades," asked one of the soldiers brusquely. "What have ya got goin' on in there?"

He was missing his front teeth, Heinrich noticed.

"It's just a little program for the children of the school," Heinrich answered. "Nothing to be concerned about."

The toothless soldier took another look through the window while his partner moved his rifle so that it pointed directly at Heinrich's face. He looked threateningly at Heinrich and Isaac Peters.

"That's not a religious gatherin' now is it?" asked the soldier with the rifle sarcastically. His nose was running and had caused icicles to form on his large moustache. "Cuz if it is, we've got orders to arrest anybody who's holdin' a religious meetin' in the school."

Heinrich's knees felt weak.

"No, the students are merely reciting some poetry they wrote," he responded. As a man who told the truth on principle, Heinrich was amazed how easy it was to speak the half-truth.

The soldiers looked as if they might become impatient.

"Listen, comrades," said Isaac Peters as an idea struck him. "You must be hungry! A cold evening like this, you've been making your rounds. It's a quiet night; nothing is going on. Why not take a break from your patrol? Would you be interested, perhaps, in a meal?"

Startled, Heinrich looked at his friend as he made his audacious offer.

"My home is just around the corner. Would you like to get out of the cold for a while? You can put your feet up by the fire and enjoy some good hot food. My wife happens to be at home." Isaac paused briefly as he watched the soldiers' reaction to his proposal. "She's a great cook!" he finished.

While Isaac was talking, the two soldiers looked at each other and pursed their lips. Slowly they grinned and their eyes lit up as the thought of a warm fire and hot food captured their interest.

"Ya know, comrade," said the toothless soldier, "I think we'll take ya up on yer offer."

"Yah," said the other gleefully. "Comrade Lenin's work can wait for an hour or two. And I'm famished!"

"Then follow me," gestured Isaac Peters as jovially as he could. He rebelled at the thought of bringing these two brutes into his home, but there didn't seem to be any other option. Something had to be done to remove them from the schoolhouse.

Later that evening, when Heinrich wearily returned home, he told Katy how the Peters had given the two Bolshevik soldiers the royal treatment. While Mrs. Peters prepared a feast of boiled potatoes and roasted pork cut from the frozen side hanging in their attic, the soldiers had lounged by the fire and devoured a platter of her Christmas baking. Hoping to make them more comfortable, Heinrich knelt and removed their heavy army boots. He quickly saw that the soldiers' feet were in bad shape. Their socks were rotting off of feet that were covered in sores. Hiding his revulsion at the smell, Heinrich removed their old threads while Isaac brought two pairs of his wife's newly knitted socks from the bureau in the bedroom. Seeing the sad condition of their feet, Isaac hurried to the stove and poured some hot water from the kettle into a basin. Snatching up a towel, he quickly brought it and the basin of water to where the soldiers were sitting. Kneeling on the hard, wooden floor, Isaac tenderly washed each of the soldiers' feet. At first they balked and asked him if he was crazy, but the sensation of the hot water on their cold, ruined skin soon had them closing their eyes in pleasure, though they also occasionally winced in pain. As Isaac finished, Heinrich daubed healing ointment on each foot and carefully wrapped it in a new sock. The soldiers sighed contentedly as their feet, warmed in the comfort of their new socks, rested on the hearth in front of the fire. After their meal, when one of the soldiers noticed a pair of silver candlesticks on the sideboard and spoke admiringly about them, Isaac Peters promptly presented them as a gift, giving each soldier one. It was late in the evening before the soldiers picked up the guns they had left by the door and finally departed from the Peters' home, waving a good-natured farewell. By then the program at the Kulomzino Mennonite School was long over and everyone was safely at home, having joyfully, and safely, celebrated their Savior's birth.

It would be the children's last Christmas program at the school. The next year, the Mennonite teachers were unceremoniously replaced by teachers supplied by the State. Alarmed by the communist propaganda being fed his children,

Heinrich pulled them out of the school and from then on, as best he could, taught them himself at home.

Hard Times

1

It was a Tuesday morning in late February 1922. Heinrich Rempel was in his back yard chopping wood for the ever-ravenous Russian oven. The wood had been delivered during the previous night by a wizened, stooped Uzbek leading a tired mare pulling a small, rickety wagon. Heaven only knew how he had come by the cords. The communists had instituted strict controls on the amount of firewood allocated to each family. It was never enough. But there were always those who sought to profit from the needs of others and Heinrich was unapologetic as he circumvented the law. His family's needs must be met. In the dark, the wood had been quickly piled against the back wall of the apartment under a small lean-to Heinrich had built to keep the cords dry and out of sight.

Heinrich's breath created a fog about his fur-capped head that froze white onto his beard and moustache. After days of heavy snowfall, the weak sun shining low on the horizon held the promise of a brighter day but would do little to warm the frigid winter air.

Heinrich swung the axe down with all his strength. It bit into the dry pinewood but the log wouldn't give. He used his sledgehammer on the axe head to drive it through the wood, splitting the log and releasing the axe at the same time. He stacked the split pieces on his growing woodpile and paused, looking over at the plot of land that until the previous year had been his family's precious garden.

Underneath the snow, Heinrich knew the garden was a tumbledown collection of weeds and overgrown plants. The unpruned raspberry and currant bushes created a barrier against which the snow had collected in long drifts.

One day in spring two policemen had appeared at their door.

"The garden on this property belongs to the workers of Russia," the incredulous Rempels had been told. "As of today, the local soviet has taken over its management."

"But, it's on my land," Heinrich had argued.

As a result of his protest, Heinrich had been arrested. He was taken to the local police station where he was roughed up for having the audacity to question the will of the people's soviet. He had returned home the next day bruised and rebuffed.

A week later, some workers appeared on the Rempels' yard. They built a tall wooden fence around the large garden plot. A gate was installed and locked with a heavy padlock. Thereafter the garden had sat, untended throughout the entire growing season. No one had come to work the soil. No one had planted any seeds. The Rempels' raspberry and currant bushes had grown wild and unkempt, and then shriveled in the summer heat for lack of water. Weeds had grown where vegetables should otherwise have ripened. Katy had wept at the sight of it.

"What a waste," muttered Heinrich to himself. "But not this year. This year we will plant and tend our garden. The Bolsheviks be damned."

The loss of their garden had created a serious hardship for the Rempels and their tenants. Food they would otherwise have grown themselves had had to be bought. Money was scarce. They had had to tighten their belts. Fortunately, the meager rent collected from their tenants had helped the Rempels make it through the winter.

Over the past couple of years, tenants had come and gone. Sergei and his mother had left one day and never returned. The Ulyanovs had moved to a flat closer to the hospital where Dr. Ulyanov worked tirelessly amongst the sick locals as well as the constant throng of refugees fleeing the famine in the Ukraine. Many were diseased—typhus and tuberculosis were epidemic among them—and in winter many suffered from frostbite in the poorly heated rail cars.

"And I can't even rent to whomever I want." The thought rankled Heinrich. "There is no way for a man to get ahead in Russia! Everything is controlled by the communists."

Tenants were now being assigned by a government committee. Heinrich was required to inform the police of vacancies. His apartments were inspected and he was required to make repairs.

"All for a fat fee, of course," he thought bitterly.

Heinrich's thoughts turned in another direction. In response to all the government intervention and meddling in their lives, and the lack of opportunity to pursue his business dreams, the idea had recently been growing in Heinrich's mind that perhaps it was time to leave Russia. His cousin in Manitoba wrote that there were no such restrictions in Canada. Canada was a land of freedom and opportunity. But Canada was halfway around the world and it was not so easy to pick up and leave the homeland of his forefathers.

"Should we be thinking about leaving Russia?" he had asked Katy one evening. She had initially been shocked by the idea, but after discussing its pros and cons they had decided that, perhaps, it was worth exploring.

Heinrich picked up a piece of pinewood and placed it on the chopping block. As he swung the axe over his shoulder he noticed a couple of policemen walking their horses toward him along Sovietskaya Street and turn left onto Trotskaya Street. Much to Heinrich's disgust, the Bolsheviks had renamed the streets of Kulomzino to reflect the success of their revolution. Behind the policemen followed a truck. He could see a few men leaning on the slatted wooden sides of its deck. Heinrich walked to the front yard and watched as the policemen stopped in front of his gate.

"What now?" Heinrich thought.

"You there," shouted the policeman. "Get your shovel and your pick, if you have one, and join our little parade. Hurry now, the day's short."

Heinrich knew there was no way he could escape this conscription. When he asked where he was being taken, the policeman said he would see soon enough. When Heinrich asked if he could inform his wife that he was leaving, the policeman said he would be back before she'd miss him. Heinrich had no choice but to get his shovel and climb onto the back of the truck with the other dispirited men.

The truck bucked and sputtered as it pulled away from Heinrich's yard. They stopped almost immediately in front of the Sarkovsky's where Ivan was forced to join their cold ranks. After a few more stops, the policemen must have decided they had enough recruits for the truck took them directly to the Kulomzino Trans-Siberian Railway Station. They bumped across some railroad tracks and finally came to a large shed. Another small group of men were already there, huddled together in a tight knot. A couple of wagons with restive horses stood waiting by the building. The drivers sat huddled in their greatcoats and smoked cigarettes while their silent, steaming horses stood with drooping heads. Heinrich noticed the drivers' cigarettes had long curling rolls of ash hanging from their ends. To discard the ash would have meant removing gloves and though the day was warm, relatively speaking for February, the drivers had no interest in exposing their hands to the frigid air.

For a few moments the conscripts were left to stand in the cold. Heinrich leaned on his shovel and waited to see what would unfold.

A policeman went to the shed and opened its door.

"Over here," he growled.

Heinrich joined the men peering into the shed. What he saw left him sick with dread. The shed was stacked with corpses piled like cordwood. They were the bodies of refugees from South Russia, who had died of starvation, or typhus, or of exposure on the long, frigid train journey to Siberia. They had been removed from the train cars and stored in this shed. Some were frozen in positions that indicated they had died while huddled on the floor; others were straight as a log. There seemed to be a preponderance of the elderly and the young. They had died and frozen solid in the overcrowded, under-heated wagons.

"Load 'em onto the wagons and the truck." The policeman's voice broke into the silent horror of the mesmerized men.

One by one the corpses, large and small, were carried out of the shed. The men tried to treat the bodies with some sense of dignity and respect, but soon gave up as they numbed to their job and were pushed to work more quickly. When the shed was empty, the men stood about miserably until they were led away from the station and down another road. The somber conscripts walked in silence, their eyes fixed on the icy ground before their feet, as the laden wagons creaked and groaned in front of them.

They stopped at a field outside of town. There the corpses were unloaded to form a long pile. One of the policemen stood nearby and used his rifle to point to where he wanted the corpses buried. The wagons drove off as the men, swinging picks over their heads, began the difficult task of breaking through the frozen earth.

Heinrich could not help but think of the field by the river where, three years earlier, he had been forced to perform this very same task. He stole a glance at a policeman.

"Different faces behind the guns, same inhumanity," he said under his breath to Ivan Sarkovsky who was struggling to break the unyielding earth beside him. "Whites, Reds, they're all the same!"

Heinrich tried to say a prayer for the unfortunate men, women, and children he buried. But his soul was as frozen as the tears that strayed slowly down and stuck to his cold pale cheeks.

Finally the job was done. What daylight the weak February sun had conjured had already fled and it was dark. The men were told they could find their own ways home. Depressed after what they had been forced to do, Heinrich, Ivan, and the others wearily plodded off, gripping their tools like walking sticks or letting them rest heavily on their shoulders.

3

Heinrich became more and more convinced that his family's only hope of a better future lay in emigration. Increasingly, his dealings with the police were becoming disconcerting and even hostile. When he encountered the soviet officials in matters relating to his apartments, they would treat him with disdain and call him a kulak.

"How is our little landowner doing today?" they would mock.

Heinrich heard the sarcasm and resentment in their voices and wondered how long it would be before they brought an action against him. Could he get permission for his family to leave Russia before some local communist official arrested him, or worse? He knew of other families who had experienced the fickleness of Bolshevik 'justice.'

One day Heinrich was accosted on the street by Fyodor Lepinov. Fyodor had reappeared in Kulomsino about six months after the fall of Omsk. As it turned out, after the abortive rebellion in November 1918, he had been found and nursed back to health by members of the militia, which he then joined. He fought in their ranks until one day his unit had been disbanded. Upon his return home, when he discovered how Heinrich Rempel had sheltered his son from the Cossacks, he swore his unending appreciation and debt to his German neighbor. So, on this day, he took it upon himself to warn Heinrich.

"Comrade Rempel," he said with a sly look. "I hear the police have got their eye on ya. Ya've been branded a capitalist, a kulak. Yer a landowner, ya see. Ya've got all these folks payin' rent. Yer gettin' rich off the sweat of other people's brows. That's counter-revolutionary." Lepinov gave a quick wink and nodded his head. "Ya'd best get yerself an honest job, if ya take my meanin'." Lepinov looked sternly at Heinrich and sauntered off.

Shaken by Fyodor Lepinov's warning, Heinrich looked for ways out of his dilemma. But he was born and bred a businessman. What else was he to do?

It was his old friend and neighbor, Ivan Sarkovsky, who suggested a solution to the precarious situation in which Heinrich found himself. They were talking in the back yard, 'over the fence' as it were, and Heinrich suddenly found himself confiding in Ivan.

"What you need, my friend, is an occupation," Ivan said. "You need a job where you earn your own living. Now, I have an idea." Ivan looked to see if anyone was within hearing distance. "Once the Reds took over," he continued, "my job at the railway station was terminated. It's the workers who are in control now," he added sarcastically. "Not that they have any idea what should be done. I've heard it's a shambles over there." Ivan paused. He took a deep breath and let it out. "So, Heinrich, I've become a farmer. Me, after twenty years at the railway!" He shook his head in disbelief and chuckled. "I've taken what money I had saved and rented some land on the outskirts of town. Five *dessiatines*. I'm planning to have the owner put in a crop of oats.

"So here's the thing. The owner has another five *dessiatines* beside my land. Why don't you rent it? We can help each other out keeping the weeds down; in fall we help each other with the harvest. It's simple. After giving the owner his share, the rest of the harvest is ours. What do you think?"

And so, that spring, Heinrich became a farmer. Heinrich had laughed at the thought.

"What do I know about farming?" he had asked himself.

That summer the weather was ideal for growing oats. The Rempel children and Sonia Sarkovsky spent endless hours in the fields pulling weeds so that the precious oat crop would not be choked for lack of space or be forced to compete for the soil's limited moisture.

In autumn the oat harvest was bountiful. Happily, Heinrich sold his portion of the crop, being careful to keep enough seeds for next year's planting. These he stored in a pile in the attic where it would add insulation against the winter's cold.

The Rempel's garden also produced a bumper crop of fruits and vegetables. It was as if the soil was rewarding them for the rest it had been given the previous year.

That spring Heinrich had used the sledgehammer to remove the lock the local soviet had put on the garden gate. With only a little trepidation, the family had worked the weedy soil and planted a garden. All through the summer, when not in the oat field, the family had carefully tended their growing plants. Now, neighbors regularly stopped by to purchase berries picked fresh off the bushes. Vegetables that Katy deemed extra were also sold to passersby.

One day the family was working in the garden digging potatoes. By noon a few full sacks were gathered in the rows. Heinrich loaded a couple of sacks onto the wheelbarrow and wheeled them to the cold cellar. Thinking to help carry the potatoes to the cellar, Katy crouched and lifted a sack. As she struggled upright under her heavy load, she suddenly experienced a sharp pain in her groin.

"Hsst!" she gasped.

The pain took her breath away. She could not hold her balance and dropped the heavy sack. Breathing quickly, Katy sat on the sack until the pain subsided somewhat. After a while, she stood up intending to carry on with her chore. But as she struggled to pick up the sack she soon realized that it would be impossible. The pain returned full force and Katy began to feel nauseous.

Heinrich was nowhere to be seen, but Henry was close by.

"Henry," she called. "Son, I need your help."

Tears filled her eyes as the pain intensified.

"Mama, what's the matter?" Henry could see his mother's distress.

"I've hurt myself," Katy responded, "and I need your help to get back to the house."

Leaning on her son for support, Katy began the painful journey from the garden to the apartment. She groaned with each step and with each groan, Henry grew more and more concerned.

"Mama, what happened?"

"I don't know, Henry. I was picking up a sack of potatoes and felt a sharp pain. It won't go away."

Henry guided his mother to her bed and Katy sank heavily onto it. Henry lifted her legs onto the bed as his mother lay down and helped her to get as comfortable as possible.

For a few weeks Katy had noticed a small lump on her right side, where her abdomen met her thigh. She had occasionally felt some pain with it, but since the pain was bearable, she had regarded it as something to be ignored. Aches and pains always came and went.

Over the next week, though, the pain in Katy's groin did not go away. She often felt nauseous and frequently vomited. Finally, Heinrich decided that his wife must see a doctor in Omsk. A friend came by with a *droshky* and drove them to the ferry. They took the ferry across the Irtysh River, up the path on the embankment and passed the great brick tower that overlooked the river. It was filled with water that was used for fighting fires.

Once at the doctor's office, it did not take long for the doctor to come to a diagnosis.

"Mr. Rempel, I will be frank with you. Your wife has a strangulated femoral hernia," he said as Katy looked on fearfully. "We must do surgery immediately to repair it. Otherwise the pain will only increase. The results of inaction could be fatal."

And so, Katy Rempel spent a week in the hospital in Omsk. The operation to repair her hernia was a success and she recuperated quickly in the bright room she shared with one other patient, a kindly, diminutive Russian woman named Mrs. Stamkova. Mrs. Stamkova was in hospital for a serious cough. Lying in their beds, the two women chatted amiably as they passed the time together. However, often in the middle of a sentence Mrs. Stamkova would begin to cough uncontrollably so that her whole small body would shake. At the end of her coughing fits, invariably the cloth she held to her mouth was stained with blood, but she was too fastidious to allow Katy to see the extent of her illness.

Too late, the doctors realized their mistake and removed Mrs. Stamkova from Katy's room. She had tuberculosis and she was highly contagious.

4

After Christmas Katy Rempel began to feel unwell. She had recovered with no ill effects from her hernia operation in September, but as the time went by she began to feel lethargic and had no appetite. Her skin was pale and wan. At night she often woke to find her nightclothes soaked with sweat.

One day in February while preparing a meal for relatives who had come for a visit from Barnaul, Katy suddenly felt faint. She reached for a chair to steady herself but instead tumbled onto the kitchen floor. Katy was carried to her bed where she awoke embarrassed at the fuss she had created.

"I'll be fine," she insisted. She was soon back in the kitchen, stirring the soup and making cheerful conversation.

As the weeks passed, Katy's strength continued to decline. Heinrich became more and more alarmed. The smallest tasks seemed to exhaust her. Then Katy developed a nagging cough.

Another trip was made to the doctor in Omsk. The diagnosis: Katy had contracted aggressive tuberculosis in her lungs; it was called consumption because of the rapid weight loss that accompanied it. No, there was no cure, the doctor said.

The Rempels were devastated.

By May, Katy was confined to her bed. Nine-year-old Joanna and three-year-old Agnessa were forbidden to enter her room for the disease most threatened the young, the weak, and the elderly. It fell to Katarina to tenderly care for her mother's every need. Frightened, she watched Katy's pale skin fall limp around her bones as her flesh melted away.

Katarina became mother to her siblings, and if truth be told, father as well. For, as Katy slid ever further into the depths of her illness, Heinrich grew pensive and increasingly morose. He sat for hours by his wife's bedside and seemed incapable of contributing to the day's responsibilities. He was short-tempered and lashed out at his children with little or no provocation. He demanded that the house be perfectly quiet lest any noise should disturb Katy. Unable to see their mother

192

and afraid of the man their father was becoming, the children retreated into themselves going about their daily chores and activities all the while walking on eggshells for fear that they should awake their father's gloomy wrath.

One morning the family woke to screams coming from Katy's room. She was burning with fever and delirious. Nothing Katarina tried had any effect on her mother's high temperature. Heinrich looked on in panic as Katy, her hair and bedclothes soaked with sweat, shook uncontrollably from head to foot upon the bed. Her anguished cries drove him from the room and outside where he wandered the streets blindly crying again and again, "Oh God, save my Katy! Oh God, have mercy!"

It was lunchtime when Heinrich found his way back home. No one was hungry. Katarina gave Agnessa a piece of cold sausage to nibble. The family sat around the table in silence, dreading the coming hours, fearful of what was happening in the parents' bedroom.

The moans and screams from the bedroom had died away. A weak voice called out, "Heinrich, are you there?"

Heinrich rose from the table and went to Katy's bedside. The fever seemed to have abated. She lay still; her skin was grey and pale as death. He knelt and took her hand.

The words came slowly to Katy's lips. "Heinrich, you must promise me something," she whispered.

A fit of coughing took her. Heinrich gently held a cloth to her mouth and when she finished coughing, the cloth was stained red. He tenderly dabbed the corners of her mouth and her lips to wipe away what was left of the bloody sputum.

Katy looked into Heinrich's eyes. "Promise me that you will marry again. Soon."

Heinrich leaned in close to Katy for her soft words were difficult to make out. "What is it you say, my darling?"

"Promise that you will marry again soon. The children will need a mother."

Tears welled into Heinrich's eyes. "Oh Katy, my dear, beautiful Katy!" he murmured. "There will be no need. You will recover from this; you will get better!"

Katy looked at him with determination.

"Promise me." She began to cough again.

Heinrich's heart felt like lead as reality dashed away wishful thinking.

"Yes," he whispered with a sob, "I will find the children a mother."

And he buried his face in her weak embrace.

Katy seemed to gain a little strength.

"Good," she whispered. "Now get the children so that I may say good-bye to them."

It was July 5, 1923. Late that afternoon, the neighbors listened sorrowfully as a keening voice rose in abject grief above the weeping of the children in the Rempel apartment at the corner of Sovietskaya and Trotskaya.

Despair and Hope

1

Heinrich Rempel was a broken man. The loss of his dear Katy cut him to the depths of his being. After all the years of turmoil and disappointment they had endured together, her death became the last straw and he was unable to pull himself out of the despair that left him morose and listless.

The days following his wife's death were a blur of activity. Friends from Tschunayevka arrived and the men helped Heinrich build a casket of pine boards while the women sewed its lining and trimmings. A simple funeral was conducted at the Tschunayevka Mennonite Brethren Church after which a procession followed the open coffin as it was carried on a horse-drawn wagon to the local cemetery. After more prayers and a hymn, the coffin was lowered into a hole dug deep in the Russian soil. Small bouquets of flowers were thrown onto the coffin by Katarina, Henry, Joanna, and little Agnessa. The men of the church shoveled the piled soil into the hole while Heinrich stood bowed and empty beside his disconsolate children watching the dirt and rocks crashing down with many a hollow thud atop the forlorn wooden box.

In the absence of their mother, the children now needed the support of their father more than ever. But over the coming months Heinrich seemed incapable of sharing in even the simplest of his family's daily routines. Instead, he sat for hours at a time outside on the porch, his hands folded on his lap, and stared into the west, following the course of the setting sun as it sank in brilliant washes of red and gold below the evening horizon. He thought about how his life had been buried with Katy beneath the earth in Tschunayevka. If the children came to him for help, he was at times unresponsive, and at other times irritable and angered quickly. They soon learned to steer clear of him. It fell to Katarina, with Henry's help, to run the household and to bring in the harvest from the family garden.

It was in the fall that Heinrich finally was able to articulate the thoughts that were plaguing him. The family was in Tschunayevka at the home of David Regehr, a prosperous dairy farmer, following the Sunday morning worship service. Pastor Ewert and his wife, Maria, were also invited. Elizabeth Regehr had served lunch. The day was hot and the men had retreated to the yard where they were now sitting under the shading branches of the massive mulberry tree that stood in its center. The large manor house, with its many six-paned windows and two brick chimneys was to their left. The windowless implement shed sat at right angles to the house. Nearby a hired man was hitching a horse to a *droshky* so that the young people could travel to a neighboring farm for a visit with friends. The air was perfumed with the smell of drying hay, the last cut before the first frosts of autumn. Birds called to one another in the branches among the browning leaves, as if announcing that the time to flee the coming cold was close at hand. But the calm and beauty of the day were hardly noticed by those deep in conversation.

"Aside from the death of Christ, the Gospels paint only a rosy picture of the life of faith," Heinrich complained. "Jesus always heals those who entreat him. Miracle follows upon miracle. The storm is silenced, the waves calmed, Jesus rescues the perishing, and feeds the hungry. Why didn't the writers record the storm where the boat sank and all the faithful were lost to the wind and the waves? I'm sure there must have been such an incident. What about the sick people who crowded nearby but were unable to meet with Jesus and went home disappointed? Where is the record of their experience? That would be a truer picture of reality."

Heinrich was talking quickly as his thoughts tumbled about and began to crystallize.

"Yes, Jesus said that we would have trouble in this world, but he also said he had overcome the world. He told us to ask and we would receive. Well, the storm has not ceased to rage around us for how many years now? Civil war, famine, disease, poverty, a government that restricts our every move.

And where is our salvation? Have we not asked and asked and asked again?"

Heinrich looked at each of his companions. When neither responded, his shoulders slumped and he stared at the dusty, trampled grass at his feet.

After a few moments, Pastor Ewert gently suggested, "It is true that we walk in the valley of the shadow of death, Heinrich. And as you say, Jesus suffered; we can expect nothing less. But we know, too, that God is close beside us, walking with us through the darkness that surrounds us."

Heinrich looked at his pastor with a pained expression on his face. "Where is God? I do not see Him! I do not feel his presence!"

"Nevertheless God's Word promises us. Jesus said, 'Behold, I am with you always.' He also promised that where two or three of his followers are together, he is there in their midst. Though we do not see him, he is here with us," persisted Pastor Ewert.

"All right. So God is here with us," argued Heinrich. "What good is He? He does nothing! We pray and nothing changes." He paused a moment. "Why did our Lord teach us to pray, 'Save us from the time of trial and deliver us from evil' when he himself was not saved from the time of trial and he certainly was not delivered from evil? He was tortured and died at the hands of murderers! Evil is rampant and our lives are trial upon trial. The prayer makes a mockery of God who remains silent and distant as the stars. I cannot fathom it."

Pastor Ewert pondered how best to respond to his dear friend. He suspected that he knew where this conversation was coming from and where it was going. "God is not unmindful of our suffering. Jesus wept at the loss of his good friend Lazarus. He weeps with us in our times of sorrow."

Rather than being comforted by his Pastor's words, Heinrich was incensed. His voice rose in anger. "Yes, Jesus wept at the death of Lazarus, but he had the luxury of having the power to raise him from the grave! My Katy is dead and nothing will bring her back! She is cold and rotting in the ground! It is little comfort to me that God weeps with me. I cannot see his tears but my cheeks burn with my tears day and night!" His voice trembled as he began to weep. "I do not know what to do. My children avoid me because all I can do is grieve and mourn my loss. My Katy was my life and she is gone! How could God take her from me?"

And his body shook as he broke into inconsolable sobs.

2

One day in late spring of the following year the family was finishing up at the breakfast table when Heinrich announced that he would be leaving the next day for the Ukraine.

"I will be gone for a number of months. Katarina, you are eighteen years old now and Henry is seventeen. You are old enough to be responsible while I am away. Agnessa and Joanna, you must obey everything Katarina says. When I return, I will bring with me a new mother for you." He spoke tersely, as if he found the whole undertaking distasteful.

Truth be told, the children were not sorry to see their father go. His absence lifted a dark cloud that had hovered over all of them since their mother's death and heralded a time they would, in other places and later years, celebrate as a summer of joyful independence.

A large garden had already been planted so their main responsibilities lay in its upkeep. This was no chore for Katarina who loved gardening. She had a particular interest in flowers and so, in addition to the vegetable garden, she had planted large beds of tulips, hyacinths, and other perennial spring and summer blooming flowers. The girls picked the flowers and then walked to the railway station where they sold their fresh, colorful posies to passengers on the trains. Since their Siberian neighbors weren't interested in growing flowers, neighbors and passersby also stopped by the house and bought bouquets. As soon as the garden's fruit and vegetables began to ripen, the children added these summer delights to their baskets and happily returned home from the station each day with their earnings. When they were not working, the children played with friends and basked in the glow of the freedom they enjoyed in the absence of their father.

It was during this time that Henry and Sonia Sarkovskaja discovered a new level of intimacy in their friendship. Together with their good friend Anatoly Lepinov, they spent long evenings lounging in the lush grass amongst the willow bushes on the bank of the Irtysh River. They talked and laughed about little or nothing at all, as only three friends who have grown up together during hard years can. One evening Anatoly left early. As Henry and Sonia sat close together in silence, listening to the river and the call of the night birds their hands touched. Henry's stomach leaped within him in a flight of butterflies. After a few moments they looked at each other, eyes probing beyond thought to feeling. Suddenly it seemed as if each became aware of the other in a profoundly new way. They leaned closer and their lips touched in a light kiss. They separated briefly before falling clumsily into each other's arms in a kiss that was long and deep. And as Henry's heart beat in his chest so that he worried it might explode within him, his fingers caressed Sonia's silky skin and he thought that he had never felt anything so soft or so smooth. The evening breeze flowing off the river chilled the air around them, but the warmth of Sonia enveloped him in her strong embrace. As she gazed at him with shining eyes Henry told her that he loved her.

3

At the end of August, Heinrich and his bride returned to Kulomzino. With the help of a matchmaker, Heinrich had found a young, single woman prepared to leave everything she knew—home, parents, friends—and take on the task of mothering a large family. The promise of immigration to Canada had figured large in her decision. The wedding was in the village of Halbstadt, in south Russia. The children greeted their father and his bride at the train station.

"Children, this is your new mother," Heinrich said gruffly by way of introduction.

"My name is Lena," their stepmother added with a smile. "But I would be honored if you called me Mother."

The children all agreed that Lena was very beautiful. They resolved amongst themselves to make their new mother feel as welcome as possible.

With Lena in the home to care for his children, Heinrich now began in earnest to make enquiries about the possibility of emigration from Russia. He learned of a large group of Mennonites who were seeking permission to leave Russia—rumor had it that it numbered close to three thousand—from the area around Slavgorod, five hundred kilometers to the east. Heinrich wrote to the Department of External Affairs in Moscow and requested that his family be included in that group.

Thus began months of waiting for the wheels of the Communist bureaucracy to turn in his favor. Finally, in June 1925, the good news arrived that their application to be included in the Slavgorod group had been accepted.

4

"Heinrich," Lena's voice trembled. She was standing in the kitchen about to begin making breakfast when a commotion on the street caught her attention. "There is a police wagon parked on the road. The police are coming through the gate. What could they want?"

It was autumn and the cold heralding another Siberian winter was slowly gaining its stranglehold. The nights were growing chillier and the wind blew the crisp leaves from branches in sometimes lazy and at other times frenetic dances till they landed on the ground and then blew away in whirlwinds of browns and greens. This morning the wind was calm and there was a beautiful hoar frost covering everything so that the world outside appeared pristine and sparkled in the first rays of morning sunlight.

The Rempels were ready for winter to begin. Their garden had once again supplied them with most of what they would need to eat during the dark months and the crop of wheat planted this year on their rented land had produced a satisfactory yield. There was money to purchase the necessities of life and even a few luxuries besides.

And, Lena was pregnant. The family was looking forward to the birth of another child early in the new year.

Heinrich went to the window and cautiously peered out. Nervous, he watched as two policemen marched up the walkway to his porch. He hesitated a moment after the knock was heard before going and opening the door.

"Citizen Rempel, you will come with us," commanded one of them, a tall man with a large moustache and piercing black eyes. He held a paper in front of Heinrich's eyes, as if it explained everything, but Heinrich could not read it, nor was he given time to try.

Of course, Heinrich had no choice. Reluctantly, he put on his coat and hat and followed the policemen to the black wagon while his stunned family anxiously watched through the windowpanes of their home. He climbed into the back of the wagon. One of the policemen followed him so that he was chivvied over to the other side of the hard, wooden bench. The remaining officer slammed the door shut. Heinrich heard a lock click shut. Putting the key in his pocket the policeman climbed up to the drivers seat. He flicked the reins and the horses set off.

Heinrich glanced past the policeman by his side. He saw his house, through the barred window, and the worried faces of his family framed in glass.

"How easily we can be broken," he thought fearfully as the wagon pulled away.

The policeman drove until they came to the ferry landing on the Kulomzino side of the Irtysh River. It was not long before a ferry arrived and they drove onto its deck with the other waiting droshky's and farm wagons, and were carried across the river to Omsk.

While being driven into the city, Heinrich's fear increased. What could the authorities want with him that warranted bringing him to Omsk? His alarm grew as the wagon drew up to the gates of Omsk Prison.

Without a word, the big policeman led Heinrich through the tall barred gate and into the prison. Doors were unlocked and then locked again after they passed through them. Heinrich was directed down a flight of stairs to a cement corridor in which iron doors were set every couple of meters. One electric light tried feebly to illuminate the long narrow space. He heard no sounds except for his nervous breathing, the scuffing of his shoes on the floor as he walked, and the creak of the policeman's leather boots. The policeman stopped in front of a heavy iron door. A jailor appeared from behind Heinrich and unlocked it.

"In," directed the policeman. He roughly grabbed Heinrich by the arm and pushed him into the cell.

The cell was dark but for the faint glow of light that showed through a small opening in the iron door. Fearfully, Heinrich placed his back against the cold cement wall and waited for his eyes to adjust to the semi-darkness. Gradually he was able to see that the cell was very small and that he was its only occupant. There was a strong smell of excrement. Heinrich soon discovered the source of the smell, a bucket sitting in one corner. There was no furniture in the cell; no bed, no chair, no table. Miserably, Heinrich slid down the wall until he was crouched against it. He hugged his legs tightly and felt at that moment as alone as he had ever felt in his life. He bowed his head until his forehead rested on his knees.

"Oh God," Heinrich whispered. "What is to become of me? Have mercy on me and my family." After a moment he repeated, "Have mercy."

It was hours later—or perhaps it was minutes, Heinrich had no sense of time in the dark cell—when a key rattled in the iron lock and a wash of dim light swept over the floor as the door was opened.

"Come," snarled a guard. He was a rough-looking man with a huge scar across his left cheek. Where his left ear should have been there was nothing but a hole in the side of his head, most likely the handiwork of a Cossack sabre, Heinrich guessed. Heinrich had trouble standing up because his legs were stiff from the awkward position in which he had been crouching. The guard grabbed his collar and hauled him to his feet. He pushed Heinrich so that he flew out of the door and slammed into the wall on the other side of the corridor. "Move, that way," the guard growled as he pointed to the end of the corridor opposite the end from which Heinrich had entered earlier.

Heinrich was taken down two more flights of stairs to a small, brightly lit room. A wooden chair stood before a metal desk behind which sat a well-dressed man who greeted Heinrich with a pleasant smile.

"Comrade Rempel," he said genially. "I am Comrade Major Yushakin, please sit down." When Heinrich had taken his seat, Yushakin continued. "I apologize for the inconvenience you have been subjected to. I'm sure there has been a misunderstanding. You must forgive our poor hospitality. We can sort this all out in a few minutes, I'm sure, don't you think?"

Major Yushakin looked sympathetically at Heinrich and for the first time that day, Heinrich began to feel some sense of hope. Perhaps his prayer was being answered. Here was a reasonable man.

"Yes," replied Heinrich, encouraged by the friendly speech. "There must be a misunderstanding. I have done nothing to deserve prison. I am an honest, law-abiding citizen."

"Of course you are, naturally."

The Major paused a moment while shuffling some papers on his desk. He picked a piece of paper up and held it out across the desk to Heinrich.

"Please read this document, Comrade Rempel, and sign your name at the bottom."

Heinrich looked at the document. It was a confession of guilt. He read it carefully. He could not believe what his eyes were telling him.

"This is not true!" he said, indignant. "Who told you this? Where did this information come from? It is a lie! I did not plant ten *dessiatines* of wheat. I only planted five!"

"Really," said Major Yushakin quietly. His voice took on a menacing tone. "Do you dare to call me a liar? You may wish to choose your words more carefully."

"But I only harvested five *dessiatines*, really."

Heinrich thought for a moment that he would tell Yushakin to get confirmation from Ivan Sarkovsky. He would vouch for Heinrich. He knew the truth. Looking at Yushakin's eyes, though, he thought better of it. There was no point in dragging his neighbor into this mess.

"I'm afraid the facts prove otherwise," hissed Yushakin. "You declared only five *dessiatines* of wheat when you actually harvested ten."

"But that's not true," Heinrich stubbornly insisted again.

Major Yushakin folded his hands on his desk. His friendly demeanor was gone.

"I am disappointed in your recalcitrance. Perhaps you need some time to collect your memory before we continue this conversation."

He briskly rose from his chair and went to the door.

"Guard!" he shouted. "Return the prisoner to his cell."

Heinrich was roughly escorted back to his cell where the iron door again clanged shut, locking him in the cold, rank darkness. As before, he slid down onto the clammy floor. Disoriented and afraid, he could make nothing of the false allegations being made against him. It made no sense. Who would accuse him of harvesting more than he had? Why?

Later, when Heinrich was again made to sit on the wooden chair in front of Major Yushakin's desk, Yushakin ignored him for a long time. He fiddled with the papers on his desk, reading some, making notations here and there. Eventually he sat back and stared coldly at Heinrich but said nothing. Though it was cool in the room, Heinrich was sweating profusely. His heart beat rapidly in his chest.

Finally the Major broke the silence.

"Citizen Rempel, let us not play games. You are a kulak, a useless capitalist, a member of the old order and a scourge on the workers of the Soviet Union. You are only playing at being a farmer. I'm right, yes? It is plain to see. And furthermore, you are a liar and a cheat. There is no place for you in our Soviet Socialist Republic. I repeat, we don't need people like you; we don't want people like you." Yushakin ground his teeth; his voice rose to a shout. "For too long people like you have pressed the workers of Russia under your heel. Well, that is now in the past." He paused, breathing heavily. Wiping some spittle that had gathered at the corners of his mouth, he continued in a quieter, though more threatening, tone. "What shall we do with you? Shall we leave you to rot in this prison for the rest of your miserable kulak existence? What do you say to that? Why should you be allowed to breathe the fresh air of our beloved Soviet Union? Why should the workers whom you have exploited all you life eat less bread so you can fill your bloated belly?"

Heinrich sat in mute silence, too shocked to make a response.

Major Yushakin slammed his fist on his desk. In the small room it sounded like an explosion.

"Answer me!"

Heinrich jumped from fright in his chair.

"I am a simple farmer," he cried. "I am none of those things you say."

"Well, Citizen Farmer," Yushakin sneered sarcastically. "Let me tell you how things stand. The fact is, the record shows you failed to declare five *dessiatines* of wheat and in so doing you robbed the Kulomzino Soviet of its rightful taxes. This is an offense punishable by fine and imprisonment. So, this is what is going to happen. You are assessed a fine of 1000 rubles. You have thirty days to pay. If you fail to pay, you will return to prison and be held there until the fine is paid. Is that understood?"

Heinrich nodded his head numbly.

"Guard," hollered Major Yushakin, "get this piece of German turd out of here!"

The iron cell door slammed shut behind Heinrich a third time.

When Heinrich finally returned home he discovered two days had passed. His family wept with relief, for their uncertainty had led them to imagine the worst.

Heinrich tried to return to a normal routine, but found it impossible. In the dark of night he was filled with torment. His sleep was disturbed by nightmares about reeking prison cells, frightening guards with rifles, and angry men who threatened to take his family away. He broke into sweats and woke to find his night clothing soaked. Unable to fall asleep, he paced the small apartment, going over and over in his mind the interrogation by Major Yushakin. Was there something he could have said differently? Why had the Bolsheviks concocted the ridiculous charges against him in the first place? And, how was he ever going to pay such an exorbitant fine?

Finally, one evening a week later when the children were all asleep, Heinrich told Lena what had happened to him in prison.

"Where will we ever get 1000 rubles to pay such a fine?" he cried.

"Heinrich," Lena said cautiously as she suddenly remembered a conversation she had had the day before. "The neighbor was telling me yesterday that the family living in the little house have said they would like to buy it. Are you willing to sell the little house? Surely the price would cover most of the fine." She paused briefly. "And, if need be, I have some jewelry that, I'm sure, will bring a good price. We will raise the money somehow."

Lena's words proved to be true. The little house was sold, only a little of her jewelry needed to be bartered, and the 1000 rubles was raised.

With trepidation Heinrich paid a visit to the Kulomzino Police Station and paid the fine. Before he could turn to leave he was given a sharp reprimand and a warning to watch himself in the future. Afterward, as Heinrich slowly plodded down the dirt road to his home at the corner of Sovietskaya and Trotskaya, his mood was heavy. He realized that in all likelihood, this would not be the end of his troubles. Leaving

Russia was becoming more and more imperative. Yet, he began to doubt that permission to emigrate would ever come.

In February Lena gave birth to a son, Johann. The baby brought a spark of new life and hope into the Rempel household. Katarina and Joanna doted on Johann and little Agnessa competed with her sisters to be allowed to hold her new brother. Even the dour Heinrich broke into an occasional grin at the sight of his contented son's happy smiles.

Departure

1

Heinrich Rempel stood naked in the kitchen. Gingerly he climbed into the large wooden barrel that served as the family's bathtub. Lena had filled it to the halfway mark with steaming water heated on the stove. No longer as hot, Heinrich nonetheless crouched down and relished the warmth of the bath. He was not the first family member to use this water. Because of the time and effort required to heat enough water for the barrel, the bath was shared by the whole family. The cleanest among them bathed first, the dirtiest went last. As always, the rest of the family made themselves scarce while the kitchen was being used for bathing.

Soaking in the bath, Heinrich felt the chaos of butterflies in his stomach as he remembered what the next day would bring. Tomorrow the Rempels would be traveling across the Irtysh River to Omsk. As Heinrich thought about it, he realized these were perhaps the two most important appointments his family had ever kept. Certainly the first appointment was. The family was going for medical examinations by a doctor from Canada, Dr. Drury, who was in Omsk for one week. His examination would determine if their request to immigrate was given approval by the Canadian government. Fortunately, Heinrich thought, everyone appeared to be healthy at the moment. No colds, no obvious illnesses. Appearing before the doctor with clean bodies could only help to make his decision easier. The family's second appointment was with a photographer to take the family's photos needed for the precious documents that would be their passport out of Bolshevik Russia.

Heinrich's heart sank as he thought about his dear Katy and the merciless disease that had taken hold of her body, now nearly three years past, and quickly killed her. He still missed her terribly and mourned the fact that it was not she whom he could hear rummaging about in the next room.

His thoughts returned to the present and the challenges of the morrow. He murmured a prayer as he slowly began to scrub his hair with a bar of soap.

The next day dawned bright and clear. Afterward, Heinrich would always remember the date: May 8, 1926, a Saturday. As the family got ready, through the windows they could see the sun highlighting the tips of green on the branches of the budding bushes in the front yard. The grass along the fence was greening up as new shoots pushed last year's brown and crumpled detritus aside. It was a beautiful day for an outing! The children could not remember the last time they had visited the city across the river. Was it on the Tsar's birthday all those years ago?

Lena made sure that all the children were dressed in their best clothes. She was an expert seamstress and had sewn new dresses with white lace collars for the girls and dark pants and matching shirts for the boys. She had despaired at the plainness of the fabric she used for the girls' dresses. It seemed that since the Revolution, good, colorful fabrics were almost impossible to find.

The air in the house sparked with nervous energy. The baby began to fuss and Lena, who was helping Agnessa with her buttons, called, "Katushya, are you dressed? Could you look after Johann?"

"Yes, Mama," answered Katarina as she hurried to attend to her baby brother.

"Hurry, children!" urged Heinrich impatiently. "We mustn't be late. Lena, can't you move any faster? We've got to go!"

"I'm moving as quickly as I can," Lena retorted. "It would go faster if you helped, you know."

By way of an answer, Heinrich opened the door and went outside. Henry soon joined him in the front yard. They had waited in the chilly morning air for only a few moments before Heinrich ordered, "Go see what is taking the others so long."

As Henry walked toward the front door, he was met by the rest of the family coming outside. Quickly they filed into the street and began the trek to the river where a ferry would take them across to the city of Omsk.

2

Dr. Drury's temporary office was in a luxurious mansion on Atamanskaya Street that in better times had housed a trade mission from Great Britain. When the Rempels arrived at its gate, they saw that a few families were already in line, waiting for their appointments with the doctor. As the morning wore on, more families appeared, some from outlying farms and villages. All were hoping for the prized declaration that they were fit and acceptable for immigration to Canada.

While they waited the Rempels visited with a family they were acquainted with from Tschunayevka, the Heidebrechts, who stood immediately in front of them in the line. The whole family was there: parents, grandparents and children. As they were chatting in cautious anticipation, the call came for the Heidebrechts to proceed into the doctor's office. While the Rempels waited their turn, the children craned their necks about as they gawked at the ornate plaster scrollwork and colorful murals on the ceiling of the waiting room. They had never seen such beautiful artistry.

After what seem like ages, the Heidebrechts finally emerged from the doctor's office. The women were softly weeping and the men looked dejected. The children appeared confused and alarmed.

"What happened?" asked Lena.

"My father has glaucoma," wept his married daughter. "He will not be allowed to go to Canada. And if he cannot go, what about the rest of us? What will we do? I don't want to leave him behind in this godforsaken country." Sobbing, she turned and hurried after her family, through the door and outside into the sunshine.

Lena and Heinrich looked nervously at each other. Would they pass inspection?

And then it was their turn to see the doctor.

210

Dr. Drury turned out to be a tall, bespectacled man with a trimmed, wispy silver beard and moustache. The top of his head was balding, but over his ears lay a thin mat of fluffy grey hair. He was dressed in a long white coat with a stethoscope draped about his short neck. As the Rempels apprehensively filed in front of him, he looked carefully at each one before he began his closer examination.

For no apparent reason he gestured to Agnessa. With a twinkle in his eye he said, "Why don't we start with you, young lady?" An interpreter translated his English words that sounded strange and foreign to the family's ears.

Soon it was Joanna's turn, then Katarina's, then Lena's. She carried Johann to the doctor and watched fearfully as he examined the baby from head to toe. Finally, it was Henry's turn and then Heinrich's.

When he had finished examining everyone, Dr. Drury made some notations on a writing pad. With a smile he turned to the Rempels and spoke some words.

As one, the Rempels looked to the translator to find his meaning.

"You are all healthy. The doctor is recommending you all for acceptance into Canada," repeated the translator. There was no smile on her face; she was all business. She was mightily bored by her duties in the clinic. Furthermore, she was unhappy that so many people were trying to leave the utopian workers' state.

"What is wrong with them?" she thought at the end of each day. "They should stay and help us build the workers' paradise."

She was a dyed-in-the-wool Communist.

Beaming, the Rempel family took their leave of Dr. Drury and headed down the sidewalk to the photographer's studio on Lyubinsky Avenue. As they walked Agnessa began to complain that her feet hurt. Her shoes were too small and her crushed toes were rubbing raw against the leather. Heinrich's response was to simply hold her hand in his firm grasp. She had no choice but to keep up with his long strides. This only increased Agnessa's frustration and pain, until finally, Henry offered to carry his little sister. She nestled her head on his shoulder and, as he held her tightly, she wiped a small tear from her rosy cheek with one pale finger.

By the time they arrived, the weather had turned cold. The sun was hidden behind a grey film of high clouds. A bell overhead rang as Heinrich opened the door to the studio.

"You might as well wait outside," shouted the photographer from a back room before Heinrich had a chance to announce their arrival. "I'll be right there. The light's better outside so that's where the pictures will be taken."

"You can't be serious," said Heinrich. "We want proper pictures taken. They should be done inside where it is warm and comfortable."

"Nevertheless," returned the photographer as he appeared carrying a large tripod at the top of which was attached a camera, the likes of which Heinrich had never seen. "The light is better outside and that's where the pictures will be taken. If you don't like it, comrade, you can get your pictures taken somewhere else. It's all the same to me."

Taken aback, Heinrich quickly acquiesced.

"So, you're planning on doing some traveling are you? Take my advice." The photographer was talking as he gathered up a few more items he needed. "Get out of this country while the getting's good. Get out and don't come back! You think things are bad? You haven't seen anything yet! Mark my words."

The photographer looked around as he stepped through the door onto the sidewalk. He winked at Heinrich who was surprised and uncomfortable with the photographer's words. Not that he disagreed. He simply wanted to avoid trouble. Who knew what ears were taking in the photographer's careless comments?

It was as if the photographer was hearing Heinrich's thoughts. As they stepped outside he lowered his voice, "And don't tell anyone I told you so. Be careful, it's getting to the point where even the walls are listening. In fact, I've probably overstepped my bounds. I've said too much. Just forget it. I'm only here to take your picture."

The photographer quickly set up his camera on the sidewalk, hung a backdrop on the front of his building, and began taking pictures of each member of the family.

"Hold still, now," he reminded each one in turn. "We don't want the picture to be blurred. If you move, even a very little, that's what will happen and the picture will be ruined. So don't move." Each one waited patiently while their image was exposed onto the camera's film.

When the individual pictures were done a family photo was to be taken. By this time Agnessa had lost all patience, what with all the poking and prodding she had been subjected to earlier, then the long walk with her aching toes, and now all the motionless posing. As the family was arranged for the picture, parents seated, Lena holding Johann who was snuggly wrapped in a blanket, the older children standing behind, Heinrich wanted Agnessa to be seated on his lap. However, she kept trying to wriggle off before the photo could be taken. Finally the photographer suggested she stand beside her father. With an annoyed look on her face she stood still for a moment and the picture was taken.

"I'll send your photos to the passport office," said the photographer, after Heinrich had paid and the family got ready to leave.

The photographer pulled Heinrich aside.

"Just to make sure everything goes smoothly," he murmured as he held his hand open in blatant expectation of a bribe.

Heinrich glared at the photographer as he handed him some extra rubles.

"Thank you comrade," the photographer smiled. "You will be notified when your passports are ready. When the time comes, you can pick them up at the Russkapa Office on Nicholsky Avenue. Good-bye."

3

"How's the farmin' goin'?" said a jovial voice.

213

Heinrich looked around to see who had spoken. They were on the ferry returning to Kulomzino. Everyone was exhausted after the long day in Omsk.

A hand nudged his arm from behind as Heinrich turned around.

"Surely you've not forgotten me, my clever kulak comrade," came the mocking voice again. There stood Fyodor Alexandrovich Lepinov with his son Anatoly.

They greeted each other warmly and Anatoly went off to find Henry who was standing by the railing on the opposite side of the boat.

"My crop is planted," said Heinrich noncommittally. "Wheat this year. We hope for a good harvest."

"Ah, my friend, that is good. But, really, let's be honest. If yer a farmer then I'm yer fairy godmother." Fyodor paused and winked. "Make that yer fairy godfather!"

He laughed, impressed with his own joke.

"Yet, I am a farmer," replied Heinrich defensively. "That is how I make my living."

Fyodor looked about them and pulled Heinrich to a spot on deck where they were more or less alone.

"My friend, I'm glad that we've met here today." Fyodor was speaking quietly. "I saw somethin' the other day and didn't know if I was goin' to do anythin' about it. Now that yer here in front of me, well . . ."

Fyodor shrugged and paused. He looked over the side of the ferry at the swirling water flowing toward the stern and into its wake. He seemed to come to a decision and smiled at Heinrich.

"I have always been in yer debt for yer kindness toward my son and my wife during the darkest days of the civil war. However, my capitalist comrade, I cannot continue forever ta shield ya. I risk danger to myself and my family. These are tricky times. But let me give ya this last warning."

Fyodor glanced right and left to ensure their privacy.

"There are those on the local soviet who are not as favorably inclined toward ya as I am. Yer name is on a list. How long ya will be left alone, I dunno. But be warned. They will act one day, probably sooner than later. And when they do," the words died on Fyodor's lips as he shrugged. "Well, I'll leave it at that."

Heinrich was shaken by Fyodor's words. His legs felt like they were turning to water. His stomach rolled and his breathing quickened. Fyodor's meaning was clear. Flashes of his prison experience flooded Heinrich's mind.

Fyodor was speaking again. "With this, I consider my debt to ya to be paid."

With a small bow, Fyodor turned and disappeared into the crowd of passengers who were waiting at the bow to disembark. The ferry bumped into the landing and the Rempels joined the tired throng as they made their way home.

4

The Russian Canadian Travel Agency, or Russkapa, was set up cooperatively between the Russian government and the Canadian Pacific Railway to facilitate the emigration of Russian citizens to Canada. In June the Moscow office of Russkapa confirmed by mail that the Rempel family was registered to emigrate from Russia with a group from Isyl Kul.

With a mixture of mounting excitement and anxiety, Heinrich and Lena began to make preparations for their departure. Heinrich's biggest concern was the sale of their warehouse suites on the corner of Trotskaya and Sovietskaya. While the sale of the land was not allowed, the building could be sold. He was counting on the rubles he would get from this sale to finance their journey out of Russia.

The difficulty was that Heinrich did not want to let it be known publicly that they were leaving. It was too dangerous; the local authorities could not know of their plans. Fyodor's last warning on the ferry haunted his dreams at night. He had not told Lena what his friend had said, lest she, too, be burdened with worry. But any time a police vehicle appeared on their street, Heinrich's heart thundered in his chest and he watched to see if it would slow to a stop in front of his gate. Memories of his prison experience would cause him to break into a chilly sweat and he would quickly hide from view when a police car passed by. Because of all of this, Heinrich relied on word of mouth by his friends and close acquaintances to sell his building.

As they waited for a buyer Heinrich would often fret, his fear bubbling to the surface and putting the lie to his usually stoic countenance.

"Lena," he would say when they were alone. "What will we do if we are unable to sell the apartments? We do not have enough money to even get ourselves to Moscow. I don't know how I'm going to pay for the passports, never mind the train tickets. The Bolsheviks have bled us dry. Thank God we can at least sail to Canada on credit."

In response Lena would shrug and insist, "The building will sell. You worry too much."

And she was right.

In August a buyer was found. A friend knew of an aristocrat who had sold his estate in the silver birch-forested hills above beautiful Lake Tavatuy northwest of Ekaterinburg. He was moving his family to Siberia in the hopes of finding the anonymity that would help him escape the ever-increasing scrutiny of former landowners by the Communists. The aristocrat paid in cash. He counted out a large pile of rubles onto the Rempels' kitchen table; enough to pay the fee for the Rempels' passports, their train tickets from Kulomzino to Moscow, as well as from Moscow to Riga, Latvia where they would board a ship; and, all things going well, there would be a little left over for a small nest egg to be changed into Canadian dollars in Moscow, to help become established in their new country. Heinrich rejoiced in their good fortune as he hid the money behind a loose board in the wall of his bedroom.

The Rempels were given until November 1 to vacate their home.

5

In late October Heinrich received word that the family's passports were ready to be picked up. He removed the board in the bedroom wall and stuffed the inside pocket of his coat with rubles. He had been told the fee for the family's passports would be more than 1100 rubles. And then, of course, whoever served him would likely expect a hefty bribe as well. That was the Russian way: whether Communist or Tsarist, everyone seemed to think it their right to a few extra rubles for services rendered.

As always, Heinrich dressed in his three-piece suit and tie. He took his precious gold pocket watch from a drawer in the bureau. He looked affectionately at the watch before slipping it into his vest pocket. It had been a gift to him from his dear Katy on the day of their wedding. Saying good-bye to his family, he stepped through his gate and onto Trotskaya Street. Heinrich walked briskly to the ferry landing on the bank of the Irtysh and took the boat across the river to Omsk.

When Heinrich arrived at the Russkapa office on Dvortsovaya Avenue, he discovered it was around the corner and just a few doors down from the bank he had used all these years. A vacant office had been transformed into the communist government's official travel bureau. The line of people waiting for passports stretched down the sidewalk. Heinrich pulled out his gold watch and looked at the time. He sighed as he thought of the hours he would waste standing in the line. He hated waiting.

Two people standing in front of Heinrich suddenly got into an argument. They talked loudly and one pushed the other into Heinrich. Heinrich nearly toppled over. He was only saved from falling by the quick action of another gentleman who grabbed and steadied him.

"Sorry, comrade, that was clumsy of me," apologized the instigator.

Heinrich looked around to thank the man who had prevented him from falling onto the sidewalk, but he seemed to have vanished.

When it was finally his turn to approach the wicket, Heinrich adjusted his tie nervously and cleared his throat.

"I have come to pick up the passports for the Heinrich Rempel family of Kulomzino."

The clerk standing on the other side of the counter had a long face with a heavy brow and close-set eyes. His unruly grizzled moustache and beard were dyed a dirty yellow from years of heavy smoking. As if he had all the time in the world, the clerk slowly opened a drawer and removed a flat box piled full with large sheets of paper. Each paper, Heinrich saw, contained a picture and was covered in writing and official looking stamps. The clerk began to casually shuffle through the papers. He muttered to himself and paused for a moment to take a puff of a cigarette that lay in an ashtray on the counter. Heinrich wrinkled his nose in disgust at the acrid smell of the smoke that was blown his way.

"No, I don't see any passports or any other documents here for any Rempels from Kulomzino," said the man when he had gone through the whole box."

Heinrich's heart skipped a beat.

"Please look again. We've been notified by post that the passports are ready. They must be here."

Heinrich showed the clerk the letter he had received. The clerk pretended to scrutinize it, making a point of adjusting his glasses two or three times so that he would appear to be reading more clearly. Finally he handed the letter back to Heinrich and took another drag on his cigarette.

"So, comrade," he said quietly, blowing the smoke in Heinrich's direction. "Why do you need these passports anyway?" He looked intently at Heinrich and, with a slow wink, continued. "I'd like to take a trip. When I used to live in Moscow, I'd take my family to the Black Sea for vacation. Lovely place, in the springtime. It's expensive taking trips, though, don't you think? Who can afford to travel in these days when we're all called to make sacrifices for our glorious leader, Comrade Stalin?"

Heinrich thought, "Here it is. He wants a bribe, but how much will be enough?"

Without saying anything, Heinrich put his hand in his coat pocket and pulled out a wad of bills. He counted out a few ruble notes and slid them across the counter.

"Comrade, I have a large family," the clerk muttered petulantly with a look of disappointment and hurt on his face.

Heinrich counted off several more ruble notes and slid them under the clerk's hand.

The clerk quickly slipped the rubles into his pocket. Without another word he pulled the box of travel documents back in front of him and began sorting through them again. It didn't take long before he grabbed a small sheaf of papers.

"Ah, here they are," he exclaimed triumphantly. "Funny how you can suddenly find something that refused to be found but a minute ago."

He sighed and gave Heinrich a smirk.

Inwardly, Heinrich suddenly found himself despising the man. He represented everything that was wrong with communist Russia. Heinrich felt an overpowering urge to shout at the clerk, to denounce his blatant dishonesty and his smug ability to flaunt his power over people who were powerless to protect themselves. For a brief moment he even felt like striking the man; he would wipe his self-satisfied smile off his face.

The clerk was speaking. "That will be 1255 rubles, comrade."

Heinrich gathered himself together as he stifled his rage. With shaking hands, he counted out the required payment. He handed the pile of bills to the clerk and put the leftovers back into his coat pocket.

The clerk loudly stamped a few papers and asked Heinrich for his signature on one of them. He slid the passports across the counter. Heinrich took the precious documents and hurried out the door.

Once on the sidewalk, Heinrich thought to find out if he had enough time to make another stop before he returned to the ferry. He felt in his vest pocket for his gold watch. It was gone.

A chill went through Heinrich as he realized he had been robbed. He knew immediately what had happened. He had foolishly revealed his pocket watch while in the passport office waiting line. Pickpockets were a constant problem in

Omsk; people were desperate to survive by any means. When the man had steadied him so that he wouldn't fall, he had grabbed Heinrich about the waist. It had been the perfect opportunity to steal the watch. Suddenly it dawned on Heinrich how close he had come to losing all of his money. Foolishly, that morning he had taken almost all of the rubles from the stash behind the wall. They were tucked into the inside pocket of his coat. It would have been too easy for the pickpocket to steal them, had he known they were there.

That evening Heinrich told Lena of the theft of his gold watch and how close they had come to losing all their money.

"What would have become of us if the thief had gone for my inside coat pocket and found the rubles?" mused Heinrich. "We would have been ruined. There is nothing left to sell. There would have been no money for the passports or the railway tickets!"

Lena listened silently. She shuddered at the thought of having to stay in Russia. The idea of being forced to remain was unthinkable. Worse yet, because they had sold their house, they would have been homeless as well as penniless.

6

That Wednesday, October 23, the day before their departure, Lena, with the help of Katarina and Joanna, spent the day baking zwieback and then roasted them all again so that they became rusks, golden brown and crispy all the way through. While the buns were baking the girls mixed up a large batch of kringels and boiled them. When the oven was free the kringels were baked so that they would not spoil on the journey. At the end of the day they had collected enough rusks and kringels to fill a large sack. They would be all the family would have to eat during the long train ride to Moscow.

Agnessa was not allowed to play outdoors that day. With all the excitement in the home, the danger of her dropping a remark about leaving Kulomzino was too great. Word of their departure must not reach the wrong ears.

That night Heinrich found it difficult to sleep. He tossed and turned until blackness finally came, but with sleep also came a dream that had been troubling him for the last several weeks.

Heinrich dreamed there was a loud knocking at the door. The knocking went on and on and he dreaded to answer it. Eventually he could not resist. With heavy feet Heinrich dragged himself to the door to open it. Rather than his familiar wooden front door, however, to Heinrich's dismay the door was made of heavy iron. It squealed on rusty hinges as he pulled it open. With his heart beating madly against his rib cage, Heinrich peered into the night. Instead of stars he saw a dark prison cell. Long arms reached to him and tried to pull him into the foul-smelling room. Heinrich struggled against the grasping hands, but the powerful arms overcame him. Each time he had the dream, just as the door slammed shut behind him, Heinrich woke up feeling like he was drowning, gasping for breath, staring blindly into the darkness, hoping to find a ray of light somewhere so that the lie could be put to his dreadful nightmare.

7

It was Monday, November 29, 1926, a little over a month since the Rempels had begun their journey to Canada. Heinrich and I stood by the window in the dining room of the S.S. Melita. Outside, the lazy, heaving gray swells of the Bay of Fundy gently rocked the ship. Low clouds obscured the horizon.

After telling me his story, Heinrich was pensive.

"We lost our schools, our churches, our riches, our homes. Our dreams." After a moment he added, "And some of us also lost our faith. We expected too much of God. We thought He would change our circumstances in response to our prayers. Perhaps at times He did, but we suffered the same as many of those who did not pray suffered. We thought that God could control the events of our lives and that when we suffered it was for our good. A comfortable theology in prosperous times. But, I am a father. Would I allow my children to suffer because I thought it was good for them? Would I deny them food when they are hungry? Protection from harm when they are threatened? A shelter over their heads when they are cold? Would I deny them the loving presence of their mother? Of course not! So why would I think that my God should be any different?"

He paused again, lost in his thoughts.

"I would like to believe that God is with us, that in the midst of our misfortunes, perhaps, He is like the air we breathe, present to sustain us, to give us the strength to endure and to live when our hearts are breaking and we have lost all hope. Otherwise, how could I have had the courage to go on? Perhaps from these ashes will arise a new faith that is not built on false expectations, or in the pride of being the chosen of God, but a faith that is born in humility and embraces our human weakness."

After a moment, he added, as if speaking to no one, "I have many questions." And then, more confidently, he looked at me and said, "I do know that in a world of great evil, justice must be all the greater, and mercy. And forgiveness, too.

"Dr. Benny," he said, addressing me with eyes that had seen too much, "Russia was a prison. More and more the state attempted to control every aspect of our lives; what we did, what we thought, what we believed. In the last weeks, whenever I went out, I had the persistent feeling that I was being watched. Fyodor Lepinov's final warning left me completely unnerved. I kept expecting the police to arrest me at any moment. We had heard rumors about people who simply disappeared. Was I to be one of them? The tension was unbearable.

"We swore the children to secrecy. They were to talk to no one about our plans. Not even our neighbors knew we were leaving." Heinrich paused. "I think Henry told his old friend, Anatoly Lepinov. We informed the Sarkovsky's and our long-time friend Butcher Giesbrecht. They met us at the station. We could not keep our departure from them. As long as I live, I will not forget the look in Ivan Sarkovsky's eyes as we said good-bye. There was deep hurt there, and envy, I think."

I turned to Heinrich and saw there were tears in his eyes.

"We were the fortunate ones," he whispered. "We were delivered from that country and the evil that is consuming it.

"At exactly 9:00 am, on October 27, we boarded Train Number Three at the Trans-Siberian Railway station."

He laughed, though there was no humor in it.

"It was a miracle! The train was on time! We took our places on the hard benches in what passed for a passenger car and gazed through the window as the train pulled out of the station. We had lived in Kulomzino for thirteen years, but we never looked back. We looked only forward, for behind us was nothing but sorrow and heartache. Ahead of us lay hope and the possibility of a new life."

As I pondered Heinrich's last words, our gazes went back to the sea and the sky. We stood together in companionable silence as we gazed into the west. The deep gray of the hovering cloud-cover was slowly growing lighter as the sun penetrated its thickness.

"What will happen to the crewman who violated my daughter?" he asked suddenly.

"I don't know," I confessed. "The Captain is judge and jury."

I looked into his face and saw his pain, then glanced back at the eternal sea.

"Look, Heinrich," I said, directing his eyes to the horizon. "The clouds are lifting."

As we watched, the haze appeared to part before us, like curtains on a window. In the distance we saw land for the first time in what seemed a lifetime. Beams of sunlight lit up a small patch of the shore, revealing trees and buildings growing up a long slope away from the faint white line of the surf crashing onto the beach.

"Canada," I said helpfully. "St. John, New Brunswick." I turned to shake Heinrich Rempel's hand. "Allow me to be the first to welcome you to your new homeland."

The next morning the sun shone warmly out of a robin's egg blue sky. There was no sign of the clouds of yesterday. As the passengers slowly disembarked, I happened to see the Rempels make their way down the gangway. The parents were in front. Lena carried the baby, Johann. Katarina and Joanna followed her closely, gazing about at the sights of the St. John port. Agnessa and her older brother trailed behind. She was holding tightly to Henry's hand while talking animatedly to him, obviously excited by something she saw.

In mid stride Heinrich looked back at the ship and perchance found me leaning on the railing. Our gazes met. I tipped my hat and he nodded his head in recognition before turning away. The family stepped onto the wooden pier, onto Canadian soil, and was carried away in the crowd.

Historical Notes

This is a work of fiction. Nevertheless, it is based on actual historical events and the lives of real people. I am indebted to the travel diary of Johann W. Rempel and the journals of Margaret Rempel Pump and Agnes Rempel Funk whose descriptions of their childhood and recollections of their lives in Kulomzino during the years leading up to their emigration from Russia, as well as of their voyage to Canada aboard the S.S. Melita, became the stimulus for this novel.

The recitation by Katarina Rempel at the 1919 Christmas Eve program is taken from the translation of a poem handwritten in German script by the child, Katarina Epp, which she presented to her parents as a gift at Christmas, 1883. Katarina Epp would grow up to become Johann Rempel's first wife. Her life and early death served as the inspiration for the character, Katy Rempel.

The story is narrated by Dr. J. Benny. The Gjenvick-Gjonvik Archives (gjnvick.com) indicate a Dr. J.J. Benny served as Surgeon aboard the S.S. Melita on its June 1926 sailing from Antwerp, Belgium to Montreal, Quebec, with stops in Southhampton and Cherbourg, though Johann Rempel recorded in his travel diary that on his family's voyage, the ship docked at St. John. Be that as it may, the character, Dr. J. Benny, is entirely fictional.

At the time of this story, the S.S. Melita was owned by the Canadian Pacific Steamship Line. The ship weighed 15,183 tons, and was 520 feet from bow to stern and 67 feet from port to starboard. The superstructure boasted two masts and two huge stacks. Boilers, or superheaters, generated the steam power to turn her three massive brass screws. The S.S. Melita's maiden voyage was in June of 1918, from Liverpool to St. John where she picked up troops who were needed for the final push against Hindenburg's armies. After a refit in 1925, the Melita accommodated 1340 passengers, of whom 206 were Cabin, 546 Tourist, and 588 Third Class. She was a comfortable ship with dining saloons for each class of passengers (although, to quote Johann Rempel, "I think many a dog is fed better than third class passengers like we are.") as well as drawing rooms, lounges, smoking and card rooms, a room for showing moving pictures, and a nursery where mothers could leave their young ones if they wanted an hour or so to themselves. The Melita even sported a barbershop with a quaint message posted by its doorway. "If you spit on the floor in your house you may spit on the floor here. I want you to feel at home!" In 1935, after making 146 round trips across the Atlantic, the Melita had outlived her usefulness as a trans-Atlantic cruiser and was sold for scrap. A company out of Italy then bought her to be used as a troop carrier. They renamed her, Liguria. In July 1940, the Liguria was badly damaged by fire during an air attack on Tobruk, Libya's harbor in North Africa. Six months later she was scuttled to the bottom of the Mediterranean off Tobruk. The Melita's end came in August 1950, when the British raised her and again she was sold and finally scrapped. Google the ship's name to find numerous sources of information and photos of her interior and exterior.

The story is set in Kulomzino, on the west bank of the Irtysh River across from the city of Omsk, in western Siberia, Russia. The village was known by both of the names Kulomzino and Novo-Omsk. Eventually Novo-Omsk came into standard usage, though it is unclear when this occurred. According to his daughters' recollections, Johann Rempel's family resided within walking distance of the Trans-Siberian Railway Station in Kulomzino. This meant that they lived in close proximity to the epicenter where events of great historic importance were occurring.

The first of these events was the incident of April 28 and 29, 1918, when a train carrying Tsar Nicholas together with members of the royal family and entourage was detained by Red Guards and eventually turned back to Ekaterinburg in circumstances similar to what I have described in the novel. Barely a month later the Omsk Soviet again flexed its muscle at the Kulomzino railway station, stopping and confronting an armored train, or bronevik, filled with soldiers of the Czech Legion trying to make their way to Vladivostok, where they had been promised transport by ship to Europe.

Because of the important role they played in events in Kulomzino and the civil war in general, something needs to be said about the presence of the Czechs in Siberia. During the First World War, there existed in Russia an army that came to be called the Czechoslovak Legion. At its peak over 60,000 strong, the Czech Legion was a front-line army made up mostly of Czech and some Slovak patriots that fought alongside the Russians on the eastern front. Their goal had been to win Czechoslovak independence from the Austro-Hungarian Empire. However, the signing of the Treaty of Brest-Litovsk in 1917 left the army in limbo. The Czech soldiers were stranded in a country at peace with their enemy, unable to fight, and unable to return to their homeland. Other Czech units continued to fight on in France, so the Legion's generals decided their only recourse was to somehow rejoin their brothers there. The only possible and practical route to move so many men and so much equipment was east, through Siberia, on the Trans-Siberian Railway line.

Negotiations were held with the Bolsheviks and initially the Legion was given a promise of safe passage to Vladivostok. They traveled across Russia in seventy-two armored trains. Some were formidable ironclad trains carrying machine gun nests and heavy-barreled cannons while others were made up of freight wagons that were sandbagged to protect rows of riflemen and sharpshooters riding on the roofs. The Czech Legion was soon spread out across the length and breadth of Siberia. The first train finally arrived in Vladivostok in April 1918. The promised British ships to take them to France were nowhere to be seen, leaving the army disappointed and angry.

Additionally, while the Czechs were trying to make their way eastward, released prisoners of war were clogging the railway in their own attempts to travel to their homes in the west. The trainloads of POWs were being given priority because the Germans were pressuring the Reds to disarm and detain the Czech Legion to prevent their arrival in France. The frustrated Czechs sat in their trains and impatiently waited on sidings as they watched their enemy chug by in train after train going in the opposite direction. To make matters worse, the

Bolsheviks were ultimately unable to agree on what they wanted to do with the Czech Legion. Mixed messages from Lenin and Trotsky confused the Czech negotiators. Trotsky had designs of coercing the Czechs into joining his newly formed Red Army. Lenin wanted to be rid of them. The Reds dithered over whether to allow them to continue on their journey east or to disarm and arrest them. Tensions mounted and spilled over in May 1917, in the city of Chelyabinsk. At the Chelyabinsk railway station a Czech soldier on a bronevik was insulted by an ex-POW riding on a passing train. It was the last straw. For his impudence, the German was shot. A short battle ensued. The Czechs quickly captured the railway station and then the entire city.

With negotiations between the Bolsheviks and the Czech Legion stalled, another armed confrontation became inevitable. On May 24, 1918 a Czech armored train attempted to force its way eastbound across the Irtysh River. It was stopped at the Kulomzino railway station by a contingent of Red Guards under the command of Commissar Grigory Uspensky who was acting on behalf of the Omsk Soviet. Intending to machine-gun the soldiers, Uspensky ordered the Czechs to get off their train and lay down their weapons. Of course, as seasoned fighters the Czechs were no fools. After a brief argument between the Czech commander, Captain Orlik Hanus and Uspensky, the Czech bronevik made a run for it. They threw their engine into reverse and fled back westward. Uspensky waited until more men came to swell his numbers and then soon followed the Czech bronevik in two armored trains of his own. Each was loaded with armed Red Army recruits, most of them German ex-POWs and a few local revolutionaries. The Czechs retreated until they came to the station at Marionovka, about a hundred kilometers to the west. There they met another Czech bronevik which had been waiting to see what success Captain Hanus would have. At Marionovka the Czechs made their stand. The Reds blundered into the ambush. They were quickly and soundly defeated. Commissar Uspensky's trains limped back to Kulomzino. He had lost dozens of men in the short, bloody battle. His trains were seriously damaged.

At the time the Czech Legion was the most highly trained army in all of Russia. The revolt of the Legionnaires quickly rolled eastward along the Trans-Siberian Railway. The Czech trains attempted to regroup, but the disarray along the railroad ultimately prevented this. Consequently, the Czech's simply used force of arms to take control of wherever they happened to be. The end result was that the Trans-Siberian Railway from the Ural Mountains to Vladivostok was soon under the Czech Legion's complete control. Their revolt helped to solidify opposition to and foment action against the Bolsheviks. For a while, the Legion became the backbone of the White resistance movement that instigated the civil war. In the end though, weary of a fight that was not theirs, they lost interest and negotiated their return to Czechoslovakia.

The event that would most certainly have had a serious impact on the Rempel family was the uprising of December 22 and 23, 1918. According to Col. Ward, this uprising was an attempt by both Monarchists and Bolsheviks from the 8th Regiment of the new Russian Army in Omsk to wrest control of the government away from Admiral Kolchak and his generals. Kolchak, who admired British institutions, had declared that he was in favor of universal suffrage. Neither Monarchists, who hoped to reinstate Tsarist rule, nor Bolsheviks, who had their own agenda, wanted to have anything to do with the notion of democracy. Kolchak's spies learned of the attempted coup and arrested the leaders late in the evening of the 22nd. Col. Ward describes in detail how his actions helped to curtail the extent of the action in Omsk. In Kulomzino, radical Bolshevik railway workers, aided by members of the 20th Siberian Infantry were much more successful. However, General Ivanov-Rinov's Cossacks, together with soldiers of the Czech Legion were able to break the resistance. Under the banner of Admiral Kolchak, who was bed-ridden with an inflammation of the lungs, Ivanov-Rinov declared martial law and his Cossacks ran roughshod on the streets of Kulomzino arresting suspected conspirators and mercilessly beating, raping and killing civilians throughout the day of December 23. Estimates of the number of dead range from 500 to 2500, depending on the source's political leaning.

Alexandr Vasiliyevich Kolchak was a distinguished polar explorer, writer, and a highly decorated Vice-Admiral in the Russian navy. At the time of the October 1917 Revolution he commanded the Tsar's Black Sea fleet. When the sailors of the fleet mutinied, Kolchak was spared the penalty of death suffered by so many of his peers. He was called to Petrograd where Kerensky offered him a position in the new Russian armed forces. Kolchak refused and was sent into exile. He traveled first to the United States where he offered his expertise in strategies for naval combat in the Black Sea. When he was met with disinterest, he came to England, hoping to be of use in the battle against Germany, going so far as offering to enlist. At the suggestion of the British Secretary of War, Winston Churchill, Kolchak reluctantly agreed to return to Russia where, because of his status and experience, Churchill considered him an ideal candidate to galvanize the Russian people in their fight against the Bolshevik "terrorists" who were rapidly consolidating their control of the country. He made the trip from Britain to Hong Kong from where he was transported aboard the HMS Suffolk to Vladivostok. A special train carried him on the Trans-Siberian Railway to Omsk, where he arrived on October 13, 1918, five days before the Middlesex Battalion and a month before he unenthusiastically accepted the call to become the Supreme Ruler of Russia. Britain spent huge sums arming and clothing Kolchak's army as well as sending troops to assist him. Other nations supporting Kolchak's civil war by sending soldiers included Japan, United States, Canada, France, Italy, Greece, Serbia and many others. In the end, all the effort was for nothing as the Allied soldiers evacuated from Omsk in the weeks before it was abandoned by Kolchak's government in November, 1919, to be looted by the victorious Red Army who found little organized resistance in the city.

Finally, a word about conditions in the Kulomzino/Omsk area during the years of revolution and civil war. As described in the novel, refugees fleeing fighting and famine in the Ukraine and other parts of western Russia crammed into train cars and rode the Trans-Siberian Railway east. Many died along the way. Margaret Rempel Pump recalls her father being conscripted to help bury the dead in the cold of winter. Refugees flooded the cities of west Siberia. Sources indicate the population of Omsk before 1914 was around 100,000. By 1919, it had ballooned, by some estimates, to as many as 700,000. Refugees lived and slept wherever space could be found; those left outside dug holes in the ground and built makeshift roofs for shelter from the elements. Epidemics of typhus and cholera and other diseases ran rampant among them.

Besides the many refugees in their city, the population of Omsk had to contend with the problem of skyrocketing inflation. Changes of currency by governments after 1917 and pervasive black-marketeering severely decreased the ordinary citizen's ability to buy necessities they could not provide for themselves. At the same time the price of goods made scarce by war and corruption soared.

And, of course, the experiment that constituted the implementation of communism would have profoundly affected the lives of everyone politically, economically, and socially.

Peter Rahn's book, "Mennoniten in der Umgebung von Omsk," was very informative in its description of Mennonite life and business in the pre-revolution Omsk/Kulomzino area. There are many accounts of life in pre-revolutionary Siberia available via the Internet. I found John Foster Fraser's on-line book, "The Real Siberia," written in 1905, to be very informative. Useful accounts of the Bolshevik Revolution and the subsequent civil war include the following: "The Shadow of the Winter Palace: Russia's Drift to Revolution 1825-1917" by Edward Crankshaw; "White Siberia: The Politics of Civil War" by N.G.O. Pereira; "Civil War in Siberia: The Anti-Bolshevik Government of Admiral Kolchak, 1918-1920" by Jon Smele; "The Republic of the Ushakovka: Admiral Kolchak and the Allied Intervention in Siberia, 1918-1920" by Richard Michael

Connaughton; "Churchill's Crusade: The British Invasion of Russia, 1918-1920" by Clifford Kinvig; "Evacuation" by L.R. Hiatt; and "And Now My Soul Is Hardened: Abandoned Children in Soviet Russia, 1918-1930" by Alan M. Ball. Fascinating diaries written by individuals who lived through those momentous times include the following: "Left Behind: Fourteen Months in Siberia, December 1917-February 1919" by Baroness Sophie Buxhoeveden; and the "WW1 Siberian Diary" of William C. Jones, 2nd Lt. U.S. Army Russian Railway Service. I am especially indebted to Colonel John Ward's journal of his Siberian experiences, "With the 'Die-Hards' in Siberia," whose historical account of the Middlesex Battalion's Trans-Siberian Railway journey from Vladivostok to Omsk, as well as the battalion's role in suppressing the December 1918 Bolshevik uprising in Omsk, among other things, provided valuable material with which I exercised considerable creative license. Finally, the three Russian folk tales retold in the story, "The Giant Potato," "The Foolish Peasant," and "Death and the Miser," can be found in any good anthology on the subject.

42493613R00130

Made in the USA
Middletown, DE
15 April 2017